House of Cleaving

Melissa Newman, Ed.D.

Published by
Martin Sisters Publishing Company
www.martinsisterspublishing.com
Martin Sisters Publishing ©2022
Reprinted with rights and permissions from original printing and publisher
Whiskey Creek Press ©2010

ISBN: 978-1-62553-106-3
Literary Fiction
Printed in the United States of America
Martin Sisters Publishing

DEDICATION

For my father, who taught me that perseverance
is the key to most things in life.

Everett Dozier, 1932-1997

CHAPTER ONE

Two days before the World Trade Center attacks, Annie watched her son's crushed little body gasp a last breath. He had just slapped Annie a high-five. She gave him the answer he wanted to hear. It was jacket weather, especially in the mornings. Turkey Day was close. He wanted his momma to know exactly what kind of bird he wanted, no mistakes.

"Am I gonna get my little turkey?" his squeaky voice became even more high pitched at the end of his question. He'd been learning that in school.

The year before, he set out with his momma looking for the biggest turkey he could find, but this year as they strolled down the aisles of the freezer section, his tiny eyes narrowed, focusing in tightly on one specific point of interest.

"What are these?"

Always persistent on breaking the rules, he stood in the back of the shopping cart, his chariot, as Annie wheeled him around. The moment he pointed, she rolled him over to take a closer look. He leaned over the side of the cart and poked at a frozen package, the heat from his finger dissolving the frost leaving a pea-sized melted spot behind.

When his momma told him they were Cornish hens, he

contorted his face and shook his head. He had already made up his mind before he had even asked that those were baby turkeys and he meant to have one for Thanksgiving.

He insisted on buying three – one for him, one for her and one for Grammy.

That high five was the last time Annie felt the warmth of her son's little hand on hers, and that question the last time she heard his voice. Annie hoped Ethan took his last breath looking forward to eating his little turkey on Thanksgiving Day and not scared he was dying, wondering why his mother wasn't holding him.

The doctors said it was the trauma of the accident and the fact that she hung upside down in the vehicle for so long that made Annie see the angel carry him away. The colors were vivid and warm; only they weren't colors Annie had ever seen before. The angel filled every crevasse, every space. The sorrow and hopelessness were gone in an instant as soon as the angel appeared but returned just as quickly when Annie saw the emptiness of death in Ethan's eyes.

Two days later it was as if no one cared about Ethan. The world now focused on Ground Zero, not the car crash and not the memory of the sweet, loving child who had suddenly vanished from this earth. When Annie saw the second plane hit the Twin Towers, she hoped the world was ending. How could it possibly go on without Ethan? But it did. Somehow the world managed to keep right on spinning, and Annie just kept right on breathing – waking up every day as some invisible force kept moving her forward into nothing.

Last year when the heavy fog came again for a long visit, Annie's mother died. The year before that, it was Ethan. She had let another year pass without escape, but not for long. The fog was here again. It didn't have the same feel to it this season, it was different. The smell of it, the wet of it wasn't quite the same. Still, she could feel it heavy on her skin; the dampness, the cold was about to set in. If all went as planned, this would be the last Rayes County fall she would ever have to see. It was always the smells that reminded her. Dead leaves rotting and wet on the ground broke her heart every fall morning.

Annie was anxious to leave. Only a few more days and she could give her notice, pack her bags and hide away in a town where no one knew her, where no one pitied her. She could spend her days preparing tax returns for the elderly and her evenings watching black and white movies on cable. The job opening couldn't have come at a better time. Annie couldn't bear to spend one more holiday in Rayes County. People here had known her since she was a child. Annie had heard her own mother sum up a person's life in three sentences: "Poor Sadie Jones. She just hasn't been the same since her husband died. She's going to grieve herself to death one of these days."

Annie didn't want her life summed up in three sentences by the praying matriarchs of Rayes County. She knew she might grieve herself to death someday, but she didn't appreciate others knowing it or watching as it happened. If no one knew her then they wouldn't ask her how long it had been since she had been out, how long it had been since she laughed – they wouldn't dare ask those questions of a stranger. That's what she wanted to be – a stranger – someone who could go to work every day and come home every night until she just didn't anymore one day. Then, some other poor sap could take her place, breathing in and out and feeling themselves pushed forward into the nothing that used to be Annie's.

For the three minutes it took to trek from the car to the office, Annie tried to keep her mind blank. There was a time when she enjoyed those moments before work to reflect or worry about what the day might bring, but now she didn't want to think; she didn't want to care. And mostly she didn't.

It had been a difficult year for the company; her boss had asked her time and again why she didn't seem more concerned.

"It just seems like you couldn't care less whether or not we survive this budget shortfall," Janet would hesitantly suggest to Annie every now and then. "Our investors are scared, and we should be, too."

Annie's standard reply was always the same, "Of course I care. It just doesn't do any good to panic."

Annie resented the accusation that she didn't care about the company, even though it was true. How could Janet even expect her to care; she should just be happy Annie was present and accounted for every day. She had cared too much in the past; before she realized that counting other people's money was a trivial act, unnecessary. If only other people could see how ridiculous their world really was. Annie would stew silently as committees formed to debate what color the tile should be in the new break rooms; or if the chairs were ergonomically correct in each manager's office. On the rare occasion when someone requested Annie's opinion, her standard, "It really doesn't matter to me," was barely audible. No one could hear her honest answer as she screamed it inside her head.

Saying goodbye to Natureson's Camping Stores, LLC, would be easy. No more bill paying, no more juggling bank accounts to make ends meet, no more payrolls to reconcile, no one asking for copies of pay stubs and mileage sheets that they should have kept track of themselves. Only a few more days and the closing on the house would be complete. Annie could go away forever.

As she entered the rear entrance of the building and headed up the stairs, she could hear them talking about their weekend. They always congregated in front of the conference room door each morning, but Mondays were especially active. It was a chance for Janet to brag about her shopping adventures, and the other women to talk about their perfect family outings. The guys in the office would try to sneak in a few highlights from the game, or some political debate from Tim Russert's "Meet the Press," but the estrogen-filled offices of NCS didn't allow much of that. The conversation would soon revert back to the clearance rack at Macy's.

The crowd would always dissipate soon after Annie reached the top of the stairs; the laughter would stop, and the volume of the conversation would drop to a whisper. It had been this way since the accident. Annie remembered those Monday morning gatherings and thought about how unimportant they seem now for the sake of NCS or anything else for that matter.

As usual, Annie walked in with her laptop bag, her purse and her coffee, barely balancing all three around her small frame. She smiled at the group but wanted to roll her eyes. They smiled back and then everyone seemed to evaporate, reappearing in their offices.

Annie's desk was piled with neat stacks of papers left on Friday in a fanned-out fashion; most important being on top and then so on. Her black leather chair was scooted neatly under her desk so housekeeping wouldn't have to move it out of the way as they vacuumed. On Friday, Annie placed her clean coffee cup on its coaster just next to her mouse pad. It stood waiting at attention for her Monday return, ready for work. The message light was flashing red, another good indication it was Monday, just in case anyone hadn't bothered to keep track. Annie found herself wondering, yet again, why anyone would call *her* office on a weekend. She was the controller, not in charge of retail and not in charge of wholesale. Still, they always did. Annie thought of her title as such a joke. *Controller. How ironic.*

She didn't make it to the coffee pot before Lila, and again she paid the price. Lila would stand and talk while she made the coffee. This meant that sometimes, depending on how deep the conversation was, a pot for twelve might end up having a dozen or more heaping scoops in it. Really, not fit to drink for anyone other than a veteran coal miner, with paralyzed taste buds. Annie piled in the non-dairy creamer to take some of the bite out. But it was so strong there could've been hard liquor in it and no one would have noticed. There were a few mornings that Annie could have used some extra spirit in her coffee, but not today. She finally had something to look forward to, leaving Rayes County, NCS and the September Mountain fog behind.

The first message prompted Annie to hit the delete button before the man was even finished talking. Annie hated salespeople and hated it even more when they left messages. Really, did they think she'd call them back in a panic some Monday morning because she'd run out of toner or fluorescent light bulbs? The second message she wanted to delete but knew better. It was another vendor calling about payment. Annie had a priority list and Leather Lockers, Inc. was not above number five, which meant pay them after the fifteenth.

"Message three," the automated voice lady continued in that Monday morning smart ass tone of hers. "Annie, this is Larry over at the bank. I need for you to give me a call this morning as soon as you can. There's a problem with the closing on the loan. Talk to you soon."

It had all been too easy – the new people loved the house. She had already contracted with the buyers through Stewart Realty. The new job awaited her arrival. It was shocking, really, how easy it had been to just leave – just go and not look back. The only real hang-up had been from the buyer's side. For some reason, the loan was taking longer than usual. Annie wasn't too concerned – kept telling herself first-time homebuyers usually leave loose ends for the realtors and bankers to tie up. Small repairs to the house went smoothly and weren't terribly expensive. The house was in fairly good shape when Annie moved in. She had always tried to fix problems as they came up. For an older home, it was one of the nicer ones in Rayes County. It was a small, frame, white-sided house; nothing exceptional, two bedrooms, one bath. There was no acreage; only two 100 x 100 lots put together; just big enough for the small house and a tiny garden on one side that hadn't been touched since her grandmother died. The driveway was gravel, the same as all the houses on Old Watkins Road. Lucy Cleaving, being of sound mind and body, had bequeathed Annie her house and property with a few scribbles on a hand-written will. When Mamaw Lucy, as everyone called her, was 97 years old and gave herself over to live in a nursing home, she asked Annie to go ahead and move in and "take care of the old place," until she could get back.

Annie was hesitant, at first, but grateful all the same. Although no one knew just yet, there was a baby coming – a baby with no father. With the house, she wouldn't have to worry about money nearly as much.

Mamaw Lucy died on the Valentine's Day, before Ethan was born. Two nights before her grandmother's death, Annie was sleeping soundly for a change. A young Lucy Cleaving came to visit Annie in a dream. She sat on the front porch of the Cleaving house and told Annie everything she was supposed to do for the rest of her life. The mostly one-sided conversation was direct and specific, even outlining which doorway to walk through at which time and which books to read. Annie listened as intently as she could and even asked the young woman, who Annie felt uncomfortable calling Mamaw, if she could write it all down. The reply was simply a stern shake of the head and even in the dream Annie knew better than to get up from where she sat to fetch pen and paper. Although Annie now had detailed instructions for the rest of her life, when she awoke the next morning, she couldn't remember a single thing Mamaw Lucy had told her; only that it was very specific and important.

When Mamaw Lucy died of natural causes only two days later, Annie and her mother agreed the dream was coincidence and never really talked about it again. Annie did, however, ask her mother why Mamaw Lucy, with so many other heirs, would give her the only place she'd ever called home. Annie's mother put it simply, "Your grandmother said you needed it most." Annie

had expected some gushy, proud statement about being the favorite granddaughter or some other such accolade. Needing it most made her sound inept, ill-equipped and pathetic; not at all the way Annie thought of herself. With a whole slew of Cleaving children, eleven of them still living and countless more grandchildren, the question did beg an answer. Millicent Cleaving, Annie's mother, was the exact middle child of all the Cleaving children and the only one of Mamaw Lucy's daughters to still carry the Cleaving name. The others left Rayes County as soon as they were old enough; there were just three left: Mamaw Lucy, Millie and Annie. Annie had heard people talk about a time when every time they turned around there was a Cleaving somewhere, "sometimes two or three of them deep," they'd quip.

Annie's curiosity about why Mamaw Lucy left her the house soon gave way to overwhelming happiness with her station in life once Ethan was born.

Annie's palms were sweaty, and her stomach filled with fluttering moths as she picked up the phone to dial Larry's number. She'd had a bad feeling all morning. She didn't even have to look up the number anymore. Larry had not only led her step by step through the process but approved of her plan to sell the house and make a new life for herself.

"This may be just what you need, Annie," Larry would say. "Make a fresh, new start somewhere else."

Annie didn't know about a fresh, new start but the somewhere else idea was *her* focus.

"Returning your call from this morning; there's a problem?"

"Yes," Larry drew a deep breath and let out a long sigh. "I'm going to try to walk you through this. It's new to me. In fact, I've never run across it as a loan officer. I had our attorney look it over thoroughly and it's gonna be a pretty tough nut to crack."

Annie listened carefully as Larry told her about how the property had become a life estate when Adam Cleaving, Lucy's husband, and the father of her children, died. Adam, who was 31 years older than Lucy when they married, had passed away long ago, just after their last child was born. Before he died, he made a will which stated that half the property would belong to his wife and the other half to his children. Mamaw Lucy either didn't know about this arrangement or didn't understand it and proceeded to leave her home to Annie in her will.

"So, what does this mean for the sale Larry?"

"I can't loan your buyers the money, Annie. Our banking regulations won't allow it. Just because you have a recorded deed to that property and you pay taxes on it, is evidently not a legal indication that you own it. And yes, before you even ask, I've talked to the bank president about it this morning – he said there's just no way."

Her heart sank to her stomach. Was her only way out of Rayes County to die? In that moment she was willing to escape any way she could, if not by moving van, then by whatever means necessary. Words finally came back to her.

"What do I do?"

"Our attorney suggests you do one of the following: get an

attorney of your own and call everyone in to court by subpoena and battle it out or visit all of them and get each to sign a Quit Claim deed, which will halt all their claims to the property."

Annie felt as if someone had punched her.

"You *do* realize my grandmother had fifteen children," Annie swallowed hard, counting to herself and making notes, "… eleven of them are still living?"

"Oh my God," Larry picked up quickly on the number eleven. "I was getting ready to tell you that this is not as impossible as it seems, but … eleven?!"

Annie let out a long sigh, "Yeah … you heard me, right. It's eleven."

"Annie, if there's anything at all I can do to help just let me know," Larry paused, waiting for Annie to ask but she didn't. "When you get all this mess straightened out, I'll be more than happy to grant a loan on this property."

"Larry don't hang up just yet. Which does your attorney think I should do?"

"The latter," Larry's voice was flat as if he were quoting someone else. "Visit them all. Chances are since they had no knowledge they were owners of this property to begin with, they'd be more than happy to stop any claims they may have to it. If any of these people are elderly, I'd hurry before they start dying off. Otherwise, this mess expands exponentially, and their heirs will have to sign off on the property."

Again, Annie was alone, left with only a generic website belonging to some real estate attorney she had never met.

Her conclusion, far from the perfection she had hoped for, held a small bit of encouragement. She had scribbled a quick list –

her mother at the top. For the first time since Millie died, she was able to help her daughter. Because of it, Annie now owned a bit more than fifty percent – more than anyone else on the list.

She placed a solid check mark next to the name Millie Cleaving and staunchly rose from her chair. Annie, who hadn't taken a vacation day since her mother died, walked into her boss's office and without hesitation stated her request.

"I need a month off." Annie ignored Janet's alarm.

"What?"

"A month off." Annie got a little louder this time to reinforce the point.

"When?"

"Right now." Annie let the power of her determination to get out of Rayes County drive her. "Today. Right now," she nodded her head as if helping Janet to agree.

CHAPTER TWO

Normally, Annie loved drizzly days – hiding inside, not showering and not opening the curtains or shades. She could get pizza delivered and even have the driver bring a two-liter, giving her no reason to leave the house at all – guilt-free days of old movies and books taking her away to distant places, still in her warm-up pants and wool socks. Rainy days drew just as much comfort from the outside as the inside. Annie knew if she withdrew from the world on an overcast day, the Rayes County gossip machine would shut down as well. They stayed in if the weather was bad. Annie would picture them melting in the rain or sitting in a group white-knuckled while clenching a Farmer's Almanac, planning their days. Either way, Annie was free from the sunny day comments: *"Annie, you really should get out more and enjoy this beautiful weather we're having, we were talking and none of us even saw you leave the house this weekend."* Sometimes Annie would lie and say she had gone to the movies or was out of town with a friend. She couldn't tell if they believed her or not, but they wouldn't dare accuse her of lying – that would be impolite. Other times, she just smiled and nodded in agreement.

No hiding today, though. She had to get started finding the Cleavings.

She missed the sound of crackling gravels under her tires, but the new pavement made the house more saleable. For weeks, she'd been met with neatly-stacked boxes against her living room wall, it gave her hope – hope for leaving. Now those boxes just sat there looking frustrated and hopeless. The throw and her pillow were folded together neatly on the couch where she'd left them. She eased into her usual scrunched up position and pulled the blanket up to her neck, her body barely covering half the sofa. She scanned the room, running her eyes along every baseboard, every corner, and each piece of furniture. At the entertainment center, her eyes stopped. Not one photograph of Ethan was hidden from sight. Every snapshot, every studio portrait and every drawing held a prominent place in her home. She would lie there day after day and remember where they were the day each picture had been snapped, the trip to the photo studio, shopping for Easter and Christmas outfits.

Annie, jolted back into existence by a loud pop, jumped up from the couch and ran to the door, tripping over the coffee table leg and dragging it with her part of the way. She opened the front door, "Really??!! Really??!! She screamed as she picked up the newspaper. "YOU BREAK IT, YOU BUY IT," Annie yelled as she chased the newspaper boy down the road. She threw the paper as hard as she could, chasing after him, hoping to hit him as he pedaled away. Just then, down the street she thought she caught sight of that Rosen boy coming toward her in his car. He didn't even deserve to be called by his first name – just "that Rosen boy" was enough. Everyone knew who he was, what he did. Yet, there he was again coming and going as he pleased. Sometimes Annie would catch sight of him, like today. He'd be smiling or laughing, cutting up with his "peeps" as he had called them during the trial. Every day he lived was a day Annie considered stolen from her son. The son of the Rayes County Sheriff could take whatever he wanted. People had always said that about him but now there was proof in the form of granite at the City Cemetery – a stone with the name of a precious child etched across it. She stood perfectly still in the middle of the road, like a statue, hoping he would hit her –

kill *her* too. As the car whizzed by, the driver blowing her horn, Annie realized it wasn't him.

Her pounding heart and clenched teeth were relaxing, and both began to ache with sadness again. She looked down the street toward her house. She had run a good block and a half, barefoot and crying.

"Oh, my God," she said quietly as she brought her hands to her face and began stepping backward out of the middle of the road. "What is wrong with me?"

Annie scanned the neighborhood to see if anyone had been watching. She didn't see anyone but was sure they must be peering out their kitchen windows. She was sure Rayes County phones were ringing as the gossip machine was alerted to a screaming, barefoot crazy woman running down the street. She quickly walked to the spot where she threw the newspaper and picked it up. She paused for a moment as she watched little Jonathan Mills, covered in a bright yellow rain poncho pedal to the top of Old Watkins hill and then disappear over the other side. He had carefully rolled Annie's newspaper and placed it in a clear plastic bag. The rubber band was tight enough to keep the paper snug in its rain protector but not so tight as to tear it. As Annie walked back to the house, her bare feet were now wet and had collected small gravels, dirt and some freshly cut grass from a neighbor's lawn. The mist from her hair was beginning to trickle onto her scalp and her face was wet – maybe rain, maybe sweat. She felt the world's eyes upon her as she took her walk of shame back to the Cleaving house. This walk was familiar to her, she had taken it many times before when she dated Ethan's father. Dressed in tight hot pink pants or a pleated mini skirt, she would be dropped off at the end of the road and then walk the rest of the way home. He would never bring her all the way home after a night of partying. It was too weird, he'd say. He always said it would make it feel like they were a couple or something. He was always in a hurry to get somewhere – work, to a buddy's house, or home to watch the game. Annie was always sure he'd come around and fall madly in love with her someday. The Sunday morning walks of shame came to an abrupt halt when Annie found out she was pregnant with Ethan. Noah Castle disappeared, moved away. To the people of Rayes County it was like he never existed.

When Annie got back to the front door, she checked to make sure the glass wasn't damaged. She was sure Jonathan hadn't broken it, but *she* had slammed it pretty hard on her way out. The shiny storm door and the newly paved driveway were just part of the home improvement plan Annie had undertaken over the past several months.

Annie went back to the sofa and folded the throw, placing the pillow neatly on top. With the newspaper under her arm and a cup she picked up off the end table from the night before, she walked into the kitchen, prepared a tuna sandwich and sat down at the table to read. Annie had been getting the newspaper for years even though she really only sat down to read it about once a month. The only reason she kept renewing every year was to help support whatever poor kid who happened to have her on his route. She just never had the heart to tell them no. She laughed a little as she unrolled the newspaper thinking about what had happened earlier with the little Mills boy.

"I've got to get out of here before I *really* lose my mind," Annie said, shaking her head.

As usual, when Annie did read the paper, she would start from the back. First the classified ads, *I have a new job, she thought, don't need to look at those* ... Annie had sent an e-mail to Baker, Wyatt and Wentz just before she left NSA letting them know that although she could not start in two weeks as planned, she would be there in a month, if that was acceptable. BW&W didn't seem like the kind of place where two extra weeks would make a huge difference. In fact, there was no Wyatt and Wentz, only Baker. The Ws had been dead a long time. It was a small, quiet place. Annie was looking forward to that job. Confident that Mr. Baker would hold the job for her, she wiped the worry from her mind and kept turning the pages. Sports ... "look at all these kids," she said. *I wonder if Ethan would have been a football player, or soccer player ...*

She skimmed through the other sections quickly ... marriages, anniversaries, birthdays. A picture on the editorial page caught her eye.

"Mary Joe," Annie said out loud to the quiet room.

Mary's column was on the left side of the page, as usual. Annie felt comforted at the sight of her face, even if it was just in a picture. Mary and Annie went to Rayes County High School together. They were in the same grade. They weren't good friends, but they were polite to one another and even ended up having some of the same friends over the years. It wasn't until Annie's car accident that she really got to know Mary. She remembered the day's accounts vividly – what people said, what people did ... for moments everything was clear, like hearing it all through a megaphone and watching it in slow motion. Mary was there. She arrived just as the paramedics were cutting Ethan's body out of the car. Although Annie knew her son was dead, she kept telling the EMTs he was still breathing so they would get him out first. Annie saw Mary in the distance, through a muddy side window. She had her camera at the ready position as Ethan's body was gently pulled away from the wreckage. She took certain aim, but she never took the first shot. Annie watched her step backward away from the scene and sob into her hands when she realized the little boy was not going to be a "miracle in Rayes County" headline. Annie remembered Mary's tears, they were real – visible tears and the first of many to be shed for little Ethan. In that moment, Annie connected with Mary in a very personal way. When the story came out in the Rayes County Journal, it was a respectfully written piece.

Annie felt as if Mary were writing about the death of her own child. A week after Ethan's burial, a small, padded envelope arrived at the Cleaving house, addressed to Annie. Inside was a figurine in the shape of an angel and it was wrapped in a hand-written note: "Annie, I am so sorry about your son. I can't even imagine what you are going through. Someone gave this to me several years ago to bring me comfort. I hope it helps you as much as it has helped me. God Bless."

Mary had helped Annie more than she ever could have imagined by sending the small pewter angel. She often wondered if Mary had seen the angel the day of the accident, too, but discounted the gift as mere coincidence. Annie was certain she saw Mary praying and whether Mary knew it or not, Annie was watching.

*

Finding all the Cleaving children in a month would be nearly impossible. Annie's mother wasn't close to any of them. Annie could only remember two of them, Asher and Jaygar, visiting Mamaw Lucy. When Mamaw Lucy died, her children were in and out quickly. Some came, some didn't. The one's who did, paid their respects and left quickly. Annie had no reason to keep in touch with any of them and never wanted to make contact at all, until now. Other than her one crazy aunt who lived in nearby Stig County, the Cleaving children had been scattered to the four corners of the earth, or at least the Midwest. There were a couple in Virginia, a couple more in Ohio, and at least two in Pennsylvania. But where, Annie had no idea. After reading the newspaper, Annie picked up her cell phone and punched in a number.

"This is Mary, state your purpose," the woman said smartly. "Hey, Mary," Annie said hesitantly. "This is Annie Cleaving, how are you?"

Mary's voice softened a bit as she spoke. "Annie? I am great, how are you?"

"Mary, I need your help finding some folks in my family," Annie skipped straight to the point, trying not to seem nervous. "And I don't even know where to begin."

*

Annie had to drive around the square twice before finding a parking spot, spaces were scarce downtown when it rained in Rayes County. Three blocks away, she found a spot. She took the newspaper from the front seat and held it over her head as she walked.

Annie hadn't been inside the newspaper office since she was a child. The building on the outside hadn't changed much at all. It was still the two-story, perfectly square brick structure resembling a red cracker box. Annie had only ever seen the first floor of the building. Mary's office was upstairs. As Annie approached the top of the stairs, she heard lots of people talking. She heard Mary's voice among them.

"Annie, do you have the list?"

"Yes, right here," Annie watched her shaky hand as it delivered the Cleaving ancestry.

"I'll do what I can, and I'll e-mail when I find something," Mary said. "I wish you luck, dear. Like I told you on the phone, I would start with the one aunt you *do* know something about and then see what *she* knows. And another thing I thought of after we hung up the phone – talk to your neighbors, I bet they know something about your people and where they might be now. Heck, some of them might even keep in touch with them. It sounds like a great adventure."

"Thank you, Mary," Annie said. "I know you're busy …"

Mary interrupted, "I'm glad to do it for you. Don't you worry about it. If you're on the road and you need anything, give me a call and let me know."

Annie nodded at Mary as she walked toward the staircase. "Again, thanks."

It hadn't occurred to Annie to talk to the neighbors. One neighbor in particular, Olga Rainey, could be of some help. Annie would need to go and see her anyway to see if she would look after the house while Annie was on her *great adventure*, as Mary referred to it. Annie had to laugh at Mary's reaction to the obscene number of Cleaving children. "Your little bitty grandma had this many children?!" Mary had asked eyes wide.

Annie really didn't want to talk to Mrs. Rainey. She and Annie's mother had become lukewarm friends after Ethan died. There were times when Annie would come home from work and Millie, tired of waiting for her daughter's arrival, would be sitting on Olga's porch having tea, talking. Annie never really had any idea what their visits were about, only that when she came up on the porch the conversation would quickly turn to weather or current events. Annie had to guess they had been talking about those things the whole time, although she knew deep down that Millie was grilling Olga about Annie's comings and goings. When Annie was dating Noah, her mother concerned herself with when or even *if* Annie was coming home. After the crash, she troubled herself to try and find out if Annie had left the house at all.

Still, all Annie could think about in regard to Olga Rainey was her comment about Ethan when he was born – "Not all babies have to have daddies, I don't guess. Some of them grow up and do just fine," she said when she brought over cupcakes to congratulate the newest Cleaving arrival. Annie never forgave her and if Millie had heard it, that lukewarm friendship would have turned quickly into a boiling hot battle. Annie was sure if her mother had been around, those words would never have left Olga's lips.

CHAPTER THREE

Olga Rainey's front yard was, at one time, one of the prettiest in the county. Like an old rust-belt town, it just stopped evolving sometime in the seventies. Olga had somehow managed to get her garden just right a little more than three decades ago and must have decided not to tamper with perfection. The roses always came back in the same spot each year and produced the same number of blooms, in what seemed like, all the same places. The marigolds knew their place, just in front of the porch; all lined up like English soldiers. Their yellow plumes stood ready to battle mosquitoes and other pesky insects just waiting to take a quick bite from one of Olga's fresh juicy gossip sessions. These meetings were planned but gave the illusion of being impromptu.

It was approaching the bewitching hour of the gathering, but Annie felt safe stopping at Olga's today. The rain had kept the old biddies at home. Maybe Annie had gotten it wrong all these years. Like a vampire at night, maybe she should have taken care of all her errands on hazy, rainy days. A quick jaunt over to the grocery store earlier had proven this theory. She could have thrown a rock from end to end of the IGA and not hit one member of that old grapevine or her rain bonnet. They had simply just not come out.

The azaleas were perched on either side of Olga's sidewalk, the monkey grass sat nearby waving in the misty rain. The red, white and purple petunias were packed tightly into their homes made from recycled whitewall tires. These two beds stood as centerpieces on each side of the walk in Olga's Glory Garden, as she called it. "A glorious tribute to God is a Glory Garden filled with his wondrous creations." She always said that's why she even "fooled with a garden at all." Most on Old Watkins knew better. She did it for the attention from her neighbors and the gushing that came forth from the display. Over the years, though, it had become stale – never a new color, never a new plant. Her once-glorious flower display had become as common and plain as the mountains showing their strip mining scars during a cold, Rayes County winter. They were just part of the landscape.

Annie drove the car into the driveway and began walking across the lawn over to Olga's house. The rain felt good on her face. She looked up at the sky and opening her eyes wide, felt the mist falling on her eyelashes. Taking a long, deep breath she exhaled as Olga's porch came completely into sight. Annie spent so much of her time grieving for Ethan; she was always surprised by the wave of sadness that would sometimes come from memories of her mother. She hadn't walked across the lawn to Olga's since meeting her mother here for the last time. She got butterflies in her stomach as a sudden hope washed over her that her momma might be there. For a moment, she could almost see Millie sitting there on the porch swing, smiling down at her as she climbed those four concrete steps. She wanted to go over and sit next to where Millie used to sit, pretending just for a moment that she was really there.

Millie didn't hang on very long after Ethan died. A little more than a year had passed when she was diagnosed with cancer. She went quickly after that. It was like she wanted to go. Annie's only comfort was to believe that her mother was somewhere in Heaven holding little Ethan in her arms. Nothing would have made Ethan's Grammy happier.

Just as Annie started to knock on the door, Olga opened it.

"Well, hello Annie," Olga reached out to Annie for a hug.

For some reason Annie hugged her tighter than she should have. Olga didn't look like the nosy old biddy she used to know. She was older, her wrinkles deeper and her eyes hollower and more shaded. Annie saw she was using a cane as she stepped out onto the porch.

"Oh, I do wish the sun would come out today," Olga said to Annie as she pointed her cane to the Adirondack chair next to the porch swing urging Annie to sit. "I would invite you in, but I want to see you out here in the good light of day."

Olga's eyes were cloudy with cataracts. Beneath the clouds, Annie could see where traces of what used to be a blue iris was turning to gray.

"Oh my, Annie, you are a beautiful young woman," Olga said, shuffling her feet in front of the chair to get a good aim before letting go of the cane and falling into her chair. "Just like your mother."

"Thank you," Annie said, smiling at Olga.

"I've been seeing you in and out of the house," Olga said, pointing her cane over to the Cleaving house and poking it into the air to stress her message. "I try to keep an eye on you. You know your mother used to get me to do that when she was still alive."

"I suspected she did," Annie said, laughing a little.

"She worried so much about you, child. I think she probably worried herself to death," Olga said, shaking her head and squeezing her wrinkled little lips together. "You worried your mother so … well, I guess you know that don't you?"

"Yes," Annie said. "I know she worried a lot about me. I worried about her as well, Olga."

25

Annie immediately began rebuilding her emotional armor. For a moment, she thought the old gossip bag had changed. But it was obvious now that the only motive for this sitting would be to make Annie feel responsible in some way for her mother's death.

"Olga, I came over to ask a favor of you," Annie continued to the point and ignored Olga's nasty attempt at guilting her.

"Oh?"

"I will be leaving for about a month and I need to make sure you have my cell phone number in case anything goes wrong at the house."

"A month?! Where on earth are you going for a month?"

"It's for business," Annie said. "I will be travelling for the Nature store." That's what everyone in Rayes County called Natureson's. Time and again Annie was asked – "Don't you work for that Nature store?" It was easier and took less time to just say yes than try to correct them.

"Oh, oh I see," Olga said, narrowing her eyes and lifting her head looking at Annie through the tiny slits she had fashioned to show suspicions. "Are you sure everything is all right?"

"Yes, Olga. Everything is fine. I just need for you to keep an eye on the house. There's no need to get the mail. I'll put a hold on it at the post office until I get back."

Annie could think of nothing worse than having Olga peer through the window envelopes at her mail. It was bad enough that Bob made comments about her mail, "The other day you got a package and I left it at the post office, it wouldn't fit in the box," Bob would say. "Did you get it?"

Of course, Annie knew Bob was less concerned about whether or not she got the package and more concerned with what was in it. Sometimes if she was feeling mean she would just answer, "Yes, I got it, thank you," and walk away. She knew that drove him crazy. Most times, though, she would tell him what the package contained … usually books, sometimes clothing. He was an old man. She felt sorry for him. If it made his day a little brighter to know what was in Annie's packages, then who was she to deprive him of that simple pleasure? She could just picture Olga and Bob together trying to figure out what was in each piece of her mail while she was gone – holding it up to the light, justifying their prying eyes saying things to each other like, "well, we just want to know if it's important … it might be something she needs right away."

It was just better to remove temptation all together and let the post office hold the mail until she returned.

"Well, that sounds easy enough," Olga said. "I don't mind at all. Don't you worry; I'll keep a close eye on things around your place."

"Thank you so much Olga," Annie said. "I feel better knowing you'll be looking after the house."

Annie hesitated a moment. She almost just got up and left. But this was too important. She needed some information about the family. Any nugget that Olga held would probably be helpful. Being in charge of the Rayes County grapevine, she had to have some inside information about the Cleavings.

"Before I leave, I wanted to ask you something I've been curious about," Annie tried to play off her inquisition as nothing more than innocent curiosity. "I wonder if you know anything about my mother's brothers and sisters – anything about them, when they left here and where they ended up. Do you know where any of them are now?"

"The Cleaving family. The Cleaving family," Olga said shaking her head. "If you would've asked me fifty years ago where they'd be I would have told you right here, right here in Rayes County," Olga leaned forward suddenly as if she were about to lunge from her chair. "That house has stood through tornadoes and floods – all these houses here have. But the one thing they couldn't survive was not having good work and enough of it for all of our children.

"That's what happened to my family, that's what happened to your family, that's what happened to the Joneses over yonder," Olga continued with a Loretta Lynn reverberation to her voice and a conviction Annie hadn't heard from her until now.

Annie, anxious for some answers, urged Olga to continue.

"I've heard that before, Olga. Where did they all go?"

"Most of them headed into Cincinnati for factory work, some of them to Cleveland for work in automobiles. Point is they all left."

"Your family, the Cleavings, they're spread here, there and yon," Olga continued. "Is there someone in particular you're looking for?"

"Not any one of them in particular," Annie was glad she hadn't brought the list with her. "Just any of them – where they might be now."

"Well, you know your aunt Veda lives over in Stig County," Olga said, with one eyebrow raised. "And well, you know all about her I'd guess. The state of her mind and all – still, she might know where some of the rest of 'em are if you wanted to see her."

"I'd love to see ole' Vady myself," Annie wasn't sure if Olga was waiting for an invitation to go with her or not, but she never extended one. "You know that's what we used to call her when we were all growing up. We'd say 'Vady's a Lady,' not for any reason you know – just because it rhymed."

Annie had always known something wasn't quite right with her Aunt Veda. She remembered going to her house once when she was a teenager. Her mother had to pick up some paperwork from her and take it over to the funeral home. Annie never did understand what that was all about. As with most teenagers, the curiosity passed quickly and moved onto thoughts of music, make-up and miniskirts. But the one thing Annie remembered vividly – all those dolls.

"Yes," Olga said. "You know Vady was smart as a whip. In school she could read better than the rest of us. She could do her math just right on, which was something none of the rest of us girls could do. She was even smart when it came to sports – you know baseball and such. She knew how to put a winning strategy together every single time."

Annie was now curious enough to sit all the way back in her chair.

"You know what her downfall was?" Olga asked then answered before Annie could open her mouth to speak. "It was boys, men – that was Vady's downfall. The boys didn't know what to make of her being so smart in their subjects and all. They picked away at her until there was nothing left. Then, when she got older it kept on. She married that sorry, son of a …. down at Stig and I hear he beat the smarts right out of her. I remember when he died," Olga stopped abruptly stopped her sermon, paused for a moment as if her mind needed to reconstruct the delivery of the next line. "I remember it like it was yesterday. All us ladies here on the hill, before we knew what *really* happened, figured that she had probably killed him. We decided right here on this porch that it was all right if she did and that we would stand up for her until our cupboards were bare."

Annie was always puzzled by the solidarity of the sisterhood of the old women from Rayes County. No matter what they did to each other, no one from outside that circle was allowed those same liberties. Annie never doubted they would have all been there for Vady if she *had* committed murder – might have even done it for her if they'd been asked.

"But she didn't kill him," Olga said, shaking her head. "It was natural causes – heart attack, I guess. But you know what I think it was?" Olga again answered the question quickly before Annie could respond. "… God taking him out of this world so Vady could have some peace," she said as if God himself had told her this during some secret meeting. "But it was too late; she was already half out of her mind when he died. He beat her senseless is what we say now when we talk about it."

Annie wondered how often the ladies spoke of Veda on that front porch – and, what else they said about the Cleaving family in between slurps and gulps of Olga's sweet, iced tea. Even the birds perched on the clothesline near the front porch new more about the Cleaving family than Annie did. They had been quietly listening, pacing back and forth across the sagging, wet rope.

Annie was no further along in her search now than she had been when she first stepped onto the creaky old porch.

"Do you know if the family visits Aunt Veda?" Annie moved forward in her chair and gave the active listener's signal – elbow placed on knee, fist under the chin.

"Oh, Lord, I doubt it. She gets crazier by the minute. I just don't think your family wants to fool with her anymore. They're probably just like every other family, they'll come around when they think she's going to die so they can get something."

"Yes siree," Olga said, shaking her head in shame at the family. "You Cleaving women are just cursed with bad men, it seems. I've watched over the years at the men who've come in and out of that old place ... all trash, all of them just trash."

"Well, you of all people know what I'm talking about," Olga checked Annie out of the corner of her eye to see if was safe just as a youngster would dip a toe in the lake to make sure it wasn't too cold. "You and your poor mother ..."

Olga stopped short, not finishing her statement.

"What do you mean, 'my poor mother,'" Annie furrowed her brow at Olga and demanded an answer. For years, Annie had asked and asked about her father. Millie would only say he left them, never to be heard from again. Millie told Annie he was in the military and could be just about anywhere by now and didn't want anything to do with having a family. He especially didn't want a baby.

If Olga knew something about Annie's father, she meant to get it out of her.

"Did you know my father?" she demanded.

"Well ... no, that's just what I heard and all," Olga continued on. "And then there was your situation and Vady's ... it just goes on and on."

Annie was uncomfortable with the direction the conversation was taking. She wanted to know more about her father but didn't want to talk about Noah Castle. Olga had placed the two of them in the same category – interchangeable for conversational purposes.

"You brought it up child," Olga lectured Annie, who had now crossed her arms and drew up a harder facial expression. "If you don't want to talk about it then maybe we shouldn't continue."

Annie was thinking the same thing ... end this conversation

now. She softened her approach in an attempt to get answers one last time.

"But do you know where the rest of them are?" Annie pressed on; getting the idea that Olga just wanted to keep her on the porch. It wouldn't have been in her best interest to give too much information. That would lead to a hasty visit and Annie had now been there for over thirty minutes.

"I heard tell Dorie and Asher are in Virginia and Jaygar is somewhere in Pennsylvania, around Harrisburg," Olga made a motion of putting on her thinking cap and tying it. "… I'm not even sure Billie Jean is still alive at all; you know she drank so much all the time. Her liver probably got ate up by the cirrhosis. That's about all I know, Annie. I'm sorry, but the Cleaving family has been spread so far here and yon, like I said before."

Annie hugged Olga while she was still sitting, "Can I help you back inside?"

"No, you go on. I'm going to sit out here and see if anybody comes by," Olga said, looking down the street at the neighbors' houses, as if she could see that far.

The rain was coming harder now. Annie was soggy now like the rope from the clothesline. It felt good to be sloppy wet; she felt rebellious tromping out into the rain in her nice work clothes, sweating and getting grass on the bottom of her trouser legs.

Once inside, Annie went to her bedroom and took out a ledger from her grandmother's chifforobe. Millie's old address book turned up in the hands of the funeral director. It must have come over with Annie's mother from the hospital. He gave it to Annie. She remembered opening the pages and seeing her mother's handwriting – so sloppy and nearly illegible. She was grateful to have the book, even if it was outdated. Seeing her mother's handwriting was comforting. Sometimes she would take it out just to look at it, pretending her mother had just written it yesterday like a grocery list Annie would carry as she picked up things at the store.

There it was – "Vady" or Veda's address. She had always lived in the same place in Trench, just over the Stig County line.

CHAPTER FOUR

The four-lane from Rayes County to Stig could have been a two-lane and folks would have managed just fine. The five or six people in Stig County who *had* jobs were the only ones who used the road – at least that's what everyone said. When people in Rayes County started to feel a bit sorry for themselves, they needed only look over their shoulders toward Stig; that would put everything into perspective. The new road brought a few years of false hope when it was under construction. The purpose was to bring the workforce out of Stig and into Rayes. Problem was, even people in Rayes County had a hard time finding jobs. Political promises brought only empty buildings that industry kept passing by for bigger cities with even bigger tax incentives. This, Annie understood – taxes, money and economic boons and busts. Numbers were definite, exact. She was sure of them, always. Two and two were always going to be four no matter what happened. Through war, famine and even the end of the world, Annie knew the answer would always be four. She also knew that until the mathematical formula was complete – jobs, plus workforce, plus supply, plus demand – the four-lane to Stig County would remain mostly untraveled.

The city of Trench, rightfully named, looked like a trench. Just near the highway, almost right up against the road was Main Street. If you didn't stop, you could pass the entire town in less than two minutes. Annie turned on her right signal, waited five seconds, as if she needed to, and then directed her tires toward the sign, "Welcome to Trench." Just over the railroad tracks, the first business in town welcomed travelers. Years ago, Baker Wholesale was the exact name, but time and weather had stolen parts of it away. About half the letters from the building had fallen off or disappeared – it now read __k_r Wh___s_le. One of the running jokes over at Rayes County was that when the last letter fell from Baker's they would close the town of Trench right along with their one and only business. Bakers would order everything from candy to toothpaste in bulk and then sell to various small mom and pop stores in Stig County. But with the coming of the big box superstores and club stores, places like Baker's had become obsolete. Still, Baker's continued to be listed in the Yellow Pages and its doors were open every day – even if only to give old Jake Baker something to do so he wouldn't have to spend all his time with his bully of a wife Kathleen.

The roads were shorter and narrower than Annie remembered. She would make a turn and then instantly have to make another. The streets were all named for garden vegetables. Annie had always thought this was cute. Veda lived on Pea Vine Street, which was right off Half Runner Circle. Most everyone in Trench lived in this cluster of tiny white, off-white and yellow homes. Veda's house was just as Annie remembered it, only smaller. It was a one-bedroom, white sided house with black shutters. She had a small front porch with flower beds on either side. There was the same metal glider in the same place Annie remembered it. It had been painted a light green color – pastel. Little pink and green handmade throw pillows were positioned perfectly. Annie always thought Veda's house looked like a playhouse – and it still did.

Annie started to wonder if maybe no one was home. She hadn't called ahead, and the house looked vacant and dim through the windows. Annie knocked lightly at first and then after a few seconds a little harder. There was some movement from within. A shadow cut through a small beam of light stretching through the kitchen. Room by room, lights began to shine, and Annie could see Veda clearly through the diamond-shaped window of the front door walking toward her.

"Yes?" Veda asked as she opened the door only as far as the chain latch would allow.

Annie felt her heart jump a little when she heard Veda's voice. She sounded so much like Annie's mother. Then, in an instant, she was sad for having heard it. She wondered how she would get through this visit, hearing that voice.

"Aunt Veda?"

A few seconds later, the door closed and then opened again.

"Oh my gosh," Veda said gushing. "I haven't seen you since you were a girl. Annie, you look just like your mother – I thought I had died and gone back to my young days. I half expected to look down and see those old roller skates she used to keep on her feet. What on Earth are you doing over here in Trench? Everything alright?"

"Roller skates?" Annie asked puzzled.

"Oh Lordy, she loved those roller skates – wore them everywhere, even in the house," Veda continued, smiling. "Momma would get so mad at her, but she didn't care – just kept right on. She could skate backward, spin around on one foot, jump over chairs."

"Really?" Annie said, disbelieving her ears. "Really?!" She repeated again, shaking her head.

"Oh yes," Veda said. "Your mother … Oh, your mother … I was so jealous of her – never afraid of anything …"

Veda suddenly came back from the past for a moment and realized Annie was there in the present, "What are you doing way over here?"

Annie relayed the information on to Veda just as it was explained to her about the Cleaving house deed, leaving nothing out other than the fact that she wanted to leave Rayes County.

Veda listened intently to what Annie was saying and nodded her head several times to let Annie know she understood.

"Are you following all this?"

"Yes, yes. I understand," Annie watched as her aunt's expression went from gleeful to somber. It made her uneasy – maybe this wouldn't be as easy as she thought.

Veda looked away from Annie and stared for what seemed like minutes out the big picture window. She gazed through the sheer curtains. Her eyes would at times move to the floor but always stop back out the window. Tears came and then she fought them back. Annie was afraid to interrupt.

In the living room, where Veda had finally asked Annie to sit, there were piles and stacks of envelopes and letters everywhere. Six stacks at least a foot high on the coffee table; two stacks each on the end tables – those were a foot or more tall, too. There were piles in the corners of the room, and it looked like a new stack was beginning just at the front door.

The dolls were still there, just as Annie remembered them – and there were more, too. The bride dolls had acquired their own glass cabinet since the last visit. Some of their dresses had browned in the summer sun, their faces now yellow. Veda had made scarves for the shelves out of eyelet lace and had crocheted edging around them to hang over, making poufs and droops of fancy white detail. It looked soft. Annie wanted to scoop the lace up in her hands and squeeze it, holding it to her face.

The baby dolls now had their own shelves. They wore new clothes of thick, colorful yarn – the girls in their frilly dresses and the boys in their jumpers. All of them had hats and booties to match their outfits. The girls had tiny yarn purses and the boys held footballs and basketballs made of yarn.

The celebrity dolls had their own room now; Annie could see Elvis donning his black leather suit peering out of the bedroom.

"I'm so sorry the place is such a mess," Veda's eyes darted about the small room. She had seen Annie's reaction to the piles of old mail. "But I'm going through something right now – it's just that I haven't had any time to focus on much else."

Veda pulled a used tissue from between the sofa cushions. She formed it like a lady's handkerchief who had just stepped out of a stagecoach. She dabbed at her eyes then held it close to her lips.

"The letters here in this room – I have a bedroom full of even more of them. I just really don't even know how to tell you this, Annie, I am sure God sent you here for a reason today. I've needed someone to talk to for a long time. I just feel so bad about it." "What is it, Veda?" Annie was growing impatient with the drama, "What?"

"Annie, I am seeing a married man."

Annie's eyebrows raised and her eyes widened in disbelief.

"What?"

"Oh, Annie. Oh, Annie," Veda said, shaking her head as if to relay her shame. "He's very powerful, very powerful and wealthy. He's wealthy with the spirit of the Lord and God has blessed him with money because he's such a good prophet."

Annie kept looking toward the front door, wondering if she should leave. Veda got up and began to gather some of the letters from the stacks. She then went into her bedroom and brought out a wooden box.

"Sit down here next to me, Annie, and I'll just show you," Veda was direct and certain as if to alleviate any doubt Annie might have.

Annie got up from the nearby chair and sat next to Veda on the couch. Her aunt began opening envelopes. The letters had been opened before and placed carefully back inside the wooden box. Veda was putting careful thought into the order of how the letters should be presented. Her hair was just as Annie remembered it – long hair, down to her butt. It was wavy, not curly, never pinned up. It hung long again today and even lay on the couch at her bottom when she sat down. It was almost all grey now. Annie could see a glimpse of dark color from time to time as her aunt would sometimes smooth her hair from underneath as she spoke. While she was looking through the letters and rummaging through the wooden box, her once-glorious mane hung sparsely around her pale cheek. Her face, once plump and pink, now held the look of old cotton just after the spin cycle. Her ears had grown larger over the years and her pitted and porous nose, too. Her 1960s horn-rimmed glasses were smartly perched there. Gravity had pulled her breasts closer to her waist than need be. Veda could have done herself a favor and rolled those things up neatly and stuffed them in a support bra.

Annie remembered how her mother would talk about Veda and how pretty she was as a girl. "Those big brown eyes, long wavy hair and creamy complexion took many boys to their knees as she blew by them like a fresh spring breeze." Millie would smile as she spoke of her sister. Millie always had nice things to say about everyone and that's one of the reasons Annie never put much faith in what her mother said about Veda's good looks. After all, Millie always said those kinds of things about Annie, too. All Annie had to do was look in the mirror to see that her mother was exaggerating. Still, looking at Veda today, Annie could see glimpses of attractiveness that time had faded. Annie's mother used to say there was only one escape from getting older. Annie used to fear old age – and dying. Not now, she almost wished it so during close calls in the car – if an eighteen-wheeler passed her too close, she would imagine being hit head on and closing her eyes to rest with Ethan. She would sometimes imagine falling, if she were at the top of the staircase at work. It used to take her breath away to look down from the top, but not anymore. It just seemed so easy to just fall and not get up. She didn't want to get old like Veda. It wasn't the wrinkles, the big nose or the grey hair that scared her though; it was living day after day knowing that once she had been happy and, in an instant, it was gone, never to return. To live like that for the next forty years seemed unbearable.

"Here, look at this one first," Veda shoved a letter onto Annie's lap.

Annie began to read to herself ... "Dear Sister Veda ..."

"No, read it out loud," Veda said sternly. "You can't get the full effect unless we can hear the words."

Annie was startled by Veda's sharp demand.

"Dear Sister Veda," Annie read nervously. "I feel so blessed to have you in my flock. You are a beautiful person, and the Lord has given you to this congregation to shine your beauty onto us. Never hide your light, Sister Veda, always shine it so the Lord can work through you."

"See, Annie, this is how it started," Veda sighed. "He started subtle – telling me how beautiful I was and how I shouldn't hide my feelings for him – see there," Veda pointed to the part in the letter that read: *Never hide your light* ...

In fact, Veda had highlighted it, circled it, underlined it more than once and put stars around it. Annie could tell from the different colors and the different shades of faded ink that these marks had been made at different times. The paper had begun to resemble fabric, the way parchment looks after being handled time and again.

"Then," Veda shoved another letter onto Annie's lap, this one longer. "He sent this one, too. Read it," Veda urged Annie, nodding her head. "Go on, read it."

"Dear Sister Veda," Annie started again and began scanning the rest of the page. There were more underlines, circles and stars – more highlights. Again, she noticed that this letter, too, had been handled many times. "I am so pleased you are continuing to shine your light on our congregation. Don't ever let it go out. The Lord is depending on beautiful souls like you to continue to do good works."

"See Annie," Veda began pointing to the markings she had made. "Right here, again he wants me to continue to not hide my light for him."

Veda could see Annie's faith in her was waning.

"Well, you have to read between the lines so to speak, but it's there," Veda poked at the paper with her yellowed fingernail. "Oh, believe me, it's there."

Annie was nodding her head in agreement mainly because she simply didn't know what else to do.

Veda pulled out all the envelopes from the wooden box, hurriedly tossing them on the coffee table.

"And Annie what man sends a woman jewelry if he doesn't have strong feelings for her?" Veda asked almost pleadingly, revealing a ring and a bracelet on a tissue hidden at the bottom.

"And he always signs his letters 'with love'," Veda poked her finger at the closing of the letter. "See there, see there."

Again, Annie nodded, not knowing what else to do. She wondered now if Veda had even acknowledged what she had told her about the house, about the deed.

"Aunt Veda," Annie started to speak quietly and slowly as not to alarm her aunt, who now seemed a little on edge. "All these letters, all these stacks are they *all* from him?"

"No, not all of them," Veda said sharply. "Some of them are from this other preacher; he's a fine man and all and he *has* shown some interest in me. But Brother Southerland is the more sincere of the two and he always answers me back when I write to him. Brother Eli Southerland knows my troubles. He prays for me, and he prays for us, so the Lord will make it so we can be together someday."

"Why does he send you jewelry?" Annie began to question her aunt's logic. "And what is he doing exactly to make it so you two can be together?"

"Why does any man send a woman jewelry?" Veda seemed angry that Annie was asking questions. "Because he loves me and so I will know not to give up."

Veda was out of breath now, "he says to wear it in good faith and remember him fondly in my prayers. So, I know that's what he means for me to do – remember that we will be together some day."

Annie kept nodding in agreement to everything Veda said. Her aunt was beginning to even look crazy now. Annie wasn't sure if she had looked like that from the beginning of the conversation or not – her eyes were open wider, and her brow scrunched tighter than before. Maybe she had looked crazy from the moment Annie got there.

"What would *you* do, Annie? What would you do if you were me? You know he's married, but so unhappy. I see them on the television together and you can just tell she doesn't love him; you can tell he doesn't want to be with her – wish you could see them together," Veda would stop briefly between sentences to see if Annie was going to respond.

"Well, Aunt Veda, I don't know what I would do just yet," Annie said. "May I read some more of these letters? You know, just to get a better idea of what's been going on."

"Yes, I think you should," Veda shook her head vigorously, excited that Annie wanted to know more. "You look at whatever you need to; just put everything back like it was. Can I get you something to drink?"

"Yes. A Diet Coke if you have it," Annie remembered the empty cartons of Diet Coke out on the front porch.

"Oh yes, I have Diet Coke," Veda was pleased with herself that she could fill Annie's request. "I'll be right back."

Annie was glad to be alone, even for just a moment, to wrap her head around everything she had just heard, to try and figure out how to move the conversation back to the deed, and to have a closer look at all these letters from Eli Southerland. Annie had seen him on television but always clicked on by. Had she known her Aunt Veda and he had a "thing" going on; she might have stopped to take a closer look at him. From what she could remember, he always had on a different colored suit – burgundy, green – not natural suit colors. She had at least seen those two colors. He had large, white elevated hair. The sides were his, but it was obvious the big pouf part on top was a hair piece. Annie walked around the room picking up a letter here and there from different piles; some from the floor, some from the table. She read each piece as quickly as she could and skimmed through some others along the way. It appeared that Brother Southerland was giving tokens of appreciation for sizeable donations – at least what would have been sizeable to Veda. She lived on a fixed income; even fifty dollars would have been a stretch for her. There was a definitive pattern, the bigger the donation, the larger and more personal the token. On one of the brochure-type mail pieces, Annie saw where a "Love Ring" was offered as a token of appreciation for a one-hundred-dollar gift as an "Opportunity to join him in love with the Lord." From what Annie could see around Veda's house, there was no way she could afford to give a hundred dollars to Southerland.

Annie took one of the letters and put it in her purse. She wasn't sure what she was going to do with it, she just felt someone had to try and do something.

"So, what did you find? More of the same I s'pose."

Veda gave Annie the glass, peering over her and looking at the letter she was reading. She seemed confident that her niece had come to the same conclusion – Eli Southerland was in love with her.

"Yes, Veda, more of the same," Annie wasn't sure she wanted to get involved but wanted to at least try and reason with her. "But you know, Aunt Veda, I've been thinking about this while you've been in the kitchen, and I've been reading some of these letters. I just think that if Eli Southerland was a truly good Christian man, he would leave his wife and get an outright divorce from her before starting anything up with you."

"Don't you think I've heard that before?" Veda was taken by surprise that Annie still questioned Eli's motives. "You all just don't understand him. If he left his wife, then who would take care of her? You know she's just not very bright. You would think that common sense people like you and Leslie could see that. And what about the flock? The Devil has made sure that this is so complicated that the congregation wouldn't understand. It would just never do to tell them, to tell his wife …," out of breath, Veda stopped talking and wiped her mouth with the tissue she was still holding.

Leslie – now that was a name Annie hadn't heard in quite some time. He was Veda's only living son. The other one was killed in service in some foreign country – Chester was his name. Leslie, the lady's man, liked his women trashy and for that he had paid a price. He had been shot twice by either ex-husbands or boyfriends; Annie couldn't really remember which. He spent time in jail for everything from assault to terroristic threatening.

Annie's mother always said, "A man who thinks he's pretty will only be pretty and not much else." Annie never really understood what her mother was trying to tell her with this ridiculous saying, until she met a man who thought he was pretty – Ethan's father. Everything passed him by while he was busy looking in the mirror – to him, perception was everything. Veda's son, Leslie, was much the same. Annie remembered him vaguely – strong cologne, curly blonde hair and colorful silk shirts unbuttoned almost down to his belly button. Jewelry hung from his neck onto furry, bare chest. Looking back, Annie understood completely what Millie was trying to tell her. Pretty had cost Leslie his whole life and that's really all he ever had to show for his efforts – what he considered to be his good looks – until he got older. Annie had noticed the family photos as she came into Veda's house, but she had been too busy thinking of how to approach Veda regarding the signing of the deed, to worry much about them. She was struck by the picture of Chester in his uniform right away. It was hard to miss. He had the look of a Rayes County boy, rugged and leather-skinned from summer days gone by. After more in-depth observation, while Aunt Veda was still trying to explain to

Annie why Eli Southerland could never leave his wife, Annie decided that the other photos were indeed Leslie. He wasn't pretty at all – graying around his hairline and quite a bit overweight. It appeared as if many years of drinking had finally caught up with him – he had a Santa belly to go with his white, curly hair, even looked jolly sitting there with his wife and children.

"What does Leslie say about Eli Southerland and you?" Annie interrupted Veda's rambling.

Veda stopped talking for a moment and then continued after she had thought about what her response should be.

"Your cousin Leslie doesn't understand," Veda said, looking concerned. "We've tried to talk about it, but I just think he can't stand the thought of me being with another man other than his father. That's the only reason I can come up with why he is so opposed to it. He even telephoned Eli – boy that could've been a disaster if his wife had found out – and told him to stop writing to me. Well, I knew what he did, and I called Eli's staff and told them to continue Eli's letters to me."

Annie was relieved to hear that someone was trying to stop this man of God from taking Veda to the cleaners.

"How is Leslie? Is that his family?" Annie asked pointing to the picture above the sofa.

"Yes, that's his wife and son, Jamie," Veda said proudly. "He finally settled down and found him a nice girl. Oh, Annie, she's so sweet. Takes care of me like I was her own mother. She brings me magazines and yarn and sits and talks with me when they come around to visit. I really like her."

"Well," Annie said. "It sounds like Leslie really straightened right up. I know Momma used to say he was quite the lady's man."

Veda laughed and nodded, giving Annie's knee a slap. "Yes, yes he was. It got him into some trouble a time or two. I was so glad when he found my little Glenna – that's his wife's name."

"I knew she was the one right away," Veda was very normal now, like any doting mother. The transition had been seamless from the crazy talk of Eli Southerland. "Only he didn't, at first. It took a little help from me and your mother to make him see it that way."

"My mother?" Annie knew her mother was no match maker. "What did the two of you do?"

"If you ever tell a word of this, I'll deny it all," Veda was twisting a bit as she spoke, like a kindergartner with a secret. "Aww… just kidding, I know you won't tell. You're a good Cleaving girl; that means *you* know how to keep a secret."

"Leslie and Glenna had just started dating," Veda stared straight at the wall where the picture hung as if she were pulling the memory straight out of the photograph. "Oh, I really, really liked her and I wanted to keep her – well, in truth, *all* of us wanted to keep her. I mean compared to some of that trash he was bringing home all the time, my little Glenna was a saint."

The woman in the photo looked a little rough around the edges but Annie could see how she could still be considered a saint by Veda.

"Well, of course, Leslie was starting to get a bit restless after a month or two of courtin' – you know he always did get antsy real easy," Veda delivered the explanation with a certainty only a mother could carry. "Leslie had started hound doggin' around with the mayor's wife – Ella Westerly. She was sleeping with one of the lawyers here in town – and don't ask me who – I can't tell you and I won't tell you," Veda scolded Annie though she hadn't even asked who. "Well, it was that night that the mayor and Ella were at dinner at Conley's – used to be a fancy place to eat over in Trace on the other side of Stig County. A hired man came in and shot John Westerly. Killed him dead right there."

"It never came out who paid that man to kill Westerly but we all know who it was," Veda said whispering to Annie. "It was the lawyer his wife was cohortin' with. Well, you know, they're married now. Have been nigh on seventeen years or so."

"Well, I called your mother just a bawlin'. I just couldn't take no more. I was at my wit's end with the women and the partyin' and goings on around here. And when I heard that man had been shot and I knew that Leslie was courtin' around his wife, I just went crazy."

"Well, Millie called up her old beau Buck Rosen – you know the old sheriff over there in Rayes?" Veda never missed a beat and intended to go right into the story.

"My mother never dated Buck Rosen. You have that wrong, Veda." Annie scooted close to the edge of her seat and gave her aunt a look of pity. Now, she was sure this story was made up – had to be.

"No, they dated," Veda said nodding vigorously. "They were real sweethearts, those two. Everybody knows that."

Veda seemed so sure, but then again, Annie thought, she is also sure Eli Southerland is sending her love letters.

"No, Veda – I really don't think you've got the right person." Annie dipped her head a little as if she were trying to find something hidden in Veda's eyes.

"Nothing ever came up in all your dealings with that Rosen boy?" Veda was sorry the second the question left her lips. She put her hand up to her mouth, but it was too late – the words had already been spoken.

Annie's blood ran cold, and her chest was suddenly tight. She could only take shallow breaths. The room was starting to spin.

"You all right?" Veda said, grabbing Annie's arm as she swayed. "I'm sorry, Annie. I didn't mean to say …"

"Yeah. I'm okay. I just need to use your restroom." Annie moved quickly out from behind the coffee table, scooting as she did.

Once inside the bathroom and away from Veda, Annie soaked her hands with cold water and then held them to her face, her hands so hot the cold water felt warm as she touched it to her skin. Veda was mistaken – confused, crazy even. Annie would just get the deed signed and pretend Veda never said them. Someone would have said something after the crash if that were true – Annie's mother would have told her. No one ever mentioned it, not even during Jacob Rosen's trial.

"Everything okay?" Veda asked as Annie sat back down on the couch.

"Yes. I'm fine. It's just something I ate earlier that didn't agree with me."

"Do you want to lie down? You look a little pale."

"No, no. I'm fine. Please Aunt Veda go ahead and finish the story," Annie wanted to hurry and get out of there.

"Okay, okay – Buck Rosen," Veda seemed to be grasping for her memory, looking at Annie for permission. Annie nodded to let her know it was fine to continue.

"Yeah, he and Millie got some serious when she was younger, but it didn't work out because of this or that … you know. I would've thought your mother would've mentioned it to you – Buck is nothing to be ashamed of, you know, he was an awful handsome fella in those days."

Annie felt sick again but was consoled by that fact that Veda was a delusional nut case. She was convinced now more than ever that the man who gave life to a monster could never have dated Millie Cleaving. Buck may have helped Millie straighten out Veda's wayward son, but they never, in a million years, dated. Annie was sure of that.

"Anyway, Rosen came over here to Stig County and pulled Leslie out of this very house," Veda looked around as if someone might be listening. "Put a bag over his head and took him to the police car and out into the woods. He told Leslie that he was arresting him for the murder of Mayor Westerly."

Annie looked shocked at Veda; her eyes open wide.

"Now, don't go and judge an old lady just yet," Veda mistook Annie's disbelief for disapproval. "I know it sounds a little harsh, but it was the only way. Me and Millie knew Buck would never hurt Leslie. And we knew that if something wasn't done, Leslie might be the next one with a bullet in his chest. He was headed that way you know – hangin' over there at that bar with all those married women. It was shameful and downright dangerous." Veda slapped her fist into the palm of her hand with each syllable of her sentence. She looked like a damnation preacher, maybe like Brother Southerland. Annie thought it was ironic Veda wasn't aware that her current predicament with the married Eli Southerland might be shameful as well.

"Buck told Leslie, while the bag was still over his head," Veda continued, looking around again as if someone might be eavesdropping. "That he was going to let him go even though he was the prime suspect in the murder. He also told him that if he ever caught him over at the Sunrise Room again that he would arrest him on the spot and charge him with Westerly's murder."

Veda leaned in toward Annie, crossing her arms. "It scared him straight. It wasn't too long after that the Sunrise Room was closed – thank God in Heaven for that. And, not two months later, Leslie and Glenna were married. Straightened him right up – your mother probably saved his life. I guess she knew after I'd lost Chester, I couldn't stand to lose another son."

Veda got quiet for a moment then spoke, "That's something me and you have in common, you know, Annie. We both know what it feels like to have our hearts ripped from our bodies. You just don't get over that."

Annie gave a smile of doubt and gratitude that this story had included her mother, but she knew Millicent Cleaving would never have been party to something so unethical, so illegal.

As if Veda were reading Annie's thoughts, she leaned over and whispered, "You know your mother wasn't always so quiet. She used to be anything but quiet. I miss her so –but even when she was here, we all missed that person she used to be. Our good ole' Millie was gone way before she died."

Annie felt sorry for Veda. Maybe it made her feel better to say her sister was "gone" before she even died. The irony in her statement was almost comical.

Veda stopped talking abruptly then stared out the window for a few moments. Excusing herself from the living room, she returned quickly with the deed Annie had given her when she arrived. Annie scanned it quickly – it was signed. Veda also handed Annie a little black address book.

"You're going to need this," Veda said, tapping the address book with her index finger to illustrate its importance. "Without it, you won't get very far trying to find that ole Cleaving clan."

Annie flipped through it quickly.

"Thank you, Veda," Annie was relieved. She was beginning to think that Veda had forgotten all about why she came there in the first place.

"No need to thank me child." Veda stroked Annie's hair as she spoke.

Veda went over to the cabinet where the baby dolls were kept and pulled one of the little boys off his shelf.

"Here, I've been saving something for you."

He was wearing a light brown shirt and a pair of shorts made of the same thick yarn, only in dark brown. His little yarn tennis shoes were laced with light tan strings. Everything matched – right down to his crocheted ball cap. He carried a baseball, also made of yarn. He had big brown eyes and long eyelashes.

Veda cradled the doll for a moment as if to say, "goodbye," then gave him a little squeeze and placed him in Annie's arms.

"Oh, Veda, he's beautiful."

"I named this one Ethan," Veda patted him on the head.

Annie's eyes got hot and wet as she watched her aunt fiddle carefully with his hands and then tie up tight his loose little bootie.

Veda was always very protective over her dolls; everyone knew better than to ask for one. She kept them all, never gave any of them away and never let anyone hold them. Annie remembered as a little girl trying to play with one. Veda had come and quickly grabbed it away almost as if it were a real child. She then carefully dusted it off. Millie explained to Annie that Veda's dolls were like her own children. To have them on the shelves, safe and warm and where she could see them, made her feel the same way Annie felt each night when Millie would tuck her in and kiss her goodnight.

"I never knew what your little baby looked like," Veda looked deeply into Annie's eyes. "I never laid sight on the little angel. I only saw that mangled car in the newspaper after it happened – that awful, mangled mess of a car. And to think that Buck's son did that is just awful. I am surprised you survived it, Annie. Your mother was so sad that Ethan died but so happy you made it through. I sent flowers to the funeral home you know. But, Annie, I just couldn't bear to come to his service. I just couldn't. If anyone could understand why, I know you could."

Annie thought for a moment about what Veda was trying to tell her and *did* know exactly what she was talking about. Since Ethan's death, Annie couldn't bear to attend a funeral. She even took the back-road home from work to keep from passing the funeral home where Ethan's service was held.

"Don't worry about it, Veda," Annie hugged her aunt. "I do understand. No apologies are necessary. And, I *do* remember the flowers, they were beautiful. And the baby doll – I'll treasure it always."

Annie folded the deed and placed it carefully in her purse, said her good-byes and got in her car. She took little Ethan and put him in the seat beside her. She even buckled him in. It brought her comfort to see him sitting there in the car.

Maybe, she thought, Aunt Veda isn't so crazy after all.

"You'll bring that address book back when you've found everyone," Aunt Veda hollered to Annie as she was getting ready to pull out of the drive. "And when you find new addresses and phone numbers add them in there."

Annie nodded and waved, "I will."

CHAPTER FIVE

Annie placed the little Ethan doll carefully on the couch, pulled the deed and address book from her purse and went into the kitchen. Everything had to be perfect before she opened that book – coffee within her reach, phone on the table in case she needed to contact someone in a hurry and a legal pad and good pen. She also grabbed the phone book as a backup.

She began fingering through Veda's little black book, slowly this time, so as not to miss anything. Veda's handwriting was a lot like Annie's mother's – lots of points and jags. Many women Annie knew from that generation had that same type of handwriting. The women at work penned notes with those same familiar disarrayed marks.

Since most of the addresses and phone numbers from Veda's book were all Cleaving family members, the first few pages were empty except for some notes. When the Cs began, so did the chaos. There were lots of different types of ink and some of the pages were torn and then taped back together. Addresses and phone numbers were marked through, and new ones added in the margins.

Since most everyone in the book was a Cleaving family member, Veda's alphabetical system was just about non-existent. Annie could see Veda's beginnings of a structured system. The Cs began with those Cleavings whose first names began with A and so on. She could tell that after so many years and changes to the book and to the Cleaving family, Veda had given in to the disorder of the listings and just went with it.

Annie turned page after page, examining all the different places the Cleaving children had been – Cleveland, Pittsburg, Atlanta …

Then, there it was, the listing for Millicent L. Cleaving, with several lines under her name that had been marked out. Annie tried to make out what they said but these had all been marked through thoroughly.

By this time, Annie had discarded her old list of the Cleaving children, opting for a new, more organized list – this one by location. She drew a make-shift map of the US on her yellow legal pad. She had always been good at geography and loved maps – had a collection of old maps – state by state. On her hand-drawn map, she began to plot points. She began with Veda and marked Trench, Kentucky as close as she could get it next to Millie in Rayes County. She made a list of her mother's brothers and sisters, putting her mother and Veda on the list just so she could put a check mark by their names. It made her feel she was making at least some progress toward her plan, which was plainly stated at the bottom of the page in big blocky letters, "PLAN FOR LEAVING."

It wasn't that Annie had to remind herself of why she was going to all this trouble; she simply wanted to see it outright. If she could have put it on a spreadsheet and then imported the data into a pie chart or line graph, she would have; and then measured her progress daily. For her purposes, she decided a plain list would do just fine.

Virginia – 4 hours away; Harrisburg – 14 hours away; New

Jersey – 12 hours away … she kept on until she was finished …
Louisville – 3 hours away …

Annie's list was coming together nicely with one exception,
Asher Cleaving. Annie remembered the one time she'd met Asher.
He came to Rayes County and stayed with them for about a week,
then just left. He mostly slept. He had long hair, with some gray in
it. He wore a split leather vest over a silk shirt with little round
wire-rimmed glasses; they were cracked on one side across the top.
Annie was in high school when Asher came to visit. In some ways
it seemed like he was there forever – it was prom week at Rayes
County High School and every time Annie needed the bathroom, it
seemed like her Uncle Asher had it all tied up. She did remember
how much more comfortable she felt when he was gone. Her
mother had told her to make him feel welcome because he was
family. Annie tried but instead opted for making herself scarce,
volunteering to stay after school for prom decorating and cleaning
up the gym for the big event. Just seeing Asher's name brought
back memories of high school, junior prom and her heartbreak
over not having a real date. Annie went with one of her friends
who didn't have a date either – the two of them bought matching
dresses – Annie's was pink, Sherry's was blue, but other than that
they were exactly the same. After graduation, Sherry went to
college and Annie never knew what became of her. Sherry's parents
moved away several years ago. Annie remembered seeing their
house for sale and then hearing through the Rayes County
grapevine that they were retiring – going to Florida.

Annie's map was full of all the Cleaving offspring, except one
– Asher. His address was listed: Asher Cleaving, Sunshine Family
of Peace – camped in Rayes County then to Blue Ridge State Park.

"Sunshine Family of Peace," Annie's voice broke through the
silent Cleaving house. It sounded odd to her to hear it. She rarely
spoke at all while in the house – there was no one to talk to – only
the dishes in the cupboard, the old furniture and appliances to hear

her sarcastic one-liners. "Figures."

Frustrated, Annie got up and poured herself another cup of coffee. She walked around the kitchen a bit, pacing and wondering where to begin. She thought about going all the way north and then working her way back, then she thought about going south and working her way north. That didn't help her where Asher was concerned. Annie picked up the big-mouth ceramic frog from the top of the sink. It belonged to her grandmother and for as long as Annie could remember, its place in life had been right there on Lucy Cleaving's sink holding her sponges and scouring pads in its big oval-shaped mouth. It reminded Annie of what her favorite accounting teacher used to say, "Eat your frog first," Mr. J.R. Landry would sometimes say to the class before they left each day. He had explained to them at the beginning of the semester to always do the hardest problem first when approaching the homework, or "eat the frog." That was his metaphor. "That way," he'd say, "you have the guts and the glory to finish the job."

That's exactly what Annie was going to do – eat her "frog" first then maybe the guts and glory would emerge. Ironic that the glory would be finding Asher Cleaving.

Annie had made her split-second decision, picked up the phone and dialed, "Mary in the newsroom, please. Yes, I can hold."

Annie listened to the hold music – old 70s hits from WRAY in Rayes County. It was taking a long time. She was nervous thinking Mary might be too busy to help her. Maybe, Annie thought, she was just being nice when she had offered to help before.

"Hello, this is Mary."

"Hey, Mary, I hate to bother you, but I need some advice."

"Annie?"

"Yes, Mary, it's me, Annie. I forgot to tell you who I was. Sorry."

"No, Annie, that's perfectly fine. I was just going to call you today."

Annie stopped pacing with the phone, surprised that Mary would be planning to call her.

"Yes, I found the two addresses you needed in Pennsylvania, and I e-mailed them over to you," Mary always talked fast like she was in a race to get the words out. "I was going to give you a call and make sure you got them."

"I haven't had time to check my e-mail yet – just got back from Stig County visiting with my Aunt Veda. And Mary," Annie was excited. "I got my first deed signed."

"That's great. You're chipping away at it already."

"Yeah," Annie said. "I do feel like I've made some progress. Aunt Veda also loaned me her little black book, inked full of Cleaving addresses. I'll cross check the ones I have in Pennsylvania with the ones you found, and we'll see if we get matches."

"How accurate do you think the little black book is?" Mary talked about the book as if it were evidence in a courtroom trial.

"I think it's going to be dead on," it seemed abnormal for Annie to be having what sounded like an every-day conversation, but she was enjoying it. "I can tell that she's updated it several times over the years. That was another reason I wanted to call you was to tell you that I think I have all I need other than maybe some help finding my Uncle Asher."

"Oh?"

"Yes, he is listed in Veda's book as camping with the Sunshine

Family of Peace in Virginia. Can you help me find out what this is?"

"Oh my God, you're kidding?" Mary sounded as if Annie had just located Deep throat from the Watergate scandal.

"You've heard of this thing?" Annie was surprised.

"Oh, I've heard of them. They're quite the phenomenon around the country."

"Phenomenon?"

"Yes. It's all very Bohemian," Mary said. "It's a group of old hippies who basically don't want to work so they claim they are spreading peace by example. They've chucked away all their worldly possessions, as if any of them really had that much to begin with, and they camp on federal lands for thirty days at a time. Federal law allows anyone the right to stay on federal property for thirty days, believe me, I think in some year's past they tried to run them out of Rayes County over by Lake Curry, couldn't do it until the thirty days were up. Anyway, they camp ..." Mary stopped. "I can't believe you have an uncle who is a Sunshiner!"

"Sunshiner?"

"Yeah, that's what people call them," Mary was extremely excited and pleased to have so much insight regarding the Sunshiners. "They go from town to town and when they get there, they usually end up causing a lot of trouble – stealing from local stores, burning in the forest when they shouldn't and in some cases, they've been caught selling pot to locals."

"Wow," was about all Annie could get out at this point. Trying to picture the Asher Cleaving she remembered as a hippie wasn't a stretch. "So, how do you know so much about them?"

"I've got a friend who is a reporter over in Virginia. It sounds right that your uncle would have been there with them – there are so many state parks over there and federal forest land – anyway, my friend has told me about them. They go there, to Virginia, a lot I gather."

"So, how do you know when they will be ...?"

Mary interrupted Annie, "They have a schedule. It's quite organized; and they have a website too. It has a few photos and a sketchy list of where they're going to be. I have no idea who puts all this together for them."

"Do you really think it's the same people?"

"It has to be," Mary said with certainty. "There's only one group of them ... it *has* to be. There's no way it could be anything else. There is the question of whether your uncle is still with them. How old do you think the black book entry is?"

"Well, it's hard to tell," Annie said. "But maybe if you can find where ..."

"I've already done it, Annie – just looked up the Web site ... and yeah, they're in Virginia again right now. They must really, really like it there. It looks like they've been all over the state this summer and it looks like they're heading south for the winter. So, take your pick – it's Virginia now or Florida near the Everglades this winter."

"Where?"

"Blue Ridge Mountain State Park, where else?" Annie knew Mary must have been laughing at the idea of a bunch of hippies communing in such a revered tourist destination. Annie could see the humor as well. "I see from the list you gave me that you have a Virginia visit anyway – Cleda Cleaving?"

Annie quickly flipped through the little black book and found

Cleda. "Yes, she still lives there. It's a small city around the beaches – Goldbug. I remember her from when I was a little girl. Me and Momma used to visit her."

"Well, there you go, Annie," Mary seemed proud of herself for being able to assist. "If I was you, I'd start with the Sunshiners while I was on my way to see Cleda. I wish *I* could go see the Sunshiners, you're so lucky. I've heard so much about them. Interesting, interesting stuff. I just can't even imagine ditching everything in my life and running off with a bunch of hippies – living day to day. Sounds fascinating."

While Mary's enthusiasm for the Sunshine Family of Peace made Annie laugh, Annie was a little less thrilled with the idea of looking for a bunch of hippies out in the wilderness of the Blue Ridge Mountains even if she could relate to "ditching everything and running off" as Mary put it.

"Are you sure you don't want to go with me?" Annie asked half joking to Mary. She would have loved for someone to go with her, but she and Mary just didn't have that kind of friendship.

"I would if I could," Annie could hear Mary being distracted by a nearby co-worker. She was whispering and Annie knew she needed to get off the phone. "But I want you to let me know all about it when you get back. In the meantime, I'll stop my sleuthing on your family since you've got your aunt's little book. But you give me a call anytime."

Mary paused for a moment in admiration for Annie's courage.

"Annie." Mary emphasized with a long moment of silence. "Good luck to you and God Speed. I hope you find everything you need out there."

"Thanks, Mary; I appreciate all your help."

CHAPTER SIX

Annie knew what leaving the Kentucky and Tennessee
borders meant; she would have to slow her driving to a crawl – 65
miles per hour. Virginia residents were tamed to drive the speed
limit and every so often she would see signs of just how that
taming had been achieved, "Speed Limits Monitored by Air."
Annie had heard of people getting tickets in the mail from air
traffic enforcement" monitoring systems. It seemed unlikely that
someone would bother with poor little Annie Cleaving driving ten
miles per hour over the speed limit, but she didn't want to take any
chances.

Fall was even more colorful in Southern Virginia than in
Rayes County, if that was possible. She rolled down her windows
and felt the cool air swirling around her. Driving a little slower did
have its advantages – the windows down didn't give her that wind-
battered feeling she got at 75 or 80 miles per hour in Tennessee
and Kentucky. Virginia legislators must have made the speed limit
60 and 65 – so people would slow down and enjoy the cool air and
colorful scenery. As Annie continued this line of thinking, it would
certainly make for happier residents come voting time. Finally, she
was beginning to relax a little. The Cleaving scavenger hunt – it had
all a happened so fast, Annie had barely had time to consider what
was going on.

That was a good thing; not having too much time to think

about it. If she'd had days to ponder it over, she might have decided not to do it at all. Sometimes just doing nothing was the only decision Annie could come to. Annie's mother always said she shouldn't fool herself into thinking she wasn't making a decision; deciding to do nothing was still a decision with consequences.

Millicent Cleaving was full of wit and wisdom. Annie often wondered who had told her all these wise one liners. Maybe she read them in books – Millie was always reading. Maybe Lucy Cleaving had enlightened her to the Yen and Yang of life. No matter where she got them, Annie had heard them all her life, "When the grass looks greener on the other side, go home and water your own," and "Pretty is as pretty does." This one was to remind Annie that her beauty needed to come from within. Millie truly lived that last saying. She was beautiful in her own right – even when she was older Annie still could see it. Old pictures revealed only the same – Millie's coal black hair and big, bright blue eyes ready for adventure – skin like porcelain and a smile that mimicked laughter you could almost hear. Everyone said she was one of the prettiest girls in Rayes County, or anywhere else for that matter. She stayed that way right up until she got pregnant with Annie. Then, as Annie had heard the story, Millie met her father while travelling. They were about to get married when he went off to the military and never came back. Annie had asked time and again about her father, why Millie and he never married and what happened to him. Annie could see that talking about it bothered her mother, so she hardly ever asked when she was a little girl. As she got older, she eventually just stopped asking all together. After Ethan was born, it just simply didn't matter at all to either of them. It seemed that when Ethan came, the hole in Annie and her mother filled instantly; the missing piece to the puzzle formed perfectly around their empty spots.

Annie often wondered why her mother never left Rayes County. Millie would say she had spent her whole life taking care of her mother. When Annie was old enough, she began to realize that

Mamaw Lucy wasn't feeble when they lived with her. Annie remembered as a little girl, working with her grandmother in the garden – hoeing, planting and harvesting vegetables – not easy work for an old woman. It wasn't until a few years before Mamaw Lucy died that she began to get feeble and old looking. After that, Millie still just stayed right there in the same house doing all the same things. Annie never remembered her mother dating at all. She was so much prettier than the other mothers of Annie's classmates. Even though Annie didn't have a lot of friends, she would see the other mothers in the car lane. Those mothers were never as pretty as Millie. As Annie got older, she would hear folks in town refer to her mother as "simply stunning."

Miles and miles of Interstate 81 had dragged on at 65 miles per hour. Annie had been so wrapped up in thinking about her mother, Ethan and finding the Cleaving children, she hadn't even bothered to turn on the radio for the entire trip. Annie had no idea what she was going to do when she got to Blue Ridge. She was almost there, now, and she knew she'd better figure it out soon.

Roanoke and the surrounding area didn't have many radio stations to choose from. Annie would've thought that a big city like Roanoke would have more. She wasn't happy having to settle for news as a distraction.

"Local businesses are complaining once again about the Sunshine Family of Peace," the radio reporter said. *"Reports of shoplifting have increased by twelve percent since their arrival two weeks ago. While police cannot confirm the shoplifters are members of the Sunshiners – as they are referred to here in Roanoke, they have stated that most of the new incidents involve people with no addresses or identification. This, however, is typical of this group – no identification and no known address. They tend to use names like Joey Joseph or Stanley Stanleyson when they are arrested. In the meantime, business owners are stepping up security in their businesses and keeping an eye out for shoplifters. The most recent reports include an incident where an individual was caught at a local department store parking lot, siphoning gas from a customer's*

vehicle."

"What on earth have I gotten myself into?" Annie flipped the radio off again opting instead for the hollow sounds dusk settling into the mountains.

Annie had gone deep into Blue Ridge before stopping for gas. She saw several older cars and vans on the parkway; some with hand-painted graffiti – mostly peace signs or rainbows. Shrinking behind the most distant mountain, she could see the sun's orange glow fading fast behind the evergreens.

Crackling gravel alerted Annie to an old Volkswagen van, painted with every color of spray paint imaginable – dots here, lines there – no order to it at all, just a mish mash of colors all running together. A man stepped out of the driver's side, a woman out of the passenger's side. Annie felt she'd been transported back in time to the 1960s. The man wore his salt and peppery hair long with a bandanna around his head. Wispy and wiry, the woman's hair was held in a ponytail with a simple leather strap. Dressed in what used to be a white, cloth drape with a leather band tied at her waist, the woman wore old, brown work boots with laces missing that hung loosely around her feet. As she raised her arm to close the van door, Annie could see a mound of hair. When she shuffled her feet in the gravels, her garment swayed in the evening breeze and Annie could see she was wearing no underwear. Her bare butt was muddy at one point but had been wiped off. She was dusty looking and her hair greasy. Her man didn't look much better. The two had been "wollering in the same hole," at least that's what Lucy Cleaving would have said if she'd seen them. The other customers pretended not to notice them.

From the windows, as Annie pumped her gas, she could see the woman move to the back of the store, stuffing candy bars and sodas under her dress, tying the leather strap tight to hold them tight. Annie hurried so she could get inside, never taking her eyes off the hippie woman. Annie was entranced as she followed in the woman's footsteps, watching her every move. Just as the cashier was about to confront the hippie lady about her overstuffed dress, Annie spoke.

"Oh, I'll be paying for their items," she shot a defiant look to the woman behind the counter.

The bleached blonde's hair was teased to the Heavens. Upset with the interference, she shot Annie a look of anger letting her know there were no friends behind that counter.

"If you insist ma'am," the cashier tapped her long nails on the counter as the hippie woman removed the items from underneath her dress. "But *only* if you insist," she looked at Annie for assurance before beginning to ring in the items on the cash register.

"I insist," Annie motioned for the hippie lady to push her items closer to the register.

The hippie lady's man grinned at the cashier, standing taller now, happy to have won the battle before it had even begun. Annie remembered her grandmother talking about "kyarn" – "filthy as kyarn, nasty as kyarn, stinks like kyarn." Annie asked her once what "kyarn" was. Lucy said it was hard to put into words, but you'll know it when you smell it. Annie was sure this was the "kyarn" she'd heard about all her life.

Annie didn't get a thank you or even a gracious smile, the hippies headed straight toward their multi-colored van.

"I am looking for the Sunshiner's gathering," Annie yelled and lunged forward as if the hippies were going to escape. Now, the customers gave some recognition to the hippies as they looked over at Annie's brand-new Toyota and then back at her.

"Can you help me find the place?" The couple shuffled to a

pause and turned.

"I don't know what you're talking about," he projected his voice so everyone in the parking lot could hear his denial. The hippie woman subtly motioned Annie to come closer.

"Follow us," her whispery breath so rank that it made Annie's eyes water. "Come on, follow us."

Annie drove deeper into the forest, the only certainty of direction coming from the dingy tail lights on the van in front of her. Then, like stars appearing in a black sky, just across the hillside in front of her, she could see small glowing dots – campfires.

As they parked in a grassy field, Annie could see just below the hillside, a bunch of small lights. It looked like an RV camp without the RVs.

"Don't worry," the hippie woman said, appearing from out of nowhere to meeting Annie near her car. "Your eyes will get used to the dark."

"Thank you. My name is Annie, what's yours?"

The two of them walked side by side toward the lights. Annie didn't see the man again; he had either gone on ahead, stayed behind or was taking a different path.

"I am Reena; it means raining love," the woman spoke as if she had been high since the 60s. "What does Annie mean?"

"I don't know," Annie was annoyed with Reena's simple mindedness and certain a pertinent discussion as to why she was there in the first place would never be addressed. "I really don't know."

"Oh, Okay," Reena's voice was silky.

As they reached what looked like an entrance to the camp, a small naked man came running out of a tent straight toward Annie. She froze. He grabbed her, squeezing her so tightly it was hard to move. He picked her up off the ground and slung her from side to side. His skin was filthy, and his hair matted. Immobilized by the shock of his naked body against hers and the smell that lingered around them, she felt herself about to vomit.

"Kyarn" again," she thought.

He was one of the nastiest creatures Annie had ever seen, smelled or felt near her – even more filthy than the dogs after a dip in Higgins Creek back home; most knew it was a makeshift sewer for that houses on that road. The little hippie was hugging her like a long, lost relative would but only if they had been stranded on a deserted island for twenty years. He kept saying over and over, "Welcome sister, welcome sister, your earth has missed you."

When he was finished hugging Annie and slinging her around, he ran around her like a wild man and began to chant.

"Earth is our mo-o-ther, come and join our mo-o-ther; Earth is our mo-o-ther, come and join our mo-o-ther ..."

Annie was done being frozen; now, she was angry. The smell of body odor hung in her nostrils. Even the fresh Blue Ridge Mountain air couldn't clear the stench of dirty hippie from her clothes. She had been hugged and hugged good, by one of the dirtiest creatures on Earth – this earth he seemed to love so much.

So much for eating my frog first, Annie thought, this is more like eating a skunk.

"I am looking for Asher Cleaving. Is he here?" Annie was yelling. She didn't want to have to repeat herself. As much as the little naked man would chant, Annie would state her purpose over and over again. "I am looking for Asher Cleaving. IS HE HERE?"

Annie could now see someone else coming out of the tent. It was an older Asian lady. She made instant eye contact with Annie.

"Can I help you, lady?" she was oddly calm as the little wild naked man continued to dance around Annie. "In the tent, Sunray ... get in the tent," the woman raised her voice on the second demand.

He danced to the tent, still chanting, but more softly.

When Sunray went back into the tent, Annie stated her purpose again, "I am looking for Asher Cleaving. Is he here?"

"Old girlfriend? Ex-wife? Need child support? He ain't got it." The woman dismissed Annie's request as pathetic. "He just ain't got it."

For the first time since Annie left the little grocery store with Reena and her man, she felt hopeful.

"He's here?!" Annie came immediately to attention.

"I don't know if he's here or not. What do you want with him?"

"I am his niece and I need to talk to him about a property matter with my house," Annie started to take the deed from her purse but changed her mind, the old woman was shaking her head "no."

"What do you mean 'no,'? He's here isn't he?" Annie demanded.

"Asher, or as Earth knows him, Ashes, has no possessions and most likely doesn't want to speak to anyone who *has* any possessions," the old woman fiddled with some beading on her sleeve.

Annie took a much-needed deep breath. She was just starting to smell the fresh air again.

"Let me start at the beginning," Annie looked deep into the old woman's eyes trying to connect with her on some level. "Asher – I mean Ashes is my uncle. He is my mother's brother. Tell him Millicent's daughter is here to see him …"

"Stop right there," the woman gave Annie a disapproving look. "Are you telling me you are Millie's daughter?"

"You know – knew my mother?!" Annie's hope for finding Asher dwindled. She was doubtful this woman and her kyarn-y little minion ever knew Millicent Cleaving.

"Yes, yes I did," the woman looked deeper into Annie's eyes as if to see something in there.

"Ashes – or your Uncle Asher," she corrected herself. "– is at the Mill tent," the old woman pulled the tent flap back to reveal an eager Sunray waiting to be invited back outside. "Sunray will take you there. SUNRAY, SUNRAY," she yelled at the tent. "Put something on and take this woman to the Mill tent."

Sunray disappeared for a moment then emerged wearing a pink polyester skirt with nothing else. Fashion sense or not, Annie was grateful his dirty body was finally covered.

Once he was outside, Annie could see he was holding a strand of flowers he had tied together," For you, for you," he pushed them into Annie's midsection.

"It's a gift," the Asian woman scolded Annie for not accepting right away.

Annie bent down as Sunray placed the flowers around her neck and then kissed her sweetly on the cheek. The Asian woman shot Annie a final skeptical look as Sunray began walking with the new Sunshine guest trailing close behind. She watched him shift from side to side as he walked determined to get Annie to her destination. His arms swung far behind him as he tackled the sloping and rocky landscape. Annie was trying to keep up but there was so much to see.

"You comin'?" Sunray turned to Annie.

"Yes, yes, I'm coming," Annie smiled at the little hippie who, since the presentation of the flower necklace, looked more like a child than a man.

She followed Sunray through the trails and passed many tents. People, some naked, some clothed called out to her as they chanted songs. The chant that she was first greeted with by Sunray was the most prevalent.

"Earth is our mo-o-ther, come and join our mo-o-ther; Earth is our mo-o-ther, come and join our mo-o-ther …"

Most were sitting on the ground. Annie kept finding herself tripping on rocks and stepping into holes because she just couldn't stop staring at everyone.

"MILL TENT," Sunray yelled up to Annie's face and pointed to a rather nice place, in comparison to the others. He then quickly walked away, but not before hugging Annie one last time.

"Thank you for my gift," she fondled the flower necklace.

"Pretty lady," Sunray turned and wandered off.

Annie reluctantly pushed the tent flap open, relieved to see the man inside was fully clothed but startled that he looked so familiar.

"Uncle Asher?" Annie squinted her eyes hoping to get a better look at him.

"Millie? Uh, I mean Angel, Annie?" Asher Cleaving answered back. "Oh my, oh my," he got up moving around the tent trying to find Annie a place to sit.

"Do you live here?" Annie looked all around the inside of the tent.

"Yes, well here and there," Asher laughed nervously.

"What are you doing here, Annie – what are you doing here, Annie?"

She was curious about many things and wanted to ask questions, mainly how that woman knew her mother. But Annie thought it best to get the deed business out of the way first just in case some insane hippie came in chanting and dancing.

"I have an issue with the house, Uncle Asher," Annie pushed her purse strap back up on her shoulder. "Do you remember when Mamaw Lucy gave me the house several years ago? Well, she didn't really own all of it ..."

Annie explained it to Asher Cleaving just as it was told to her.

"Got a pen?" Asher, who was already holding the deed in his hand throughout Annie's explanation, signed on the X immediately, dated it and handed it back to Annie.

"We have a notary here if you need one," Asher nodded with excitement.

"Really, you have a notary here?!

"No, we don't, just kidding," Asher laughed a raspy smoker's laugh. He then coughed for a moment and laughed some more. "You're just like your mother the last time I saw her – so serious. Lighten up; you're going to die of a heart attack. So young – so serious."

"You came all the way out here just for that?" Asher conveyed his displeasure for societies need to own things with that one small question.

"Yes," Annie folded the deed and placed it in her purse. "Just for that."

As if he had been searching for something he'd lost, he had been looking at Annie's face and through her face at times.

"God, I miss your mother," Annie couldn't tell if he was about to cry or if he was just high.

"How did that old woman at the entrance know my mother, Asher?" Annie looked her uncle directly in the eyes as if expecting he would tell her a lie.

"Everyone here knows Millie," Asher moved some blankets and sat down on a cot. "Here, we called her Miera. They thought she was our miracle."

"Did … did, she stay here? When? Where was I?" Annie was searching for an answer, looking at Asher as if he were lying. "Miera? That's just crazy," she rolled her eyes and shook her head.

"Not so crazy," Asher poked at a hole in his shoe so he wouldn't have to look at Annie. "Everyone here knows you too, Annie – Angel. You were born right here in this tent. Not on this land, of course, but in this tent – the Mill tent; named after your mother. All her things are still in here, see," Asher pointed to trinkets, cups and jewelry placed all around the tent. "I kept them all in here. We tried to get her to stay, but she wouldn't – she went back to be in the cattle herd of human existence," Asher delivered the last line with perfect pitch as if it had been rehearsed before.

Then Annie saw it – a picture of her mother holding a baby. There she was, Millicent Cleaving – beautiful long dark hair, big blue eyes. She was wearing a dingy cloth white dress just like Reena's and a bandanna around her head. Her cloth dress gathered at the waist with a leather strap, just like Reena's. The baby in her arms was sleeping, cinched up tight in a cloth that looked like it was once white.

There it was – an image of Millicent Cleaving in an old, framed photo at the Sunshine Family of Peace gathering in the Blue Ridge Mountains of Virginia in a tent named just for her. As Annie stared intently into the old photograph, hoping to get a glimpse of something that looked familiar to her, there was no doubt in her mind as to why people referred to her mother as "simply stunning."

CHAPTER SEVEN

Annie was startled to see Asher standing over her. As her vision came into focus, she saw the coffee pot he was holding.

"Want some coffee, Angel?"

"I told you not to call me that," the cot squeaked as Annie sat up.

"Sorry," Asher delivered a bit of sarcasm. "Would *Annie* like some coffee?"

Annie didn't answer she just took the cup from his hand and began to sip.

"Strong," her eyes now watering a bit.

"Yeah," Asher laughed and coughed. "It's not like I have a Mr. Coffee here in the Mill tent. It used to be worse until your mother gave me this little tin percolator. We usually don't have a lot of coffee here at all. This is a real treat from Reena."

"You mean from me," Annie took another slurp, glancing over her cup at a confused Asher.

"I met them at the store at the bottom of the mountain – they were shoplifting. I paid for their things," Annie sipped at her cup again waiting for Asher's reaction.

"Just like the herd, keeping a score card displaying who pays for what," Asher scolded his niece. "You can't just enjoy the coffee."

Annie looked at the coffee pot, embarrassed to look at her uncle. She thought she recognized it. It was made of aluminum and had a hollow glass button at the top. When the coffee was done, it would burst into the hollow glass knob. Annie remembered seeing that coffee pot as a little girl. She loved to watch it when the coffee would boil up into the knob.

Annie began looking around the cot for her shoes. She should have left last night but the darkness trapped her there. She could have driven around for hours and still never found her way out until daylight.

"I'm glad Reena and Greenbriar were able to help you," Asher touched her on the arm to make her look at him. "That's part of what we do here – help people."

Her eyes scoured every inch of the tent for any sign of her shoes. Annie couldn't believe her mother would ever have stayed here for even a day. She could feel the gritty dirt on her scalp, the dirt now even on the backs of her hands.

"I asked Momma once for us to go camping," Annie flicked the side of the tent with her finger, counting in her head the number of times she was allowed to get dirty as a child. "She wouldn't even hear of it."

"What are you looking for?" Asher looked all around, mimicking Annie's frantic behavior.

"My shoes, I can't find them."

"They're on your feet," Asher coughed out another of his loud raspy laughs.

The insects stopped clicking and the birds stopped chirping as the sound echoed outside. It reminded Annie that they were deep in the woods even if she was holding a cup of fresh ground.

"Want to come out and take a look around?" Asher rose from his spot on the ground. "C'mon, I want you to meet some of my friends."

Wiggling her toes inside her shoes to make sure they were there, Annie stood up as tall as she could still holding her coffee and even stopping for a moment to get a refill.

"Kind of grows on you, doesn't it?" Asher held the tent flap open.

Once outside, Annie could see the mountains clearly for the first time since she got there. In the darkness, they looked like large, looming clouds – huge dark giants watching her every move.

This morning they looked like old friends from home. Evergreens anchored the red and golden Maples. Oaks added splashes of color among the green, burgundy, and golden dancers, moving slightly in the cool breeze.

Annie's eyes were opening wider and wider as her jaw began to relax. It was like she couldn't help it, she wanted see everything, feel everything. She lowered the coffee cup from her face and drew in a deep breath that immediately took her back to the fall day when Ethan died. Her eyes began to get hot.

"It *is* truly amazing, isn't it?" Asher had been watching her. "I love getting to see people take it all in for the first time. You know it doesn't matter where you camp, every morning, it's the same – this view is everywhere under this mountain.

Allowing Asher his moment, she stopped herself from telling him her tears had nothing to do with his precious mountains.

"Yes, they're amazing," Annie sipped at her coffee cup, regaining control over her tears.

Annie followed her uncle down the strangely familiar path. Light from the night-time campfires were gone; some of the pits still smoldered. People were moving up ahead, coming out of their tents. The sound of smacking firewood echoed off the mountain as stacks were starting to form.

Asher waved to the people as he went by almost everyone calling his name and wishing him good morning as if he were mayor. People were staring at Annie. She hated that feeling of being watched. Some came up to Asher and asked outright who she was without even looking at her.

"Oh, don't worry, she's with me – a relative," Asher continued walking.

"I would tell them who you are but then they'd all want to meet you," Asher turned his head to Annie. "You don't really look like you're in the mood for a lot of attention this morning."

"No, thank you, I'm not," Annie agreed but then stopped herself. "But why would they want to talk to me?"

"I'll tell you later," Asher smiled and walked on ahead of her.

Annie's coffee was getting cold. It was so bitter it made her want to spit but she didn't dare. Instead, she just swallowed it and followed on. She was relieved it was all gone now. As long as it was hot, it wasn't so bad. Lukewarm and then cold was foul tasting, but she didn't want to appear ungrateful again that Asher had shared his coffee with her.

Just over a ridge on the dirt path, Annie could see two tents side by side. They looked like they had once been red but had faded into a muted pink. Traces of bright red could still be seen near the stitching and in the creases.

"C'mon over here with me," Asher motioned toward the pink tents. "There's someone in there I want you to meet."

Ducking under the doorway, Annie saw an older woman at a wooden counter with several little wooden bowls. She was mixing something. Annie could stand all the way up in this tent. She was grateful for that – to feel like she was in a normal room in the middle of the wilderness, seemed odd, but comforting, nonetheless.

Annie recognized the woman right even though here head was down. She was the same woman from last night; the one at the entrance, the one who made Sunray put on clothes.

"You knew my mother," Annie startled the woman, who had just noticed Annie and Asher coming in.

"So, you two met already?" Asher seemed pleased but puzzled.

"Yes. She said she knew my mother."

The woman reached over and took Annie's free hand. Annie flinched at first but after a stern look from Asher, she gave in and let it fall free.

"I'm sorry about last night – giving you a hard time and all," the woman took her other hand and patted Annie on the shoulder. "I had no idea that you were Miera's daughter."

"You mean Millie?" Annie annunciated every consonant to make it clear what her mother's name was.

"Yes, Millie," the woman corrected.

"Annie," Asher stepped between the two women, "meet Phoebe. Phoebe, meet Annie."

The woman nodded her head to Annie and smiled a sweet motherly.

"Annie, Phoebe was the nurse who delivered you in the Mill tent the night you were born," Asher put a hand on each woman's shoulder as if bringing them together.

"Oh," Annie looked the woman up and down and then began examining the room.

The tiny wooden bowls and the wooden counter had been put together with plywood and two-by-fours. There were four cots lined up in a row.

"What is this tent?"

"Phoebe's Med Tent," Asher held his arms in presentation. "We put it together for her a long time ago when she came to join us. We were very glad to get a nurse here."

Phoebe stood a little taller, maybe a whole five foot two, flashing a wide smile.

Annie nodded her head, still taking a skeptic's look around the tent.

"Phoebe's an expert as piecing people back together," Asher pointed to a scar over the bony part of his thumb.

"Surgery?" Annie scanned the room for scalpels.

"No *real* surgery," Phoebe jokingly pushed Asher's hand from Annie's view. "A stitch or two here and there – a splint sometimes there and again."

No expert at sewing but knowledgeable enough to recognize a worthy stitch, Annie lifted Asher's tanned and leathery hand. The scar from the stitches was white in contrast.

"Looks like pretty good seamstress work," Annie gave no credence to Phoebe's nursing skills.

"You a seamstress?" Phoebe was pleased to find something personal about Annie.

"No, but my mother used to do some nice work," Annie walked over to the counter to examine Phoebe's tools. She picked up a small wooden spoon, examined the front and back then placed it carefully back on the counter.

"There's more than one way to piece someone back together," Phoebe gathered her mixing tools together and placed them in a wooden cup at the edge of the counter. "Sometimes a scalpel is not the tool you need."

Nodding, Annie let Phoebe know she heard her words but was unaffected by their meaning.

"Good to meet you," Annie walked toward the tent flap opening. "You coming?" She hesitated for a moment before stepping out.

"Yeah, I'm coming," Asher patted Phoebe's arm.

Once outside, Annie began to walk fast – to where, she had no idea. She just knew she had to get out of there and away from Phoebe's Med Tent.

Asher ran up ahead then turned to face her, "Annie, I know this is a lot to take in. I knew your mother hadn't told you about the other part of her life … life before you."

Annie demanded an answer, "What do you mean 'life before me?'"

"Come on Annie, let's go somewhere and sit down so we can talk," Asher pointed to a spot off the path and began walking toward it. "I don't want you to leave here upset or mad."

Curiosity about what Asher might say kept her following in his footsteps. He stopped at a rock overlooking the valley. Annie positioned herself so she could see his face.

"Your mother had been here before … before she came here to have you," Asher spoke to Annie as if he were explaining nuclear energy to a kindergartner. "She came here after a fight with her boyfriend," Asher waited to give Annie a chance to interrupt but she didn't. "I guess most kids run off and join the circus when they decide to see the world. Your mother ran off to join the Sunshiners with me," Asher's raspy laugh was whispery and strained. "I used to write to her all the time and let her know where I'd be. I would always expect to see her when we'd camp close to Rayes County, but I never did until that one summer."

Annie propped her elbow on her knee, "Go on."

"I should have sent her home sooner, but I thought she might learn a little something here with me," Asher picked up a stick and began writing Miera in the loose dirt.

"She stayed about a week before she went back home," Asher raised his head, looking over the valley. "Momma was happy and I know that boyfriend of your momma's was happy, too. It was Buck that wanted to get married, not your momma."

"Buck?" Annie stood up, looking down over Asher. "Buck Rosen?"

"Yes, *Buck Rosen*," Asher's voice began to smack of sarcasm. "Rayes County's fine, faithful and loyal sheriff … is he still sheriff over there?"

"Yes, yes he is," Annie sat down again anxious to see what else she could learn.

"Well, he wasn't then," Asher smoothed over Millie's name in the dirt and wrote Buck. "He was just a little crispy cop with one bullet in his gun and big love for your mother. It wasn't until he married that Jameson girl that he got to be sheriff and run the county over there."

Annie, of course, recognized the name ... Jameson's Real Estate, Jameson's Construction, Jameson's Apartments – Elizabeth Jameson Rosen, mother of a drunken murderer ...

"Then your mother came here again when she was pregnant with you – 'bout seven and a half months pregnant," Asher rounded his arms mocking a pregnant woman. She was big and looked like she was about to go any minute."

Annie took the stick from Asher's hand and dusted dirt over Buck's name, carving deep trenches after his name had completely disappeared.

"I called Momma," Asher rubbed his foot over the dirt to smooth it out once again. "She had no idea who the baby belonged to, only who it didn't belong to – Rosen. Millie never said who, either. I never met him, and your mother was glad he ran off. Good enough for me."

"I don't know why she never told me ...," Annie stood again, throwing Asher's writing stick out into the valley.

"Told you what? That she was here?"

"No, that she – well, yes. That she was here and that she and Buck dated."

"Does it really matter?" Asher stood, kicking at the now loose dirt.

"It does," Annie's thoughts went back to the day of the crash. Still slobbering drunk, that bastard was leaning against the tree.

Buck came rushing up, and helped put his son onto a waiting gurney. When he reached into the car to support Ethan's body, he kept telling Annie it was all going to be okay. He touched her arm, his hand covered in Ethan's blood.

"Are you okay?" Asher yelled at Annie. "Hey, hey – are you in there," he snapped his fingers in front of her face.

Annie came back from her thoughts and saw Asher's face in front of hers. He was smiling but looked concerned.

"Oh, I'm fine. I was just thinking."

Annie got what she came for, the deed was signed. There was no reason for Asher to know about Jacob or the trial. He was off the grid, no newspapers, no radio, no TV.

"She stayed here around a couple of months but then said the camp was no place for a baby," Asher looked approvingly around the grounds as if disagreeing with the absent Millie.

"That sounds more like my mother," Annie dusted the dirt off her pants as if her mother were watching. Asher followed her as she began walking the path back to the camp entrance.

This was the first glimpse of Millicent Cleaving that Annie recognized since her visit with Asher had begun.

"Yeah, I guess it does sound like the way you knew her," he hinted a smile.

Drug addiction came easy when the Sunshiners camped in California. Dealers and addicts, looking for a place to hide, found the Sunshiners as easy prey. LSD came with them.

"We told all of them they either had to stop using or they had to leave," Asher tugged at his nose trying to shrink his forming tears. "That was the first time we had ever asked anyone to leave but we just couldn't handle them anymore. We were starving trying to keep them in drugs. I was elected to ask them all to make the choice."

Annie kept walking the path to the entrance, watching people as Asher spoke, wondering what their eyes had seen, who they used to be.

"He'll never be right, but it gave us all hope that he lived through it," Asher nodded his head toward a fully dressed Sunray, who was gathering sticks and stacking them next to a hole in the ground. "That's why everyone here loves your mother. By saving Sunray, she really saved us all. Many good lessons that year you were born."

Asher kicked at the dirt and rocks as he walked, trying to slow their pace.

"Sweet lady," Annie recognized Reena's silky voice. "You aren't staying?"

Reena was sitting on the ground surrounded by pieces of colorful cloth. She looked much older in the daylight. Annie had mistaken her vulnerability for youth.

"Bet you didn't know Reena was a quite the collector," Asher went over to Reena and bent down next to her. "These are beautiful. New, aren't they?" Asher fondled through the pieces.

"Show Annie your work, Reena," Asher pointed into the tent.

Reena was inside for so long; Annie was beginning to think she had gotten lost in the tiny tent. As she and Asher waited, they both knelt fondling through the hundreds of tiny misshapen pieces. They reminded Annie of quilt pieces her grandmother used to cut. But this fabric was different – worn and ragged on the edges.

"Here they are," Reena spoke with her own soft level of

excitement.

Annie couldn't take her eyes off the multi-colored shoulder bags.

"All these from this," Annie couldn't help but touch them all. Reena beamed.

"I have one for you," Reena quickly disappeared into the tent and returned just as quickly.

The bag was just the right length for Annie's small frame as Reena hung it over her shoulder it reached Annie's waistline perfectly. Stitched with every color, pattern and texture – many more than Annie had ever seen before all-in-one garment. Hundreds of different types, colors and thicknesses of threads were woven into hundreds of patterns about the bag. At least a hundred tiny pieces of broken mirror were woven into the bag. Annie pulled it from her shoulder and held it up to her face – the reflections of colors inviting her in.

"This is amazing," Annie didn't know if she said it out loud or not.

"Oh, you're sweet," Reena stroked the bag and then Annie's arm. "This one belongs with you."

Annie looked at Asher as if to ask if it was okay.

"Looks like you've made a friend," he looked at Reena then back at Annie.

"Please let me pay you," Annie began digging in her pocket for change. Reena quickly grabbed her arm and clenched it tight looking Annie straight in the eyes for the first time, "No, thank you."

For the first time, Annie saw a different side of Reena, one that was more forceful – not absent.

Reena sat down near her collection and began working again, "Bye now."

Annie looked at Asher for direction. He had already started walking away.

"What's her story?" Annie walked to keep up with her uncle but couldn't help but look back.

Asher kept walking but didn't answer. He hesitated and finally spoke, "She was the worst kind of broken when she got here – we are still piecing her back together."

Asher gave Annie's new shoulder back a push with the back of his hand. Annie took another look at the pieces of broken mirror looking back at her.

"How long has she been with you?"

"She got here just after you and your mother left," Asher stopped as if he couldn't count and walk at the same time, then began stepping again after his answer.

"Hey, look over there," he pointed toward a mud hole, as if he were trying to lighten the mood on his and Annie's last moments together. "You remember those mud pies … every day you'd start on me, 'Ashes come over and make …,'" Annie looked confused and when Asher noticed, he never finished his sentence.

CHAPTER EIGHT

Annie was glad to be back on the road again – rested and bathed. Clean clothes and a moisturized face made her feel almost human again. She had often wondered about living off the grid. It sounded like something she'd like to try – no cars, no bills, no one to bother her. She never thought about how difficult it was to just exist. The Sunshiners worked harder than anyone she knew or at least anyone at Natureson's – gathering, scavenging, and building fires – stealing, or collecting as Asher had referred to it.

The sunlight reflecting in the mirrored pieces of glass pulled Annie's eyes toward the colorful bag sitting next to her. When she had first placed it in the car, the tiny mirrors fogged up immediately, as if they hadn't felt air conditioning in a while, a luxury lost when they were discarded from their former life. Annie was glad to have air conditioning in her car, and a soft seat to sit on – all things she had taken for granted until the day before yesterday.

Virginia looked so much like Rayes County she kept forgetting where she was. The tree-covered mountains were bunched together, protecting their little towns – their little people, just like back home.

The house looked the same as she remembered it as a girl. Annie was happy to find that even though she hadn't seen or spoken to her aunt in years, she still lived in the same place. Cleda's house was always fun – lots of things a little girl could get into – exotic plants everywhere and all of them edible. Annie remembered Aunt Cleda constantly saying, "eat this," or "try this," and then picking off a leaf or flower from a plant and holding it to Annie's mouth. Annie's favorite was Cleda's back yard – she fed the birds back there every day when she'd visit. She would love to stand in the middle of the back yard and let Cleda throw the bird seed up in the air. The birds would fly all around Annie trying to get at their breakfast. Annie would imagine she was one of them – waving and flapping her arms wildly as the blackbirds screeched and screamed, diving for their food.

Annie could see lights on in the house but no car in the driveway. She had called Cleda ahead of time, so Annie felt sure if Cleda wasn't home, she'd arrive shortly. It wasn't like Aunt Cleda to miss a family visit, from anyone, let alone Millie's baby – as she had always called Annie.

The aged oak tree in front of the driveway was gone now. Annie tried to stare in the exact spot where the tire swing used to be but her eyes kept focusing on the garden in the distance.

Cleda's deed from the glove box, the address book that Veda had loaned her – Annie wanted this visit to be short, to get back on the road and into a hotel. Even though she had slept well the night before at the Roanoke hotel, she was still tired from her visit at the Sunshine camp.

Annie had just opened the car door and placed one foot on the ground when out of nowhere a car skidded in next to hers. It was a big, long white Cadillac and it carried a dainty blonde woman with a beehive hair-do – Aunt Cleda.

Cleda fled the car quickly and started running toward the house, leaving the car door open and the engine running.

"Come on, Annie," she yelled, not even looking back.

Annie was moving slowly in comparison to her aunt. For an old woman, she was running pretty fast. She had on a pair of white pedal pushers, as Annie's mother used to call them, and a bright red shirt covered with black floral patterns. Her hair never moved as she ran in long, great strides toward the front door. She was holding what looked like a turnip or some other root with long strands of ragged leaves attached to it. They flowed in the wind after her as she ran.

Annie gathered her purse, placing the deed carefully folded inside, put her light jacket over one arm and walked over to Cleda's car. Reaching through the already open door and turning off the engine, she then took the keys out of the ignition and pulled her aunt's purse onto her shoulder to share space along with her own. Annie sighed when she felt the weight of Cleda's purse then saw the bag of groceries in the back seat. She managed a free finger to take the handle and carry it in.

Luckily, Cleda left the front door open – otherwise Annie might have dropped everything. She could hear water rumbling and boiling in the kitchen. It was popping and smacking with loud bloops as it was nearly boiling over the top. The kitchen windows were covered with moisture from the cool fall air outside and the steam inside. Cleda stood over the counter chopping the dirty root she had just been running with.

"Hang on dear, just hang on, I've almost got it," Cleda yelled, trying to talk over the sounds of the boiling pot.

Her face was shiny and her mascara and eyeliner moist – just about ready to smudge. One false move – the brush of a hand across her forehead to remove a bit of sweat or the flick of a finger to remove a glob out of the corner of her eye and Cleda's make up masterpiece would've looked like war paint.

"Whew," Cleda blew out a big breath. "It was *almost* garbage. I started making it this morning and thought I'd get it done before you got here. Then, I forgot the Yucca root and the lemon grass. It would have been wasted, absolutely ruined. And ... you have to add it while it's at a hard boil."

"Oh," Annie was afraid to ask what Cleda was making. Millie always said if Cleda's cooking and it doesn't smell like dinner then look out, she's potion making."

With the root and lemon grass finally chopped and added, Cleda lowered the gas flame.

"Now, we can go sit down and talk. It just has to simmer a bit, then I'll freeze it and mark the clock for the thaw time after I prick my finger," Cleda said, as if she had just chopped a few vegetables for soup.

"Want something to drink?"

"Sure," Annie kept watching the pot.

"Will iced tea be all right, sweetie?" Cleda seemed satisfied today – even giddy. "Speaking of sweetie – the tea's real sweet, is that okay? That's all I make around here. You know what they say, 'If it don't make your teeth hurt it ain't near sweet enough.'"

"That's fine," Annie almost laughed at her aunt's mountain pronunciation of tea – more like "tay."

Annie's curiosity kept pushing her toward that big pot. Cleda had used her big black and white speckled canning pot; it was filled almost to the rim with a dark brown liquid. Bits of red somethings that looked like pimentos were rolling to the top as the liquid boiled. It smelled like cow shit, peppermint and sage. In her aunt's defense, the cow shit smell might have been coming from the farm nearby. Still, whatever potion this was, it stank. The smell filled the entire house.

Cleda took the two glasses of iced tea and placed them on the kitchen table. She opened a bag of pretzels and poured them in an elegant crystal serving bowl with gold flecks around the edges.

"Let's go into the den – way more comfortable in there," Cleda took off walking, a glass of "tay" in each hand. Annie followed her aunt with the fancy pretzel bowl, watching as Cleda's curvy bottom twisted back and forth. She smelled of old perfume, hairspray and cigarette smoke. She and Edwin had been divorced for as long as Annie could remember. But for some reason, whenever any of the family spoke of going to see Aunt Cleda, they would always say, "We're going over to Cleda and Edwin's." Annie thought maybe it was because her Aunt Cleda never remarried. Or maybe it was because Cleda obsessed over Edwin to the point that he had become a permanent member of the Cleaving family whether he was ever present with real flesh and bone or not.

Most everyone in the Cleaving family knew the story well. Annie had heard it from her Mamaw Lucy, who, as it happened, hated Edwin with a generous passion.

When Cleda and Edwin first married, she was consumed by him. He was like a drug to her and nothing else mattered. She didn't call or contact the family. Mamaw would say, "It was like she disappeared from the face of the earth and that's just what that sorry son-of-a-bitch wanted." When speaking of Edwin, Lucy Cleaving minced no words and extended no pleasantries. Edwin was ten years older than Cleda; he always liked younger women. After the two of them had been married for only a few years, he began fooling around with lots of other women, much younger than his wife. When her marriage was in trouble – that's when Cleda started calling home. She would hate him and then love him; she'd leave him and then go running back to him. Two or three times a year there would be a "big blowup" as Lucy called it, because Cleda had caught him with another woman.

He fell in love with one of his mistresses and left Cleda for good. He stayed with his new wife and by all accounts was faithful to her. His new-found monogamy drove Cleda crazy. Again, she hated him and then loved him; wanted him dead and then wanted him back. She started dabbling in the mystic; at first it was only astrology. Then it turned to witchcraft and fortune telling. She spent thousands upon thousands of dollars with fortune tellers or clairvoyants trying to find the answer as to why Edwin loved this woman more than her and if he would ever come back. Annie's mother only ever had two words to say about Edwin and she used them time and again, "Good riddance."

Cleda was just dying to tell almost as much as Annie was dying to ask, "What are you cooking?"

Cleda turned to her as they were sitting on the couch, got very close to Annie's face and whispered, "It's a potion."

"Really?!" The syrupy tea had puckered Annie's tongue so she could barely roll out her l's. "What kind?"

"The best kind," Cleda spoke in an ominous tone. "It's permanent."

Annie stared at Cleda's diamond-studded fingers as she spoke. Sparkles of light were flashing as her rings reflected the sun as it broke through the sheers on the picture window.

"Well, your cousin, better known as my ungrateful son, Ed, Jr., allowed my precious little granddaughter to go on vacation with my ex-husband and that horrible fat wife of his." Cleda's voice got much louder as she spoke each word at the end of her sentence.

"So, I had this potion I used on one of Edwin's whores one time." Cleda began whispering again as if someone were listening. "I put it around her house, and it made her breath stink horrible."

Annie broke out a small laugh but then realized her aunt was not kidding.

"Laugh if you want," Cleda waved her hand in the air. "But it worked. I know," she didn't give Annie a chance to even smile at the prospect of potion-making this time. "I asked the checkout girl at the grocery store, who is still to this day a close and personal friend of mine, to tell me if she smelled anything when that old whore Kathleen Jensen came through the line," Cleda put her hand on Annie's knee and drawing in closer now for dramatic effect. "And it did! She said it stunk awful. It wasn't too long after that Edwin stopped screwin' around with her."

"Are you going to do the ...." Annie was interrupted.

"Yes, you guessed it, Annie. Only this time, I'm going one better. My group of ladies who like to make special remedies for what ails a person came up with an extra ingredient that makes the spell permanent."

Annie waited for Cleda to tell her about the secret ingredient but got the impression that her aunt wanted her to guess.

"Yucca root?" Annie reluctantly played the game.

"Yes," Cleda seemed proud that Annie was now a potion-making pupil.

"Now, when I finish the potion and pour it all around their house, Ginger's breath will be so horrible that my little Katie will never want to be around her again," Cleda looked sinisterly satisfied with her impending achievement. "And if it'll even make Edwin a little more miserable, well that's just gravy."

Annie noticed all the decanters and colored glass bottles around the room and wondered now what kinds of lay waiting inside to cry curse and claim vendetta for their creator.

"I can show you how it's done some time," Cleda reached down and gathered three thick black books in her hands. Annie was unfamiliar with the symbols on the covers as her aunt fanned them out in front of her, but she was sure these books hadn't been borrowed from the little white Baptist Church down the street.

"Everyone needs a little magic every now and then," Cleda placed the books on the coffee table where Annie could reach them once she realized Annie had no intention of diving into any of them right away. "In fact, I mixed up a little concoction for you last night just after you said you were coming over."

Annie flinched as her aunt reached over her shoulder and scooted a turquoise atomizer off an antique table behind the couch.

"It's a little protection potion we ladies like to call liquid bounce," Annie contorted her face, not believing Cleda had just mixed up a potion for her. There were bottles everywhere – Annie was sure her aunt just grabbed this one at random but attempted to play along.

"What a beautiful bottle," Annie cupped the atomizer in her hands and then held it up to the light. "This is real turquoise?!" She recognized the genuine stone right away and then realized Cleda really had made this just for her. Millie Cleaving was fascinated by real turquoise. She said it was a living rock that's why you could see the veins running through it. She passed her love of the stone on to her daughter as well.

"Yes. That was an old perfume bottle that belonged to your mother. I thought she'd be pleased if I put a protection potion in it for you. Because the bottle belonged to you mother, and she loved you so dearly, it will make this particular potion much more powerful."

"Smells like Day Lilies," Annie said, as she sprayed a little near her nose.

"It smells like whatever brings you peace, Annie. Your mother loved Lilies." Cleda seemed satisfied the potion was working.

Annie held the bottle in her hands and imagined a young Millie Cleaving pumping the atomizer, looking forward to some young man coming to see her. Annie rubbed her fingers over the smooth surface, examining the veins and where they crossed paths.

"So, about your issue with the house." Cleda sighed and shook her head.

"Oh yeah, the deed," Annie's focus had been stolen by the atomizer.

"Poor mother, she was married to such a sexist man. I bet he never told her a thing." Cleda shook her head in disgust.

Annie pulled the deed from her purse and unfolded it on top of one of the black volumes of witchery on the coffee table.

"How is the old place?" Cleda signed the deed and handed it back to Annie who folded it three times back into its original shape and carefully tucked it back into her purse.

"It's in great shape," Annie was proud of the work she'd done on the Cleaving house recently. "You should come for a visit sometime."

"Eh," Cleda shook her head no. "I don't think so."

Annie wondered what memories the Cleaving house held for Cleda, a time when she knew a younger Rayes County.

"So, you've been over to see Asher, have you?"

"Yes," Annie helped her aunt move past talking about visiting. "He lives in a very interesting place, doesn't he?"
"Well, I guess you could say that – but he really doesn't live there –

he really doesn't live anywhere. That boy is crazy, always has been," Cleda gulped her tea and then caught her breath. "He signed your deed didn't he?"

Annie nodded a satisfactory affirmation, thinking of her list and how she felt as she marked him off.

"Well, I should hope so after all he put all of us through, me, Momma and Millie included."

"I'll never forget one time ….," Cleda took her mind back to when Millie and Asher were younger.

"The Sunshine Family of Peace came to Rayes County to camp one year and Millie called her old friend Buck Rosen to come and help the Cleavings retrieve Asher. Millie suspected Asher of taking drugs – he had also written a letter with a suicidal tone. Millie heard the Sunshiners were going to be in Rayes County and sent Buck after Asher," Cleda said.

"Buck again." Annie was over the shock of hearing her mother's name in the same sentence with Buck Rosen.

"Yes, he and your mother were all the talk in Rayes County," Cleda was pleased with herself for having what she considered to be the inside scoop. "Even after he married, they were the best of friends."

Cleda either remembered that Buck's son was the one who killed Ethan or simply gauged Annie's reaction to the conversation. Either way, she stopped talking about Buck.

Asher came to the Cleaving House and stayed with Millie and Lucy for quite a while.

"You were a teenager then, Annie, as I remember it," Cleda touched Annie's hair. "Asher cleaned himself up for a while, got his old job back at the bank …"

"Bank?!" Annie furrowed her brow as if she didn't believe her aunt.

"Oh yes, your Uncle Asher is an investment genius. He's made millions for people all over the world. And I should say he didn't do too badly for me either. I had a little money to invest, and Asher turned it into a small fortune for me," Cleda rubbed her thumb and index finger together and looked around her well-furnished room. "Well, I also put together a prosperity spell ..."

"Asher did quite well when he came back to Rayes County for a while. Then, out of nowhere, he just left and went back to the Sunshiners again. But not before he planted marijuana seeds all around Olga Rainey's yard," Cleda blasted in Annie's face with laughter. "He had planted them in the spring in all her backyard flower beds and then waited until June and called the police on her."

Annie gasped, "He didn't?!"

"He most certainly did and it gets even better," Cleda's eyes were watering as she tried to hold back the punch line. "When the police tore through all her flower beds, front back, and she was charged with cultivating, she was quoted in the newspaper blaming the 'jealous old biddies' at the garden club who didn't want her to win the Rayes County Blessed Flowers of Summer contest!"

Cleda and Annie were both cackling. For the first time in a long time Annie was crying tears of laughter. Olga being taken in by the police and then blaming the garden club was priceless information for the Cleavings to have – dirt on the lady who specializes in digging up dirt – Annie didn't know if she could ever look at Olga again without picturing her in handcuffs.

"When I get back home, I'm going to the newspaper office and looking up that article, I have to have it ... I have to read it," Annie tried to talk through her laughter.

"Yeah, that Asher, he's a mess," Cleda shook her head and grinned. "You know your mother was crazy like that, too. We never knew what she and Asher would be into next. Then, your momma changed quite a bit – grew up a little after she had you, I guess," Cleda patted Annie on the knee.

When the laughter ran out of the room as quickly as it danced in, Cleda, like the other two Cleaving children, wanted to talk about Millie.

"You know your mother ... oh, I miss her so bad," Cleda started to cry. "I just wish things were different."

"How do you mean," Annie didn't know what Cleda was referring to. "Different?"

"Oh, how she loved that grandbaby of hers," Cleda moved onto Ethan and didn't revisit why she wished for something different but Annie got the idea that she was sorry for something. "She was always talking about him, sending pictures and writing about the funny things he'd do. It's hard to believe all this time has passed since your accident."

Annie didn't answer Cleda. She didn't want to talk about the crash or Ethan, and she was hoping her aunt wouldn't want force her to be rude.

"Well, you know ... I'm so sorry."

Annie nodded in acceptance as tears began to well up in her eyes.

"You know Annie, you were almost born right here in this house," Cleda changed the subject.

"But *I* was born at the Sunshine Family of Peace camp," Annie's sarcastic tone surfaced.

Cleda scolded Annie for the backhanded comment, "Your mother was a fine, decent woman and whatever she did, she did out of love and concern for you. Now, you remember that."

Annie nodded and didn't know why but felt ashamed as if her mother were listening.

"Your mother came here when she was about five months pregnant," Cleda rounded her hand out over her belly. "Oh, I was so happy to see her. I knew she was hurting but I had no idea why. We all assumed you belonged to Buck but she said no."

Annie was so tired of hearing about Buck Rosen and her mother. It was sickening to hear the two names constantly pushed together. She was so hurt that her mother never told her, not even when Buck showed up at Ethan's funeral. Annie had always assumed it was guilt that took him there – guilt for what his son had done, not because of an old flame he held for her mother.

"She didn't want to talk about it, so we didn't," Cleda shrugged her shoulders to illustrate how trivial the matter was. "It was just a nice, long visit. Well ... until Edwin showed his ass."

"Showed his ass?" Annie hadn't heard that phrasing since her grandmother passed away. Funny, she thought, how such a nasty sentence could bring back good memories.

"Well, sugar, he's always doing that, but on this particular occasion, I knew it was over between us."

Cleda insisted Annie bring her bags into the guest room and take her shoes off. Her furniture was the most comfortable Annie had ever sat in – big plush couches with tons of throw pillows and blankets. It seemed as if everything was covered in fur from the pillows to the rugs to the throw Cleda draped over Annie's legs as she refilled Annie's glass.

"Your mother was beautiful ... absolutely stunning," Cleda smoothed the back of her hand against Annie's cheek as she draped the throw over her legs. "Looked a lot like you ... one of the, if not *the*, prettiest girl in Rayes County or anywhere else for that matter."

Even as many times as Annie heard this, it never got old.

"She had been here about a couple of months and me and Edwin were having a time ... By that time Edwin had gathered long line of women and had two going during Millie's visit. Cleda and Millie would drive from house to house looking for Edwin when he would say he was working late. So many times, his car would be at the car dealership so it would look like he was there. He would even leave the light on inside his office so it would look like he was working. His office was located behind the showroom floor and the main doors stayed locked – no one could come in or out without a key. And, phone calls could never prove he was there, either. The main line was set to automatic voice messaging. Only *he* could call out and no one could call in – they'd just get the standard message.

"But we knew he wasn't there," Cleda pointed her long nail in Annie's direction. "We knew he was at that woman's house."

With Millie's help, Cleda instigated a sting operation. Millie would sit at the car dealership and Cleda at the "whore's" house. They knew they would eventually catch him, and they did.

"Your mother gave me the courage to stand up to him – to tell him to get the hell out. We packed his bags and had them waiting for him when he got home," Cleda pointed her thumb in a backward motion toward the front door. "Oh, he hated your mother for that ... hated her, loathed her.

"Stupid me, I took him back again ... only about a week after we caught him. He told me this bull-crap story about how Millie had a thing for him and how she had come on to him.

"He said she was trying to get me to throw him out so she could have him," Cleda swallowed hard and cleared her throat fighting back tears. "I believed him, and your mother and I had words – it was awful," Cleda brought her hand up to her mouth to hold it shut and then removed it to reveal one last sentence, "… the things I said to her … She left here, pregnant and no place to go … and I let her …"

"But you know she saved me whether she knew it or not," Cleda wiped her nose with a ragged tissue she retrieved from inside a one of the witch books on the coffee table. "Things were never the same between me and Edwin after that. He's just a dirt bag."

CHAPTER NINE

Annie's knowledge of Interstate travel could fit in a very small thimble. She had heard her mother use that particular phrase over and over throughout her lifetime. Annie had begun to understand it rather well, especially today. Driving around D.C. had been treacherous with eight and sometimes ten lanes of traffic. Annie found herself wishing to be back in Rayes County driving two-lanes – sometimes only one and a half.

Annie never had a reason to be in this part of the country before now. A feeling of dread and doom loomed over her as she approached the Delaware Memorial Bridge. She didn't like to be surprised – if there was a train, or an eighteen-wheeler coming at her, she wanted to face it head on – not be startled as it sidled up next to her, within mere inches of her passenger-side door. It had never occurred to her before just how much trust was involved in travel. She was trusting that everyone would stay in their own lane, and they were trusting that she would stay in hers. What they didn't know about her was that she really didn't care to die. But, if it was going to happen, she at least hoped it would be on the Delaware side and that it would happen quickly – maybe off the side of the bridge and into the cold water. She planned it all out in her mind – she would jump out of the car, mid-air, so she could die quickly, not waste time waiting for the car to sink under water. Her bones would be shattered inside her skin and death would be instant. The only flaw in her logic is that she was driving in the center lane. If she were to run off into the river, she'd have to make a few lane changes first. That was nearly impossible at this point; she was midway across the bridge and there was no way anyone was letting her over. She decided that if she were to be crushed by the cars and trucks on either side of her, she'd just have to deal with it. There would be no quick death; only a slow crushing, demeaning end as her body would be scraped up off the highway on the Jersey side by EMTs named Carmine and Vinnie.

Annie's random thoughts of death were soon replaced with thoughts of her goal. She was able to mark four Cleaving children off her list now – Millie, Veda, Asher, Cleda. It was going better than she had hoped; and quickly, too. Veda's address book had proven itself valuable and Annie started to wonder what she would have done without it. Phone numbers had been marked out over and over and replaced by new ones; addresses too. It looked like Dorie had lived just about all over New Jersey – towns were marked out and new ones added to the book. Still, she had somehow always managed to stay in Jersey.

When Annie spoke to Dorie on the phone, her aunt sounded familiar. All the Cleaving women did, though; they all sounded like voice clones of one another. There was an ever-present perfect pitch and volume to their voices, just like Lucy Cleaving. They could have all been radio hosts or newscasters if not for the Southern accent. The Cleaving women from that generation didn't stumble on their words the way Annie did. They were certain when they spoke – like they always knew exactly what they were going to say. The tone may have been sweet and calming but their words were respected upon delivery. People listened to them, at least Annie always did.

Dorie, like the others, was happy to hear from Annie and said she was looking forward to the visit. Annie knew she'd been lucky so far. Not all the Cleavings would be happy to hear from her.

The little town of Swifton was Norman Rockwell-like, the colors vivid and bold; the people coordinated. It really looked a lot like Rayes County, she thought. That is, if no one bothered to speak. Annie hated the Yankee accent. Even when talking with customers on the phone, she hated it. She felt certain that her best Elly Mae Clampett impression was what people were expecting to hear on the other end of the line. And whether she liked it or not, she delivered it time and again without even trying. "Precious" was the word most used to describe it.

Dorie's house was big – three stories, three sets of windows, a circular drive, pool in the back and a carriage house light on the front porch. Annie had no idea that any of the Cleavings had done so well. She put the car in reverse and backed down the drive just to make sure the number on the entrance was the same as the number on the directions she'd gotten from Dorie the night before on the phone.

"2252 Ransom Highway. This is it," she said as she looked at the house again, pulling forward into the circular drive once more.

Dorie and Dutch had been married for over forty years, never having any children. Annie had heard her mother say that Dutch was a good man. He came from a good family in Rayes County – the Channings, who were originally from Bangertell, Kentucky. Dutch's father was a lawyer, his mother was a doctor. They had come to Rayes County so his mother could help open the People's Clinic – a place where the poor could get free healthcare. They were both in their late forties when they had Dutch. They really looked more like his grandparents than his parents, Millie used to say. His father became quite a famous Rayes countian – one of the few who managed to overcome not being a native. Annie's mother told her that Goldie Channing, as they called him, took on cases that no one else would – old Rayes County names meant nothing to him. He went right after a few doctors whose careers ended with huge malpractice settlements. He took on a coal company and got millions for his clients and their families in a negligence suit and a wrongful death claim. That didn't make him popular in Rayes County – maybe feared but very unpopular. Dorie and Dutch started dating and were married almost the minute his shoes hit Rayes County pavement at the entrance sign when he returned from law school. Dutch's mother and father died shortly after that and Dorie and Dutch left. Dutch joined a friend from law school in a practice in Jersey. They opened several more firms all over the state. Dutch oversaw each one until the fledgling practices found their wings.

Annie stood at the front door under the big light and waited for someone to come. She had pushed the lighted button and chimes were still going off in the house long after she had removed her finger. The house looked even bigger from the front porch. It was red brick with white trim – spectacular, the landscaping picturesque. Evergreens anchored the Rhododendrons and Holly bushes; ivy draped perfectly over the eaves of the house; river rock spilled over onto the entrance. Annie immediately thought of Olga and how envious she would be of Dorie's effortless blooms.

"Annie," Dorie opened the door, immediately hugging Annie, "It's so good to see you."

"Thank you, Aunt Dorie, it's really good to see you, too."

"I can't believe you're all the way up here in New Jersey – that's quite a drive. If I had known before last night that you were coming, we could have had a plane ticket waiting."

Flying was something that didn't occur to Annie as she planned the trip. It just always seemed so unnatural to her, being up in the air with the birds.

"No, I really enjoyed the drive," lingered in the hug longer than she expected. Dorie's skin felt familiar as it squished against Annie's cheek. "I visited Cleda and Asher on the way up."

"... still with the Peace Family I guess?" Dorie rolled her eyes and gave Annie a pat on the back, ushering her inside.

"He seems pretty happy with his situation," Annie followed her aunt inside.

"I wish Dutch was here to see. Stockton and him took out to conquer the world again but I shouldn't complain; it keeps mama well," Dorie lifted her hands in the air displaying her diamond-studded fingers.

"You really have a beautiful home."

"Thank you, Annie. I have been so very, very blessed. Come on in and I'll show you the place. We don't' really live in this part of the house but it makes for a very grand entrance for company, huh?"

At that moment when Dorie asked a question, ending it with "huh," Annie felt right at home even in all the grandeur surrounding her. "Huh," at the end of a question was a Cleaving trademark or maybe even part of Rayes County's history somehow. When Annie heard it from Dorie, she no longer felt she was in a foreign country.

"Yes, it does make for quite a grand entrance." Annie tense muscles began to loosen.

The foyer was almost as big as Annie's entire house. The glass and marble tiles were elegant, the ceilings at least thirty feet high. There was a tree near the winding staircase with landscaping right there in the room. A waterfall cascaded down the side of the stairs and ran into the small pond around the tree. Small bushes and tropical plants found niches near the tree's trunk. Sun beamed in from a skylight, white puffy clouds were moving by.

The solid dark wood and brass staircase must have been

custom; Annie had never seen anything like it.

"Come on in here and I'll show you the rest," Dorie's silky dress flowed behind her as she walked.

Royal chairs filled the formal dining room, elegant cushions on carved wood and clawed feet. Cloth napkins and rings atop gold-rimmed China dotted the dark wood. The glasses were etched with gold edgings; the cutlery was gold, not silver. Annie had visions of Dorie struggling to carry this loot from Saddam Hussein's palace. A Bond spy movie couldn't have had a better set than Dorie's ballroom; just the right place to discover high-dollar and even higher security international secrets while dancing with a sexy double agent.

"Do you have parties in here?" Annie couldn't help herself.

"Yes, we do have a Christmas – well, a Holiday party here every season and an anniversary party each year as well. I had your Uncle Dutch's fiftieth birthday party here some years ago. That one was the most fun. We had some DC royalty here for that. There was even a write-up about it in the *"Post."*

Annie assumed Dorie was talking about the *Washington Post*. She couldn't imagine any other Post would be allowed entry.

At the end of the at least twelve-foot-wide hallway, there was a set of double doors that matching the massiveness of the outside entry doors. Dorie pushed one slightly. It seemed to move on its own with just her gentle nudge. She nodded her head toward the living space, telling Annie to go inside. Annie was starting to feel a little like Alice down the rabbit hole. She wondered how someone in the Cleaving family could end up living like this while the others had managed to land in swamp of Stig County. She remembered Millie telling her once that marrying well was just as much of a skill as any other trade. Millie would laugh about it, as if it was a joke, but still Annie could always see the truth in that statement. Dorie had done it; married well. Now, she was living well. Uncle Dutch had made himself a fortune and it showed in his home and his wife. Dorie looked very young for an older woman. Annie started to wonder if she'd had any work done. But Dorie's face didn't look stressed or stretched, just relaxed and happy. Just before Annie entered, she noticed another door just a few feet up the hall to her right. There was a woman carrying bags in.

"Oh, that's Janie – she lives here and helps me take care of the place," Dorie said. "It's a full-time job, believe me."

Annie nodded, "So, she's the maid?"

"Yes, but I prefer to call her an employee. It sounds less pretentious," Dorie laughed a little. "Annie, please don't think I'm uppity; I still know where Rayes County is, and I know I'm still a Cleaving …"

"No, Aunt Dorie," Annie interrupted. "I don't. I am just amazed at this house, and you have a maid. You've done well."

"Dutch does well," Dorie hesitated then smiled. "I just got lucky enough to fall in love with him."

As Annie entered the big, wooden double doors, she found herself in a normal, ordinary house – like a house inside of a house. There was a normal-sized foyer, a normal-sized staircase and to the right, a normal-sized living room. It had a television and a large green sectional. There were magazines on the end tables and a cup sitting on a coaster. A ragged looking throw lay on the floor next to the couch and the remote-control to the television was on top.

"This," Dorie held her arms out in presentation, "is where we live. That," she pointed her thumb, hitchhiker style, to the door they just came through, "is where folks think we live. I wasn't about to have a house this size without some comfy space. This is much cozier, huh?"

Annie smiled, "Yes, it is. I would have never thought this was in here."

"Most people don't and most never see it. I could live with or without the rest of it. The main entrance that we came in doesn't even really have to be there."

Dorie took Annie to the back of the house and showed her a door leading to the garage separate from the rest of the big house. It was attached only to the back of the smaller house. Annie peeked out to see the garage door open and the main drive off in the distance. The smaller garage was messy just like any other garage she had ever seen. Very normal, other than the dark blue Mercedes parked inside, Dorie referred to it as her blue baby.

"Let's go get something to drink," Dorie pointed to the kitchen. "What would you like?"

"Anything, really."

"How about an Irish Coffee? You know, it's not *really* that early."

"Fine with me," Annie imagined her aunt having the drink of the Irish every morning with her toast.

Annie sat on a stool near the bar and watched as her aunt made the coffee. She put the whiskey in the coffee water that she was about to run through the coffee maker. This not Dorie's first time making Irish coffee.

"Go ahead and get those papers out and let's get that out of the way," Dorie held her palms out giving the "come on" signal.

Annie was relieved that she hadn't had to ask her aunt again to sign them. She pulled her purse from her shoulder and laid the deed and a pen on the counter.

"Do you want to take off your jacket?" Dorie was trying to make Annie more comfortable. "You can just throw your things over on the bench."

Annie saw the bench next to the dining room wall. It was filled with books and papers some folded laundry – it was all white. She took her coat and purse and placed them on the bench next to the other things. When she turned back around, her Irish coffee was ready – complete with whipped cream on top and Dorie was busy signing the deed.

"There," Dorie handed Annie the deed. "Now, stick that in your purse so we don't misplace it in all this mess. You can tell I'm the one doing the housework in *this* place. I haven't gotten to it in a while."

"Why don't you let the lady who works here take care of it?"

"It makes me feel better doing laundry, dishes, vacuuming … you know, I can get awfully depressed if I don't have something to do. It makes me feel useful, keeps my mind occupied."

Annie wondered how Dorie could ever feel depressed or not useful while living in such a beautiful place and having so much money.

"You know Annie, all of us Cleavings are prone to depression," Dorie swirled her finger around her temple giving the international crazy gesture. "Now, there's you – even you, the next generation, have been handed the Cleaving curse."

Annie knew Dorie was talking about Ethan. She found a slight smile and took a sip from her cup.

"I know it must be painful to talk about," Dorie let Annie know she wasn't going to make it the afternoon's conversational topic.

"So, you said you had seen Asher, Cleda and Veda?"

"Yes."

"What? Are you saving the monsters for last?" Dorie cackled then stopped abruptly. "Seriously, you do realize that the hard parts are coming. I heard that Jaygar has moved off his reservation and onto someone else's so to speak."

Annie gave her aunt a puzzled look.

"Yeah – he has renamed himself some Native American name, no kidding, and is now a part of some kind of reservation; at least that's what I had heard," Dorie was proud of herself that she was still in the Cleaving grapevine.

"I hope to be seeing him soon," Annie made her aunt aware of her resolve. "He's over in Pennsylvania."

Dorie stood at the bar sipping at her Irish Coffee, "Yes, the Cleavings have had their share of pain."

Dorie drew a deep breath, "You know I really wanted to come and see your mother – I wanted to visit with her so many times. I just couldn't, you know. When you were little, I thought there'd be no way I could look at you. And, then when you were a teenager, all I could think about was what you were doing, how you were doing in school, were you going to prom … having your hair done, your nails manicured. I knew how pretty you were. Your momma sent me photos."

Annie was becoming more confused with every word Dorie spoke.

"I know you don't have any idea what I'm talking about," Dorie seemed to be looking over every inch of Annie's face.

"What are you talking about?" Annie looked down into her

cup to break Dorie's stare.

"I wanted so much to be like your mother. She was so wild and so free – free from what people thought of her, free from the convictions that the old Rayes County women put on us Cleaving girls. She didn't care. I was so envious of her – so brave, so brave," Dorie looked Annie's eyes. Annie knew her aunt was seeing Millie at that moment.

"She came here and stayed with me during the last couple of months before you were born. I could tell she had changed – something about her was different. She seemed frightened even – scared of her own shadow – jumpy, you know."

Annie remembered Asher saying her mother had stayed with Dorie before coming to the Sunshiners.

"I was so excited about you coming. I wanted the both of you to live with me and Dutch forever. I bought baby clothes, fixed up a room for you. I was consumed, really."

"Your mother was so brave," Dorie repeated herself again. "She always was. I could tell she was damaged, though. I tried to get her to tell me what happened – she wouldn't. She would only say the same old story about how your father left. Maybe that was enough to change her – but I never really believed that."

"What do you mean, something happened to her?" Annie leaned in closer.

"I don't know, really," Dorie shook her head like she was confused. "She just wasn't herself when she got here. The daredevil in her was gone, for the most part. But there was that last moment of MILLIE THE INVINCIBLE!" Dorie shouted, thrusting a fist into the air.

Annie sat back a little, not knowing what to expect next.

"Pay me not never mind – I like to get a little loud sometimes," Dorie finally sat down on the bar stool across from Annie.

"Yep, she dug down and pulled her old self back out for a day or two. She saved me, she saved Dutch, and he doesn't even know it. I don't know where I would be right now if she hadn't helped me."

Dorie held her index finger up and looked around the room as if someone had been listening, "Hang on just a second and let me make sure no one else is in the house."

Annie watched as her aunt walked room to room and then went to the front doors. She opened them, looked around in the hallway, then came back in and locked them tight.

"I want to be careful. I trust Janie – you know, my housekeeper – but I really wouldn't want to have to deal with any explanations of this. I'm only telling you now because I want you to remember your mother the way *I* do – brave and relentless when it came to protecting her family."

Annie forced a smile but was tired of being told she didn't know her own mother. She thought about how many times she had wished for her mother to be brave – stand up to people, throw some insults – even curse a little. It never happened; she never fought back.

"I couldn't believe it when she told me what Edwin did to her," Dorie looked longingly out the kitchen window as she spoke.

When Millie finally told Dorie what had happened, Cleda had already thrown Edwin out for good.

"It all made sense after that," Dorie nodded as if she had a clear understanding of the matter. "The way she was acting when

she got here – damaged, broken."
Dorie told Annie about the night when Cleda and Millie spied on Edwin. The same night when they caught him with another woman.

"What your aunt Cleda most likely and conveniently left out of the story was why Millie left there after that," Dorie hesitated, cleared her throat and took another sip of her coffee. "Your mother was packing her things to leave Cleda's house after Edwin had lied and told Cleda that Millie wanted the two of them apart so Millie could take her place. I am assuming Cleda told you at least that much?"

"Yes. That's what she told me happened," Annie didn't want to know what more could there be.

"What she didn't tell you is that she was out while your mother was packing her things. She was so mad at Millie she didn't even want to be near her again. She just wanted her out. She believed Edwin and what he said about Millie wanting to be with him – what a joke," Dorie gave a sarcastic "humpf" through her tears. "He was so conceited – he thought every woman wanted him, still does from what I hear."

Edwin came home while Cleda was gone and found Millie packing. Edwin knew Cleda would be out, trying to avoid having to look at her sister. He had convincingly portrayed Millie as the home wrecker, who was trying to break up his and Cleda's "blissful" life together.

"He came up from behind her – that's the only way he could've done it – from behind, like the coward he is," Dorie held her hands to her mouth, tears dropping down on them. She pulled a tissue from a pocket Annie hadn't even noticed on her dress and wiped her eyes. "He stripped her down and threw her out of the house. There she was pregnant, naked and trying to get back in.

She was out there for a good long while before one of the neighbors called the police."

Dorie drew her hand up to her mouth as if she were trying to keep anything else from coming out.

"Your mother was just broken after that; I just can't explain it. He had humiliated her to her very core. Talked to her like a dog and threatened to rape her right then and there – give her what she wanted, he said. He was a horrible man … cruel," Doris cupped her hand around Annie's arm as it lay on the counter.

Annie was trying not to picture someone being so cruel to her mother, but it was playing in her mind over and over again as Dorie spoke.

"Did Cleda know?" Annie begged for an explanation.

"Yes, she drove by as your mother, naked and pregnant tried to chase her down to get help and wouldn't stop."

Just like the mother Annie knew, Millie forgave her sister and never mentioned the incident again. Even so, Annie couldn't imagine what kind of person it took to drive by while someone was so helpless, so vulnerable.

"Your mother swore he didn't rape her – that he only threatened, but I just don't know. She was broken, I tell you, just broken. When she showed up here, she was bruised on her face and neck. Dutch said he's seen evidence photos of rape victims in court – their necks are usually always bruised."

Dorie said she and Dutch begged Millie to let him ruin Edwin.

"Dutch wanted to kill him, or at least ruin his life – tax evasion has always been his vice. You know he was involved in some shady financial deals through his dealership. He wasn't just a car salesman; he sold guns too – sometimes to felons. They were the ones who would pay the most for an untraceable weapon. Your mother just wouldn't let us do anything. She said he had responsibilities to his family, and they needed him to be 'whole' – financially. So, we held off."

After Cleda had thrown Edwin out, Dutch and Dorie paid Cleda a visit and told her they knew what happened.

"We were convinced that as many times as she had taken that son of a bitch back that she surely wouldn't let him come home again. We told her if she did, she was nothing more than dirt and not to contact us again for any reason," Dorie eyes were red, but she had stopped crying. "She never has to this day taken him back."

The family never spoke of it again, mainly because Millie, Dorie and Cleda didn't want the children to find out, especially Ed, Jr.

"No wonder she went to live with the Sunshiners. I think I would've too – away from this family – anywhere away from you guys," Annie was angry that Cleda hadn't told her the whole story.

"There was more to her visit," Dorie paused for a moment as if to ask Annie if she was ready to hear it. "I hate to dump all this on you in one day, but we may not get to visit like this again. And I want you to know what your mother did for me – for us. I've always wanted you to know how brave she was – how she loved me, everyone, unconditionally."

Annie had expected many things before she started on the trip – maybe the occasional angry heir wanting their part of the Cleaving property, even talk of Ethan and Millie that would make her uncomfortable. But not confessionals she didn't want to hear. What good were they now? Her mother was gone.

"I don't know where she found the strength after all she'd

been through, but before Millie told me what happened with Edwin and Cleda, she helped me do something – something necessary."

"Go ahead," Annie sounded sarcastic. "Tell me what it is – I'm ready for anything now."

Dorie crossed her arms and tightened her lips, letting Annie know her sarcasm had been noticed.

"Okay, I'll tell you," Dorie smiled and trying to lighten the mood. "But not before you agree to stay the night and let me take you out for a spa evening."

"I appreciate you wanting to treat me, but I just don't have the time," Annie pleaded as delicately as she could. "I really don't feel like being pampered just yet – I am in the midst of a real estate crisis here and I need to get all the deeds signed. Maybe I can visit again when all this is done."

Annie had no intention of returning to New Jersey – ever. They both knew this was likely the last time they'd visit in person.

"Okay. Have it your way – you don't have to know the rest," Dorie was disappointed that Annie considered her offer for a spa day trivial. "It's probably better that I leave this one in the closet where it belongs. As it stands now, there was only one other person on Earth who knew – your mother. Now, it's just me – alone with it. I guess that's how it should be."

CHAPTER TEN

Annie was a little uncomfortable at first – having people rub all over her and bring her drinks. But after the fourth Tom Collins her aunt ordered for them both, she didn't mind it so much. Every part of her body had been massaged – right down to her fingers and toes; she had been waxed, conditioned, peeled and scrubbed.

"Oh, how great it is to be me," Dorie slurred her words, holding her drink up as if to give cheers. "Now, Annie, this is the life. You should come and stay with me and Dutch permanently. Forget about that old Cleaving house. Let it sit there and rot."

Annie couldn't imagine living in Jersey – even if it was near her rich aunt Dorie. And, as bad as she wanted to leave Rayes County she was surprised at how much she longed for the familiar surroundings of home.

She didn't want to know anything else about her mother, her family. She should have just left after Dorie told her about Edwin; still, something kept her there wanting to know more.

Annie had never been to a spa, and she didn't suspect she'd ever go again. It was nice, but when Annie started to feel relaxed and happy, Ethan was the first thing that came to her thoughts. How old would he be now, where would they be now, would she be helping him with his homework? One thing was for sure, if

Ethan were still alive, she wouldn't be having a spa treatment with this rich old lady in Jersey. Annie watched her aunt gulping the drink, trying not to get any on her white robe.

"So, come on Dorie," Annie urged. "Cough it up, hand it over, spill it …"

Annie even surprised herself at the many ways she could demand answers. She and Dorie laughed until their eyes were watering.

"Shut the door," Dorie pointed a limp arm at the attendant the nodded toward the door. "I'll let you know when we're done."

Dorie's tone was ominous. Annie wiped the smile from her face, positioning her chair upright. Despite the robes, having their hair in towels and their faces being covered in mud, Annie could feel the mood of the room becoming suddenly tense and anxious.

The attendant nodded to Dorie through an almost-closed door. She placed the "Do Not Disturb" door hanger on the outside knob before the door shut completely, demonstrating to Dorie that she understood her demand.

"Thank you," Dorie yelled after her. "It's always important to be polite to those less fortunate."

Annie wasn't sure she needed an etiquette lecture from her rich aunt but took the advice and smiled.

"Go on, tell me," Annie's mind was already forming scenarios of what her aunt might tell her. "What else happened?"

"You know, you're more like the old Millie I used to know than you can ever imagine, Annie. She was always relentless in her pursuit of life. I see that in you."

Annie wasn't sure she agreed with Dorie. Life wasn't

something *she* pursued at all; it was more like living until death came for her. If one could call that a pursuit, then pursuit of the afterlife would be a more accurate description of how Annie lived.

"But all that was gone when she came to me and Dutch with you on the way," Dorie kept tugging at her robe, trying to cover her almost exposed breasts. "I knew something was wrong with her when I asked her to help me but I asked anyway. I just really didn't know where else to turn."

Annie raised her eyebrows and lifted her glass at Dorie as if to say once again, "spill it."

Dorie swung her legs around to the side of the chair and sat facing Annie. "You know why Dutch and I don't have any children? The real truth, not that we were too busy – but the real truth was that your uncle is sterile – we can't have children."

"Yes, Aunt Dorie, I know quite well what sterile means," Annie resented the fact that Dorie slowed her speech and enunciated more clearly in her attempt to educate the heathen of Rayes County sitting there with her.

Annie was familiar with the Yankee perception of Southerners. But it surprised her that a native of Rayes County thought the same thing.

"When your mother arrived at our house, I was feeling sick … very, very sick. It went on like that for two weeks. I had no idea what was going on.

"Then one day your mother asked me if there was a possibility that I could be pregnant," Dorie smiled, her face coming to life. "Your mother always knew everything; she had a keen eye or maybe it was a keen soul."

"So, you weren't, or you were?" Annie was sure she knew the

answer now.

"I was."

"But you just said Dutch was …"

"Yes, your Uncle Dutch fathered children," Dorie didn't slow her speech or over enunciate her words ridiculously this time. "Your uncle was so, so busy all the time, he was gone – sometimes for days, weeks."

"I'm not proud of it but I started fooling around with a young man who was coming by our house to do some yard work – 'bout half my age."

"Hello, Mrs. Robinson," Annie smiled and toasted her glass to Dorie.

Dorie didn't smile. Through her sad eyes she scolded Annie for the cruel joke.

"It wasn't like that, Annie," Dorie looked surprised that Annie could be so cruel. "I don't know if I did it because I was lonely or to get back at Dutch for not being around. Either way, it was the worst mistake of my life."

"Your mother and I kept trying to figure out a way that I could keep the baby," Dorie's eyes were now red and tear-filled. "But the math wouldn't work. There was no way to do it without Dutch finding out I had …," Dorie stopped in mid-sentence, looking at the floor.

"At that time, it was illegal," Dorie didn't speak the word but Annie knew what she was talking about. "You had to ask around to find one."

When she looked up from the floor, Annie could see the shame in her face, "I had been asked to join a D.C. cause to help rid the country of illegal clinics and get the doctors indicted for murder. I signed the petition but never did any real work on it – never got off the ground. I found the clinic listed in there."

Annie remembered all her life hearing about poor Dutch and Dorie, how they never had any children. What a lonely life they'd have when they grew old is what people would say.

"Oh Annie, I wanted a baby so bad." Dorie dropped her head back as if she were in pain. "I had begged and begged your mother to let me have you – to let me and Dutch have you so she could go on with her life and we could be your parents. I pleaded with her – told her we'd be such good parents to you and that we'd love you and care for you better than any parents ever loved and cared for any child."

Annie wondered why her mother never spoke about Dutch being sterile – she'd just say they never had time. That was just like Millicent Cleaving, too proper to talk about the reproductive cycle and too considerate to mention that her sister wanted a baby but couldn't have one. Annie wondered what her own reaction would have been if someone had asked if they could keep Ethan.

"She would never give you up; wouldn't even consider it for a moment, Annie. She loved you so much, even before you were born; she loved you so much …"

Dorie's tears turned quickly into sobs.

"I, on the other hand, didn't love my baby enough to sacrifice my lifestyle for her," Dorie sat rigid now, her face showing disgust for her actions. "Every time I have a spa day, every time I buy a new dress, a new car – help myself to some caviar at a fancy party, I think about the price I paid to keep my marriage, my life, untouched."

Dorie took a big gulp of her drink and lay back down in her

lounge chair as if she were resting after pulling a boulder up a mountain then letting it drop down the other side.

"This is my life, Annie – this is my life now. And the sad part is that I truly believe now that Dutch loved me enough that we could have kept that baby and our marriage would have recovered. He does, I just know it," Dorie said as if the opportunity to keep the baby still existed. "… he loves me that much, he loves us that much."

Annie watched as her aunt lay still, staring at the ceiling as if she were waiting for an out-of-body experience.

"Your mother was visibly pregnant; I wasn't," Dorie covered her face with a wet washcloth the attendant left on a nearby basket. "We walked into the building and up those stairs – those dirty stairs, looking at those dirty walls. The elevator only worked from the fifth floor; it creaked and popped. I wanted to die. When we got to the twelfth floor, I kept looking at window after window and wondering if they opened. I wanted to jump."

Annie knew that feeling well. She had felt that way every day since Ethan died. If there was an opportunity to think about jumping out of a twelve-story window, driving her car off a bridge, standing in the middle of the railroad tracks while a train was coming, she had thought about it – taking her last breath here on Earth and her next with Ethan in her arms.

"Your mother held my hand all the way up those stairs and into that elevator. She held me in her arms as I sat there waiting to kill my baby. I felt you kick so many times that day," Dorie took the washcloth from her face and turned her head, looking at Annie. "It was as if you were trying to tell us to stop – to go home. I always wondered if you and my little child had some sort of connection that day – if you comforted her during her final hours," Annie looked toward the door to avoid looking at her aunt, but

Dorie sat up then turned Annie's face toward her. "Yes, Annie, like it or not, you were there. You were there with us that day."

Annie tried to imagine her mother being at an abortion clinic or even anywhere near one. She couldn't. She just simply couldn't picture the moral, ethical, honest and forthright Millicent Cleaving participating in the demise of an infant, especially a niece or nephew. Annie wondered why Dorie kept referring to the child as a she; and then decided that must have been what her aunt had wished for.

"When it was over, your mother held me there for a long time," Dorie picked up her glass and took a sip of her drink then took a long breath and sighed. "You didn't kick anymore that day after it was over. It was like you were grieving right along with us that day. Your mother carried me to the elevator. She was very pregnant, yet she found the strength to carry me," Dorie rolled her eyes at the irony. "That was the last time I saw Millicent Cleaving the brave, Millicent Cleaving the invincible," A trace of a smile ran quickly away from Dorie's face. "She showed herself one last time to take care of me and then vanished again."

The sisters stayed two days in a hotel near the clinic, Millie feeding her sister when she would eat and carried her to the bathroom when she needed to go. Even though Dorie wasn't listening, Millie read to her from a book she had taken out of Dutch's library – Ernest Hemmingway's *For Whom the Bell Tolls*.

"I was so weak – physically weak, just drained," Dorie but both hands on her stomach as if she was hoping the baby was still inside. "My body grieved, and my mind grieved right along with it. For two days we stayed there – just the two of us, and you."

"I was looking out the window, hearing your mother's words as she read when Millie stopped reading. I hadn't paid any mind to her words at all, only heard her voice. I loved her voice," Dorie stroked her neck as if she could feel Millie's voice inside hers. "When she stopped reading, I looked over to see her packing up her things. I don't know if she came to the end of the book or just got tired of watching me lie there. She then pulled me up out of the bed by my arms as I fought her. She shook me hard. She told me it was time to go home. Her exact words were, 'this moment has passed.'"

Annie recognized the phrase and new it was her mother who had been there with Dorie during her abortion. There was no doubt that Dorie and she were there at that hotel. Those words, the same words Millie spoke to Annie when she felt Annie had grieved long enough over Ethan's death. Annie hated those words but loved them just as much. It gave her permission to move on even though she thought she shouldn't – permission from the highest power, her mother.

"She said I had to straighten up and go home to my husband," Dorie over at Annie as if to ask if she recognized her mother now. "I cried and begged her to leave me there and just tell Dutch I'd run off. That was the only time your mother ever slapped me – she had taken me that far and I gave up on her. I truly wanted to die. Do you ever feel that way, Annie, Do you ever want to die?"

Shaken by Dorie's question, Annie fidgeted nervously with the belt on her robe. She didn't know her death wish was so transparent – a readable face, yet another Cleaving flaw. All the women had one. If they were upset, you knew it; if they were mad, you knew it; and if you wanted your spleen pulled out then just let them know you saw an emotion they were trying to hide.

"You don't have to answer that question," Dorie's tender smile returned. "I think I already know the answer."

Annie shoved Dorie's pity away in the corners of her mind

where the other gibberish and horse manure lived; things like, "It's always darkest before the dawn;" "There's a reason for everything;" and, "It's all in God's plan."

"So, what happened after that?" Annie shifted the focus back to Dorie.

"I went home; lived my life and loved my husband," Dorie shrugged her shoulders, fighting back another round of tears. "But the one thing I never did again, Annie, was ask your mother to give you up; to give you over to me and Dutch. As it turns out, I was not, nor would I ever be the perfect parent," Dorie's voice was barely a whisper now. "I would cry every time Millie would mention you – every time I'd see her rub her belly," Dorie placed her hand across her stomach again. "That's why she left; she knew it would kill me to see you."

Annie rose from her seat as if some invisible force was pushing her and sat next to her aunt. Trying to lighten the mood, Annie whispered loudly, "I'm here now – not killing you, is it?"

Dorie laughed and bumped Annie's shoulder with hers.

"I remember the pictures she used to send to me," Dorie smiled. "You were there in your little hippie garb, running around there on the campsites, playing with the other little hippie kids. I still have some of them at home."

"What? What do you mean 'running around'? Annie was confused. "We left there after I was born?"

"No. Millie stayed with Asher until you were about two years old," Dorie shook her head, puzzled that Annie didn't know. "In fact, I have a picture of you celebrating your second birthday there."

"WHAT?! Annie almost yelled. "Are you sure?"

"Yes. Why are you getting so upset?"

Annie went back to her lounger chair so she could face Dorie again.

"I'm upset because I had no knowledge of my mother ever staying at the Sunshine camp, then I go there and find out she gave birth to me there. Then, Asher tells me my mother left with me shortly after I was born – still a baby. Can you explain this to me?!"

"What do you mean you had no idea?" Dorie shook her head in disbelief.

"I had no idea Dorie – I had no idea," Annie ranted. "Until a few days ago I had never heard of the Sunshine Family of Peace."

A look of panic came across Dorie's face.

"Oh, well I'm probably mistaken about that. You know your mother moved around so much when she was pregnant with you. I probably just have my dates mixed up."

"No, you don't, Dorie!" Annie leaned in toward her. "You have pictures of me when I was two. Don't you try to back out on this!" Annie pointed her finger.

Annie could tell that Dorie's brain was firing rapidly now, searching for what to say next.

"Annie – your mother has always done what was best for you. Just know that about her."

Back at the house, Dorie couldn't "lay hands" on those photos Annie was so upset about. There were unanswered questions now – a growing list in Annie's mind; questions that didn't exist a few days ago. There were a few more stops to make but Annie meant to give Uncle Asher one more visit before going home. She was sure now that the old hippie knew something.

CHAPTER ELEVEN

Annie's butt was numb from driving for so long without stopping. She stretched her arms up high and swayed back and forth in front of the mirror. She looked like a different person; she was transformed into someone else – someone pretty.

She stopped swaying and leaned in closer to the mirror. She really liked her new hair color. It was softer, more brunette and glistened under the fluorescent lights. Her eyebrows matched her hair color, and they were perfectly manicured, along with her fingernails, toenails too. She had renamed the makeup chosen for her and was now calling it Miracle Elixir. It covered everything. Her face was porcelain with a peach glow. She dug into her purse and took out the new lipstick and began applying it just as the cosmetologist had shown her – dab, dab bottom; dab, dab top; then, press lips and rub together in a frontwards motion then sideways. If the desired affect is not reached, then repeat. Annie only had to do it once; it was plenty dark enough with just one application. She inspected her eyelids and eyeliner. She was proud of herself for remembering exactly how the cosmetologist applied it the day before; exactly as she was shown. Annie checked her teeth – not lipstick on them. She was told that was important. They were at least two shades whiter. Annie tilted her head from side to side and let her hair touch her shoulders. She looked new. She hadn't realized how dull she had become until yesterday. It was like someone had found the right size ladder and cleaned the windows inside and out – the colors were vibrant and vivid – Annie was vibrant and vivid.

She was glad to finally stop at a gas station with a store and a restroom – one that didn't look like the crime scene tape had just been rolled up and put back on the shelf for future use. This station looked like it could have been in Rayes County. It was clean, colorful and had just about everything a girl on the road would need. The coffee station was spotless, the lids and cups stacked and even the cappuccino machine wasn't sticky. Annie touched it on the way in just to be sure. She had already spent at least twenty minutes in the bathroom, and she was about to spend at least another fifteen looking around the store. It was nice to be off her butt and on her feet and to have something to look at other than pavement, signs, and billboards.

The aroma of vanilla roast coffee was ghosting its way up to Annie's nose. She closed her eyes and sniffed just a little as she reached for a cup. What sounded like falling ping pong balls brought her out of the vanilla haze.

"Oh, oh gosh," Annie began picking up the foam cups and plastic lids she had just knocked over. She looked over at the casher, who was not paying attention, and then continued trying to correct the coffee cup chaos she had just created.

"Here, let me help you with those," Annie heard a man's voice and then felt a hand on her shoulder. She could smell nice cologne, even as she was just looking at his shoes.

Perched on the balls of her feet and squatted in the floor, she had been able to stack several cups together in her left hand. As she stood up to place the cups back on the counter, she could now see his back as he crouched down to pick up more cups and lids.

He leaned his briefcase up against the counter. Now, Annie could see that his shoes matched his suit – very classy, pinstriped black and gray. She watched as he bobbed up and down a little as he picked up the last of the lids. She looked over at the cashier, who was now paying attention. Annie smiled at her sheepishly and mouthed the word, "sorry." The cashier threw an excusing hand motion her way and then gave Annie a thumbs up nodding an approval at the handsome fellow cleaning up Annie's mess. Annie laughed a little to herself but then stopped when he rose up and placed the cups and lids on the counter.

"There," he turned and looked at Annie. "It's all okay, all cleaned up – everything just like it was. It happens to me all the time."

"Really?" Annie was struck by his quick wit.

"No, I'm just trying to make you feel better," he laughed and then stuck his hand out for her to shake.

"Hello, I'm David," his eyes seemed to drill holes in her pupils.

Annie put her hand forward to return the greeting; he gave it a shake. His eyes were deep brown, his skin and hair dark. His lips were thick and ruby and his eyelashes long. Annie could feel a small moth in her belly awaken and begin fluttering about.

"And you are?"

"Oh, I'm sorry," Annie came to herself and realized she had yet to say a word to David. "I'm Annie – Annie Cleaving."

"Well, hello Miss Cleaving," his voice was sure; his body language indicated interest. "It is Miss isn't it?"

"Yes, it's Miss," Annie could see David was no amateur with the ladies. "Thank you for helping me clean this up; you really didn't have to."

"Nonsense," David dismissed Annie's apology. "I'm always eager to rescue a damsel in distress."

Annie smiled, "Well, thank you." She reached for a cup.

"No, no, allow me," David took a cup from the stack he had just placed on the counter. "What is your pleasure?"

"Vanilla bean," And there it was. She sounded just like Ellie Mae Clampett at the Queen's Tea – or "tay."

When David heard her say Vanilla bean, he turned. "Your accent is beautiful Annie Cleaving," David repeated her name as if to engrave it into his memory.

"I am from Kentucky," Annie again sounded just like Ellie. "Rayes County – southeastern Kentucky."

"Ah, Kentucky," David's eyes grew wide. "Beautiful horses, beautiful mountains and beautiful women."

Annie smiled as he continued filling her cup with the fragrant coffee, almost running it over.

"May I add cream, sugar?"

"Both please," Annie couldn't stop staring at him. He was handsome – dashing is exactly how she would describe him if she were an actress in one of her old black and white movies. "So, are you from here?"

"Me? No, not from here," David talked as he added cream to her cup. "I am on my way to New York to try a case."

"Oh, you're a lawyer?"

"Yes, an attorney who is in desperate need of a cup of coffee," David handed the coffee to Annie just after putting a lid on it. "Lucky I ran into you. Otherwise, I wouldn't have known that what I needed was Vanilla bean."

David put his own cup under the coffee spout. Annie stood there awkwardly, not knowing if she should wait until he was finished or go and check out. Seeming to sense her tension, he asked her to hold his briefcase while he added cream and sugar to his coffee.

"What brings a Kentucky girl to the Philly area?"

"Going to see a relative in Pennsylvania," Annie caught herself bouncing like a child as she spoke.

"Oh, I see," David's dropped his head slightly to show Annie how sad he was. "I was hoping to hear that you were travelling my way so we could stop and have lunch together later."

Annie really wished she were travelling David's way. Of all the places, the stupid Cleaving clan ended up, she thought, why couldn't one of them have been on the way to New York?!

"Yeah. That would have been nice," Annie felt her stomach shaking.

Now at the counter, both of them stood waiting for the cashier to turn around. She was taking her time, Annie noticed, pulling cigarettes down from their shelves and then placing them back on top – a completely nonsensical act.

"Well, since we can't have lunch Annie Cleaving, let me at least give you my business card," David handed Annie the card, touching her wrist as he did. "You never know when you might need a good attorney or just someone to help you clean up a mess."

Annie felt her moth flutter again inside her stomach. When David touched her wrist, it was like he was touching her entire body. She felt warm, suddenly. She wanted to fall into his arms and close her eyes. She wanted him to carry her away – to where didn't matter.

"Thank you. I'll keep it," was all Annie could manage to blurt out.

Annie wanted to give him her information but didn't have a business card. Writing her number down on a slip of paper seemed trashy, as her mother would have said, so she just turned to the cashier and began getting her wallet out of her purse.

"It was nice to meet you, David," Annie backed out the double doors, stumbling a bit before turning around. "Again, thank you for helping."

Now Annie was sounding more like herself. She was treating David just like an NCS customer – thank you and great to meet was always a good bullshit office reply.

"Nice to meet you too, Annie," he turned to the cashier as if he'd given up on wooing Annie any further.

Annie buckled herself in. Across many pumps, she could see David through the windows of his SUV. She watched him as he pumped his gas for a few moments. He was beautiful, poised, handsome … he had taken a manly stance as he propped one foot upon the pump platform. He ran his hand through his hair at one point as the breeze tousled his bangs over his forehead then rubbed a hand across his perfectly chiseled face. He pretended not to notice that Annie was still sitting in her car at the gas pumps.

Annie glanced for a moment at herself in the rearview mirror. She noticed the cashier inside staring at her and making hand motions.

"Oh, great, I left something in there," She looked around; her purse, jacket, and everything else was in the seat next to her. She looked at the cashier, shrugged her shoulders and held her hands up, "What?"

The cashier pointed at Annie and then over to David. She made a writing motion on the window.

Annie looked over at David and then back at the cashier, who was nodding her head letting Annie know they understood one another.

If Annie was going to give David her information, she knew she had to hurry. Thank goodness he was driving a gas guzzler; she had already wasted so much time. She quickly scribbled her e-mail address on an old grocery store receipt she found in her purse and walked it over to David, who was still pumping gas.

"Here's my e-mail address," Annie's voice now squeaked. She still couldn't bring herself to give a phone number. "Maybe you can send me a message some time."

How stupid. Send me a message sometime? Really? Is that all you can say? Annie's mind was racing.

"I will," David was confident, his smile wide now. "I will send you a message, Annie," he put a big emphasis on the word will.

Annie playfully began backing toward her car and away from David. She couldn't stop smiling.

"See ya," she turned and began walking faster.

"Bye," David yelled back at her.

As Annie was buckling her seatbelt and putting the car in drive, she noticed the cashier again. She was standing in the window giving Annie a thumbs up and nodding.

Annie smiled at the cashier and drove out of the parking lot.

"She must be from Rayes County," Annie smiled.

CHAPTER TWELVE

Annie had vague memories of her aunt Roslyn. She looked Native American – long, black, shiny hair. She was dark, not like the other Cleaving women. Annie remembered seeing Native Americans once in a children's book; that was the first time she thought of her Aunt Roslyn as being different.

She watched as her aunt shuffled about in her kitchen – her bare feet swishing around on the linoleum. A distant memory surfaced as she heard that sound – the swishing feet sound. It was here, in Roslyn's house, where she'd last heard it.

Roslyn signed the deed just after Annie had walked in the door. She wasted no time getting the deed back into Annie's purse and seemed satisfied to have done so – like marking something off a "to do" list.

Millie had always said Roslyn had "been through hell to get where she's at." Annie remembered hearing that statement time and again not just from her mother, but from other members of the Cleaving family, including Mamaw Lucy. She remembered her grandmother, in particular, talking about Roslyn's life and how she would never be fooled again by one of her daughters' husbands. Roslyn's first husband, Mason, had been dead for years. Roslyn remarried and then divorced, leaving her pretty well off but still, no fancy house slippers – just barefoot, swishing around the kitchen.

"Here you go, Annie," Roslyn handed her the tall glass of lemonade. "It's so sweet it'll make your teeth hurt – just like back home."

Annie took a sip. Roslyn was right, it did hurt her teeth. But then, that is how it's always done in Rayes County. Not just the lemonade but also the sweet tea or "tay" – just like Aunt Cleda's.

"Thank you, Aunt Roslyn. I really appreciate you doing this," Annie patted her purse, the signed deed tucked inside.
"Don't thank me, Annie. I'm just glad to help you in some way. I really never thought I'd get the chance to pay your momma back for all she did for me."

Roslyn's house was no showplace, but it could have been. She had all the right things – beautiful, claw-footed furniture, cherry wood – most of it. She had wonderfully hand-carved bar stools and a big fireplace with a hand-carved mantle. All the right stuff, just no rhyme or reason as to where it was stationed in her house. There were two bar stools placed on either side of the fireplace and two more in the living room where conversation chairs should have been. She had exercise equipment in her formal living room and then more in her downstairs de with nice formal living room furniture – a foosball table sat nearby.

Roslyn was no decorator; then again, neither was Annie. Still, she couldn't help but think that if she had access to all this elegant furniture, she'd at least be able to portion it out correctly.

Roslyn added three children to the Cleaving family – two boys and a girl. The two boys turned out fine, as Annie remembered her mother telling her. But Sophie had gotten into drugs and parted ways with her mother and the rest of the family. Although Millie never visited Roslyn much, they spent countless hours on the phone as Millie would try to comfort her sister when Sophie would be out on a drinking or pilling binge. Then, Roslyn just never heard from her daughter again. Millie said she couldn't imagine how painful it must be to know your child was out there somewhere maybe alive maybe dead. Annie's mother always had a way of putting herself in other people's shoes; almost as if completely understanding and feeling their pain might relieve them of some of it, even if only temporarily.

"Thank you anyway," Annie smiled.

Roslyn threw her hand up, "shew ... don't make no never mind. Like I said – glad to do it."

Roslyn questioned Annie about all the right things – work, home, Ethan ... And, Annie, in turn, did the same – home, kids, asking who Roslyn had been in contact with over the years.

Just as the two of them were about to run out of things to say, Roslyn upped the ante.

"Annie, have you ever wondered why me, and Dorie look so different from the rest of the Cleaving children?"

"Well, no, not really," Annie lied. "The two of you look a lot like the boys, don't you?"

"Strange," Roslyn looked at Annie like she knew she was lying. "Everyone else has."

"Well, yeah, I guess I have," Annie confessed and moved right into interrogation. "Is there a reason?"

Lucy and Hugh Cleaving had been married when Lucy was only fourteen and he was forty-something. She had been given to him by her family when Hugh's wife died. He had money and land, Roslyn said, and Mamaw Lucy's family – the Marsips had nothing. She was sent there to do the cooking and cleaning and take care of his two sons.

"As you can imagine, she probably wasn't very happy," Roslyn finally sat down. "I really can't prove it and never really wanted to try, but I do believe that me and Dorie are not – well, products of Hugh and Lucy Cleaving – you know," Roslyn waved a limp hand through the air as if to scoot an unspoken message over to her niece.

Annie didn't respond but sat quietly for a moment, wondering why Roslyn had decided to take on this topic so quickly. The round of confessionals with each visit was beginning to wear on Annie. She didn't want to know. Still, curiosity burrowed away at her like a chigger in August. After all, walking away would be rude. At least that's what her mother would say if she were still alive. Even though her only purpose for seeing these people was to claim what was rightfully hers – the Cleaving House – it seemed as if each of them was trying to connect one last time with Millie through Annie.

"So, you think Mamaw Lucy had an affair?" Annie almost choked on the words as she delivered them. Imagining her grandmother being young was a feat in and of itself but to even imagine her having an intimate relationship with anyone was teetering on disgusting.

"I try not to think of it as an affair," Roslyn scrunched her face up as if she had just smelled something putrid. "That makes it sound dirty. Since me and Dorie would have been the product of this union, I prefer to consider it my mother's big love. Doesn't every woman have one?" Roslyn shrugged her shoulders as if "big love" were commonplace discussion.

"Me, your mother and Dorie came to the conclusion that the big love of Lucy Cleaving's life was not her husband," Roslyn sipped at her lemonade and leaned back in her chair. She was as satisfied as Sherlock Holmes after solving a case. The only item missing was the pipe.

"So, do you speculate who it might be?" Annie decided to throw caution to the wind and join the investigation.

"I have, we have," Roslyn nodded quickly, excited that Annie was interested in who it might be. "We thought we knew but the family was so splintered and then your mother died," Roslyn's face saddened. "We really never felt comfortable asking anyone else about it."

Annie glared at her aunt, concentrating on trying to pull her words apart – family – ask … Then, the moment Annie was about to speak his name, Roslyn interrupted her.

"You *are* going to see your Uncle Rubin?"

"Yes," Annie waited for confirmation that she was on some sort of right track. She never got it.

"Do me a favor when you get there."

"Okay," Annie posed the word as both an answer and a question, hesitating slightly to let Roslyn know she wanted more information. "I guess I can."

"Ask him about your grandmother and if she ever had a big love in her life," Roslyn smiled, excited that the mystery might finally have a conclusion. "I think he knows. He would have to. He's the oldest of all of us that are still alive. He knew Momma when she was younger. Let me know what he says."

"Why don't you ask him yourself?"

"He hasn't spoken to me or the rest of the girls since your Mamaw died," Roslyn bit her bottom lip after she spoke the words. She was hesitating – about to say something Annie didn't want to hear. "Your mother never told you because she didn't want you to worry. But Rubin thinks the Cleaving House should have gone back to him because his father built it before he and Momma were married."

Annie had been unsure of Uncle Rubin up to this point. She had wondered where he would stand on signing the deed. Now that she knew, she wished she didn't. Roslyn could sense Annie's growing tension.

"Don't worry about your uncle Rubin, he'll sign. Just ask him the question and he'll sign."

Annie felt unreasonably reassured by Roslyn's insistence or maybe she had just grown so tired of worrying about the deeds getting signed she was happy to have someone's permission to stop. She still had a long way to go; worrying about one signature wouldn't make getting the others any easier; like Scarlett O'Hara, "she'd worry about that tomorrow."

Annie's muscles in her shoulders began to relax. She leaned back in her chair for the first time since she got there. The cool glass felt good against her lips, the lemonade moistened her dry mouth. She was tired of moving her mouth, tired of hearing her own voice. Sitting there, quietly sipping her lemonade, she thought about how many words she'd spoken in the past three days and how few she'd spoken during the months before and began to miss the quiet of home.

"Isn't that your mother's ring?"

"Yes," Annie lifted her hand, placing it in full view. "You recognize it?"

"Oh yes, I recognize it," Roslyn held her hand out to Annie. "I have one too."

Annie couldn't believe she hadn't noticed it, "They're identical."

"Yes, they are," Roslyn put her hand beside Annie's to

compare the rings. "Your mother and I wore these always. You know we were very close."

"Where did you get them," Annie looked closely at each one.

"I got them for us after Mason died."

Annie watched as a look of worry struck her face.

"I actually went out and got them," Roslyn pulled her hand away from Annie's. "Your uncle Asher used to dabble in stones a little. He told me one time what all of the gemstones represented. For example, the opal is supposed to awaken mystical qualities and enhance your intuition when you need it."

"What does the black onyx mean?"

"These stones are meant to help the wearer let go and banish grief," Roslyn was proud of herself for having such knowledge of the black onyx. "It encourages happiness for the wearer. I'm glad to see you wearing it."

Annie remembered the day she took possession of the ring. Her mother's cancer was eating her body alive. She was so thin, so frail. She tried to wear her jewelry – demanded it. But the ring kept falling off into the bed sheets. Finally, Millie called for Annie. In her frail, little hand she held three rings – a silver band, a diamond cluster, and the black onyx ring. She told Annie to keep the diamond one and the silver one safe; that she wanted to be buried with them. The black onyx, she said, she wanted Annie to have. Millie placed the ring on her daughter's finger. Annie had never removed it.

"I remember when Momma gave me this ring," Annie twisted the ring around her finger, remembering her mother's touch as she placed it on her finger. "She knew what she was giving me, didn't she?"

"She wanted you to go on and be happy – to go on with your life," Roslyn tapped the black stone on Annie's finger. "She loved you so much she didn't want you to grieve anymore for her or for the baby."

"So why matching rings for the two of you?" Annie imagined some sort of a pact between sisters. Annie always wanted a sister – someone to share things with – a matching ring would have been fun.

"You know, Annie, this is unfair to me. When I'm talking to you, I feel so much like I'm sitting here talking to your mother," Roslyn looked into Annie's face as if she'd lost something there. "I feel like you should already know everything about that ring but then I come to my senses and realize that you don't," tears began to well up in Roslyn's eyes. "I want to share something with you – how important your mother was to my family. I can't imagine what might have happened to me and the kids if your momma hadn't come here."

Roslyn and Mason met and fell in love – had a bright future. He was a good provider, a good father and never missed a day of work or church. He was proud of his family and loved his Rosie. They had a little frame house on a hill in eastern Pennsylvania. Roslyn stayed home and cleaned and cooked; put out a garden and grew beautiful flowers. He used to say none of her flowers were ever as beautiful as she was.

"I remember the day the foreman came to the house to tell me Mason had been in an accident," Roslyn spoke as if she were talking about something she'd seen on the news – a story from some distant place. "The children were all little; they had no idea what had just happened to their father. I was worried about him but I worried about the rest of us too. I don't know how, but I knew my life – our lives, were never going to be the same."

"Momma said he worked for the railroad?" Annie had always heard her family say that Pennsylvania Railroad workers made good money.

"Yeah, he did," Roslyn was talking but struggling for what to say next. "That was where it all started."

Roslyn said the foreman's most memorable words were, "He's lucky to be alive at all."

Mason was trying to manually detach two cars, something he knew better than to do. One of them began to move and he got wedged in between the two hitch bars. It was a spinal injury. Strange thing was, only one of his legs was lost completely and the other was still intact and living just not useable other than for standing. For the rest of his life, he used a crutch and his one, good stiff leg to balance himself.

"He wasn't much fit for anything after that," Roslyn shook her head. "Because he was doing something he wasn't supposed to be doing; detaching the cars manually and by himself, we got nothing. The court ruled it as negligence on his part, not the company's. They said he had enough training and enough years of experience in the railroad yard that he should have known better. They said he acted on his own and his supervisors would not have allowed or approved his actions."

Mason got a disability check for the rest of his life. He became distant and depressed and had become addicted to his prescription pain medication. That mixed with the drinking brought about the change in him – the cruelties toward his children and Roslyn.

"When your mother came here to visit, she thought our lives were the same as they'd always been. Sure, she knew about the accident, but I never told anyone about what was really happening to him – to our family."

At first, Roslyn said, she thought Mason was going to behave himself during Millie's short visit but then Millie decided to stay on.

"I didn't know your mother was pregnant with you when she got here," Roslyn patted Annie on the arm, squeezing it firmly. "I thought she was just coming to visit – no idea she ran away. She wanted to stay on for a while. I didn't want her to see what was going on here, but I could never tell my sister, no."

When Mason found out Millie's stay was going to be extended, he packed his charm away like a moth-eaten wool suit in an old attic wardrobe. For the first time since the accident, Millie saw the man Roslyn called her husband. No longer able to climb the stairs to the bedrooms, Mason made his home next to the television and kitchen. Roslyn set his bed up next to the couch. Day after day and night after night he'd lie there watching television. When he *did* go out, it was always to drink. Roslyn dreaded the first of the month. The only thing worse than Mason on a regular day, was Mason with money. His paranoia grew more sinister when he drank, sleeping with his pistol under his pillow.

"We tried so many times to act like we didn't hear him when he'd call for us to come downstairs and watch TV with him," Roslyn's voice shook as if she were afraid all over again. "That worked for a little while, but then he'd shoot through the ceiling, scaring us all to death. After that, when he'd holler for any of us, we'd all come down together. We had gotten used to his games but your mother – your mother had never seen anything like it. She came to me expecting to find my happy home." Roslyn shook her head as if her sister's disbelief had been transferred to her.

Annie tried to remember anything about her Uncle Mason; she couldn't. Her only memories of him were what her grandmother had told her – no real memories of her own would surface. Mamaw Lucy had said Roslyn was better off since he died. Annie recalled once when her mother told Mamaw Lucy to shut up about it.

Roslyn expected Millie would leave once Mason showed his crazy, but she didn't.

"I think she was staying on, at that point, to protect me and the boys and Sophie," Roslyn looked away from Annie and out the kitchen window. When she turned back tears were running down her face. "She would never leave my side – always trying to get us all away from the house at the same time so she could talk to me – impossible situation; he was always listening," Roslyn cupped her hand behind her ear. "It was like since his legs no longer worked, his ears had become sensitive to any sound, even a whisper."

Roslyn knew Millie wanted her to leave Mason; her sister had at least gotten that point across. Millie would bang pots and pans in the kitchen and clang dishes together so she could talk to her sister without Mason hearing them.

"He knew we were up to something, and it made him worse," Roslyn's voice got lower. "Michael, our youngest, was downstairs sitting on the couch next to his father," Roslyn's face contorted with disgust at the word, father. "Mason had held him there with the gun to his head and burned the bottoms of his feet with a lighter. Your mother walked downstairs and caught him. She heard him say to Michael that if he cried, he'd shoot him in the head."

"Oh my God!" Annie screeched. "Oh my God, that's awful Aunt Roslyn. How did you ever ..."

Annie stopped when she realized just how upset the outburst was making her aunt.

"That's not the worst of it, Annie. Jeffery, our oldest, was forced every night to play Russian Roulette with that same gun. Mason would tell Jeffrey, 'either you play or your mother will play.'"

Annie couldn't even imagine Ethan having to withstand that kind of cruelty. She remembered her cousins Michael, Jeffrey and Sophie. She never knew what they had been through. With the exception of Sophie, the other two turned out quite well. Jeffrey became an attorney and Michael a well-respected freelance writer. Annie tried to imagine her mother in this situation with Roslyn and her children. The questions finally began to surface over the shock.

"Why didn't you just leave him?"

"I had tried once before," Roslyn's voice became choppy between her breathy sobs. "But they made me give him visitation with the children. I *had* to stay with him to keep the children from ever being alone with him. It was awful. When I *did* come back, I really paid the price for that."

Since his injury, Mason had begun to develop heart problems, having several heart attacks which were diagnosed and several that weren't. He kept nitroglycerin close by. Doctors had told Roslyn there wasn't much else they could do for him until he stopped smoking and drinking. The suggestion for getting some exercise didn't please him so the nitro was his only lifeline. He refused any kind of surgery, telling the doctors he couldn't stand the thoughts of being away from his family. Millie knew it was because he was afraid Roslyn and the kids would disappear and never come back.

"I don't know how we managed it," Roslyn shook her head, looking up at the ceiling as if searching Heaven for Millie. "But your mother – your mother could always do anything. She was so brave. I would catch her looking at him sometimes when he was asleep. There was something inside her – angry like flames. I had seen it in myself before when it all first started happening. I don't know what happened to my fire. Maybe it was doused with fear; but not hers. The damper was always wide open."

Roslyn, hoping that Millie would help her find a way out,

never scolded her for the hatred she felt toward Mason; she sometimes even encouraged it by making sure Millie saw the scars on her body when she was changing clothes.

"I was so afraid for your mother to be there, but I was even more afraid that she would leave us," Roslyn held her head in her hands as she finished the story. "So, when she came up with the idea, I helped her."

Mason had emptied every cabinet in the house. Dishes were broken in the floor. Food was all over the counters. Roslyn said that's how she knew the plan was taking place.

"He couldn't find his glycerin anywhere. He was so mad. He kept saying we had two bottles — two bottles, 'where the hell did you put them, bitch?' Roslyn mocked a deep and raspy voice. "I told him I never remembered seeing two bottles. I only saw one and that he must have lost track of his days. He hit me a couple of times, but I stuck with the story."

When the pains started, Mason had no choice but to send her to the drug store. He would never let all of them leave the house at the same time but for his nitro he would have done anything.

"I told him Sophie was asleep upstairs and the boys were outside playing. They were waiting in the car for me," Roslyn pointed to the driveway as if she had been transported to the exact spot where it all took place. "I had told them to lie down in the back seat like their lives depended on it, because it did. I told my own children if you raise your head, you might as well plan on dying — I was so coarse with them but they needed to be terrified."

Millie had been packing things out of the house for several days. She told Mason she was leaving and going back home. He seemed relieved and didn't pay much attention to what she was packing out. She had taken all the children's clothes and even some of their toys. She took everything to an abandon building downtown, then rented a moving van for the day she had planned for Roslyn's escape.

"As me and the children were driving down the road, we passed her going back to the house. I knew what was about to happen," Roslyn stopped talking for a moment looking at Annie for understanding. "We had no choice. The courts would've still made me take the kids to see him if we divorced. We had no choice, Annie. We couldn't go on like that anymore. Your mother understood that better than anyone."

Annie was afraid to hear anymore but a little fire had begun to blaze inside her as well. It was as if her mother placed it there in that moment so she could feel, if only a miniscule, how it felt to be near the Devil himself – near Mason.

"Your mother told me she had gone inside and purposely made him angry," Roslyn drew a short, shallow breath. "That was the plan – to get him so upset, so mad that he would begin to have heart palpitations – made sure to put the bottle of glycerin tablets on the table next to him, to look like he was home alone and just couldn't get to the bottle fast enough."

Roslyn went home to Rayes County for a couple of months and grieved for her husband's death with the comfort of her mother. After a time, she and her children went home to Pennsylvania. She was questioned a couple of times by police about the death, but only because the life insurance policy was under six months old. There was no one who cared enough about Roslyn and Mason to have noticed there was a guest in the house. He had hidden Rosie and his children away for so long he ended up isolating himself as well. His death meant nothing more than five lines on page two of the local newspaper. His funeral was attended only by a couple of members of the Cleaving family who lived close enough to make a day of it.

"And just like that, my nightmare was over," Roslyn's face relaxed, her shoulders dropping. "The only thing I had to offer your mother for saving our lives was that ring you're wearing," Roslyn lifted Annie's hand to look at Millie's ring. "We banished our grief and chose to look forward."

Annie looked at her ring as if she was seeing it for the first time. Just like her mother, it was as if she didn't recognize this familiar thing, she'd looked upon for so many years day after day. Annie had never seen even a small flicker of anger from her mother and certainly not rage. While Annie was seething with hatred when Ethan died and fire could have burst out at any moment from every orifice of her body, her mother was calm, almost accepting. This other woman the Cleavings knew – admirable and strong – a vigilante for the oppressed, the abused, the downtrodden, was someone Annie had never even met.

CHAPTER THIRTEEN

He looked like a pig drying himself in the sun – just like Annie remembered him when she was a little girl. His fat spilled out over the edges of his aluminum lawn chair he had crippled underneath him. He was rubbing his belly protruding from his undershirt, his feet propped up on a tree stump. As she looked at each of the neighborhood home, it came as no surprise that his was the one with the most trash around the yard and on the porch.

Unlike the vague memories of the other Cleaving siblings, Annie remembered her Uncle Jay vividly. It was like she had seen him just yesterday. He had come to her house once to visit Mamaw Lucy. Annie woke up one morning and he was just there – must have come sometime during the night. That happened intermittently at Lucy Cleaving's house; people would just come and go whenever they felt like it. Annie's grandmother never seemed bothered by all the dropping in and out. She was always happy to see her children, but she always snickered when said she was just as happy to see them go.

Sitting in Annie's chair at the breakfast table, Jaygar seemed to be having a serious conversation with Mamaw Lucy. Millie was scuffling about the kitchen, making sure Annie had breakfast before school. All Annie could focus on was a bit of egg hanging on her uncle's unshaven face. It was the shape of a small triangle and was hung up in his whiskers. Annie couldn't eat that morning.

The sight of him with egg on his face, watching it dance as he talked with his mouth full made her sick. For the rest of her life, Annie couldn't eat eggs. She couldn't even see an over-easy egg without remembering her Uncle Jay. Even the word "egg" made her think of that moment. She had sometimes wondered if her memory of him was a bit skewed because of the terrible things she had heard about him from some of the other Cleaving children. But seeing him now validated what she had always believed. Growing older had in no way endeared him to anyone or anything God ever created.

She remembered her mother saying that he had been married once, to Marge. Annie had never met Marge. She did, however, meet their one son a few years ago. He was passing through Rayes County and stopped to visit. From the few hours Annie spent time with him, he seemed very normal and not like his father at all. Annie's mother seemed interested in talking to Jay Junior. He kept asking to be called JJ. Millie kept apologizing every time she forgot to call him that, which was often. Annie remembered finding it hard to believe that he was the offspring of Uncle Jay. JJ was well spoken, mannerly and clean shaven. Annie suspected that he must have taken after his mother. He was kind to Ethan and rolled a ball around the floor with him for a few minutes. Annie remembered her mother talking about how lucky Marge was to have gotten away from Jay; and how grateful she was that Marge didn't have to raise Jay Junior in "that" environment. It was hard to imagine that anyone would have married Uncle Jay in the first place and even harder to believe that some woman out there had chosen to procreate with him. Annie figured Marge must have been a decent person to have raised a son like JJ, in spite of her husband.

The sun pierced the clouds from time to time with quick transitions making Annie's eyes burn and water. The sparse clouds brought moments of shady comfort to an otherwise miserable, steamy day. She smiled a little when she saw buzzards circling not too far off in the distance as Jay relaxed in his warped aluminum lawn chair. Its legs dug at least four inches into the ground; he had obviously enjoyed many afternoons sunning in that exact spot.

Annie thought she had made a lot of noise as she pulled her car into the drive. The gravels were big and the crunching sound they made could be heard even over the car's motor, radio, air conditioner and even through the rolled-up windows. She was sure he had heard her pull in, yet Jay never moved, never looked up. Maybe his hearing had gone in his old age or maybe he really *was* sound asleep there in his chair. Even when she slammed the car door he didn't twitch.

Slowly, she walked closer to his chair. She had no idea why she was trying to be so quiet. After all, she was going to wake him up anyway.

"I hear you over there," Jay grunted, still not moving an inch. "I seen you pull in."

Finally, he opened one bloodshot eye and looked up. Standing directly over him, Annie was afraid to speak. She just stood there.

"I knew you'd be up here sniffin' around sometime," Jay rose from his chair.

The rickety lawn chair was about to collapse under his weight as he wiggled to free himself from its weak grip.

"Uncle Jay," even Annie's bravest voice quivered as she spoke. "I don't know if you remember me or not ..."

"I know who the hell you are," Jay was annoyed by Annie's presence. "The question is why the hell are you here to see me – as if I didn't already know."

"What do you mean?" Annie hardened her voice trying to regain some ground.

"I'll just bet somewhere on you, you're carryin' a long, folded, blue piece of parchment?"

Jay began bobbing back and forth from one side of Annie to another and acting as if he were reaching around her on either side.

"Where is it? Where is it? I know you go it."

Jay was grinning a half toothless smile. His one good eye was bright and glowing. He was gleeful. Annie imagined this was probably the same look he got each time he tortured small animals and other helpless things.

Annie took a long look at him, top to bottom, as if sizing him up. She then looked at his lawn chair and behind him at his trailer sitting up on concrete blocks. Her eyes then moved to the trash strewn about on the front porch. She could feel her disgust for him rising to meet her outward expression. His situation was pathetic, even more so than his attempts to intimidate Annie by dancing around her like a patient in a mental institution.

"So, you know why I'm here then," Annie grabbed her anger thrusting it forth at her uncle. "Well, at least I don't have to explain it to you – or do I? I take it you're not in the stages of dementia yet?"

Jay's crazy grin left his face. When it did, Annie could see traces of evil deep into his face, no longer hidden by the joy he had initially gotten from his bullying. Like so many others, he had mistaken Annie's initial kindness for weakness. Death was uglier than Jay and more evil and she had stared it in the face twice. She wasn't that scared little girl he remembered.

Annie grabbed the folded deed from her purse. It was just as Jay described it, long, blue and folded.

"You can either sign this or you can own a patch of Cleaving property in Rayes County that's about the size of your nasty foot," Annie nodded toward Jay's dirty foot was sinking into the ground with his weight. "All the others have signed."

Annie made her threat sound certain, even though she was lying. All the others hadn't signed; she only suspected they would. Jay, she knew, would be one of the exceptions. She rehearsed over and over in her head how all this was going to play out once she and Jay were standing toe to toe.

"*All* the others have signed? *All* the others have signed?" Jay repeated himself to make his point as if he knew something.

Annie knew the only person he hadn't alienated was Billie Jean, the one and only sister who still cared enough about him to keep in contact.

"Billie Jean would have told me if she signed," Jay's squinty eye twitched like it was trying to open. "But as of last night, you hadn't been there to see her. Don't be so shocked that I know where you've been. Dorie called Billie trying to get her to feel sorry for you – to not give you a hard time when you got there. Billie told me what you were up to."

"Fine, fine – that's fine with me," Annie gave a convincing performance of aloofness. "The two of you can own a piece of property the size of both your nasty feet. But know this: everyone else *has* signed."

Jay plopped back down in his chair as if he could make a last stand by sitting down hard. The aluminum lawn chair creaked loudly as if crying out in pain. Annie sat directly in front of him on the tree stump.

"Well?" she said, holding the deed up to his face. "Here's a pen."

Annie felt as if she were standing face to face with a demon. He glared at her with a harsh, bloodshot eye; the slit where the other eye used to be nervously jerking.

"You know I came here to be left alone," his voice raspy and aged. "I just don't want to be bothered by you or anyone else – especially anyone from Rayes County."

"Then sign the deed and I'll be gone from here. I can promise you that."

Annie held the deed in one hand and the pen in the other and offered it to him again. She was proud of herself for not backing off – she wasn't giving an inch; this was too important.

"My name is not Jaygar Cleaving. So, you're barking up the wrong tree, girl."

Annie was puzzled. Now, he had caught her off guard.

"A few years ago, I went to New Mexico to find a wife. While I was there, I converted to full Native American. I have the documentation to prove it. My name is no longer Jay Cleaving. I left him there on that reservation and my Native American family prayed him away up into the sky."

Jay wiped the spit from his chin. It had landed there in spatters as he spoke. Annie rolled her eyes.

"Oh, make fun if you want," Jay notices Annie's reaction. "But it's true. They gave me a wife – one of the finest women in the world."

Jay pointed backward with his thumb, "She's back there."

Annie saw a woman behind the trailer hanging clothes on a clothesline. She had noticed her earlier but thought she must have lived in one of the other trailers.

"She's mine," he was rather proud of himself. "We've been together almost five years now."

She had long, dark hair and was thin. She looked young – a lot younger than Jay.

"I changed my name and became one of them 'cause I wanted her so much," Jay brought out his torturous grin again. He licked his lips. "I wanted her so bad, you just can't imagine. There she was being offered to me. All I had to do was agree to become Native American and I could have her right there, that very night."

Annie didn't think she could be more disgusted by her uncle than she already was but hearing him describe this pre-marital courtship made her want to vomit.

"I read about it and went over there," he boasted. "It cost me but the way I figured it, it's no different than paying for a whore or a housekeeper three or four times a year. After a while it all adds up to big money. This way, I just paid it all up front."

"Poor woman is about all I have to say," Annie looked at her uncle with disdain.

"Oh, she likes what I give her; she likes what I give her," he said with the same devilish grin he revealed when taunting Annie over the deed earlier.

"So, sign the deed," Annie pressed him. "And I'll leave so you can get back to it."

"Oh, you'd like that wouldn't you?"

"Actually, yes I would, please."

"*'Actually, yes, I would please','*" Jay repeated her in a mocking voice. "You think you're so smart, do you? You're stupid; as stupid as your mother. I am trying to tell you that as a member of a

165

be difficult, she had expected that, but this encounter had been downright bizarre. She began walking back to her car, deed in hand, keys at the ready. She saw the dark-headed woman coming toward her. She was carrying an empty laundry basket and was walking far away from the trailer toward Annie. The woman motioned with her arm for Annie to follow her into the wooded area.

Annie hesitated for a moment but then opened the car door. The woman waved her arms wildly; Annie's curiosity led her away from the car.

Once there, just inside the tree line, the woman began to speak. She was much younger than Annie thought. She couldn't have been over thirty. Jay was at least sixty now. Her skin was a brownish yellow color – hardly any wrinkles. Her hair was black with a few white strands around the edges. Some women pay big money to get that at the beauty parlor, but you could tell hers was quite natural. As beautiful as she was, this woman was just as broken. Annie saw the signs – a deep scar across the bottom of her jaw was proof she had been cut, possibly almost killed at some point in her life. The pale-yellow bruises on her cheekbones appeared when she moved her head as she spoke. Her nose had been broken before, maybe more than once. Annie could see the crook in it as the full sun hit her face. She was sweating and was out of breath but not like someone who had run a long distance. It was fear taking her breath, broken with moments of helplessness – the same fear Annie felt just moments before. The same helplessness Annie had felt after Ethan died.

"Meet me at the store down the hill," she whispered in nervous breaths as if someone would hear them. "Do you know the store?"

"Yes, I just passed it coming up here," Annie pointed in the general direction. "But why do I need to meet you?"

"Just do it, please," the woman pleaded. "Please go to the store and wait for me."

Her English was clear but had a few breaks. Annie wasn't sure if the breaks were due to a Native American dialect or because she was so afraid. Either way, this woman was the real deal. She could have stepped right out of the history books.

"Okay, I – I will," Annie stammered a bit but agreed to go. "I'll be there."

"WEEKO! WEEKO! WHERE THE HELL ARE YOU? GET YOUR ASS IN HERE!"

Annie heard her uncle screaming from the back of the house.

"Weeko? Is that you?" Annie looked quickly at the house and then back at the woman.

"Yes, yes, I am Weeko," the woman looked toward the house and then turned to run. "Now go."

Annie waited in the parking lot for almost an hour. She started to leave several times but the curiosity of what Weeko wanted, kept her there staring at the hill, waiting to see someone walking over. She found herself worried about this woman; she seemed so afraid, so shaken. Annie stared intently at the top of the hill as if to will Weeko to come over it. Finally, Annie could see the top of someone's head bobbing up and down and then there she was.

Annie watched her as she walked, looking over her shoulder frequently. As she approached the car, Annie could tell she had been crying. Her face was red, and her bottom lip busted.

"I am so sorry I took so long," Weeko wiped sweat from her head. "Your uncle finally let me go. I told him I would go and fetch him some more beer."

"That's okay. I would have waited longer."

"You are so sweet," Weeko touched Annie's arm.

"Do you want some water?" Annie gave Weeko her half empty bottle. Weeko quickly gulped it down.

"Thank you."

"What is the matter?" Annie began asking Weeko, as if she didn't already know.

"I need for you to help me. I need your help," Weeko was nodding her head as if that would make Annie agreeable.

"You can drive, and I want to drive too," Weeko pointed at Annie's steering wheel.

Annie was expecting Weeko to tell her to take her to the police, take her away, take her to a battered women's shelter – not to drive.

"You want to drive?" Annie spoke slowly to make sure she was clear on what Weeko wanted.

"Yes, yes, show me please," Weeko seemed desperate. "Drive me somewhere, now."

Annie put the car in reverse and pulled the car to the edge of the parking lot. "Which way?"

"Show me how you came to town," Weeko pointed out to the street. "Show me how you drove here."

Annie turned toward the Interstate, not too far from the store where they were sitting. Weeko didn't say anything. She sat close to the dashboard, facing Annie and watching her every move, as if she were absorbing everything Annie was doing. She nodded her head many times as if taking mental notes. She kept looking around at the windows and praying a whispery line, "Please, please God – please, please God."

Annie never heard any other words, but she had a pretty good idea of why Weeko was praying. Like Annie, she was desperate to get away and Jaygar was standing in her way, too.

Annie drove, waiting for the right moment to speak.

"I came from over there," Annie pointed at the Interstate. "Weeko, why are you wanting to drive? Are you running away? Is everything okay?"

"Oh, yes," Weeko spoke quickly, giving Annie an odd look. "Why would you think everything is not okay? I am wanting to surprise your uncle and drive him for his birthday."

Weeko had a bizarre look on her face. She was smiling but also looked terrified. Annie knew she was still distrustful of her. She wanted to say something that would let her know that Annie was not on Jay's side, but hers.

"You know lots of men go to jail for hitting their wives?" Annie was talking now but Weeko wasn't paying attention. She was focused in on Annie's driving. "Does Jay hit you? Does he beat you?"

"Oh, this?" Weeko touched her split lip and shook her head. "No, no, no. I fell. I am so clumsy. Jay would never … no, not never."

Annie didn't know what to say. If only she knew her a little better, she might be able to help her. She kept trying to find a way to connect.

"You know women throughout history have been abused by their husbands," Annie felt as if she were about to give a lecture. "Many men's wives ended up leaving them and finding much better lives."

Weeko nodded, finally acknowledging what Annie was saying but still not comprehending.

"I'll drive now," Weeko demanded. "You are going to teach me how to drive now."

Annie pulled over and gave Weeko some basic instructions for driving – brake, gas, gears. She let Weeko sit in the driver's seat for a long time and get a feel for the setup. Annie pulled the car around to what looked like an abandoned factory parking lot. There was plenty of room for mistakes there. At least Weeko could go a pretty good distance before finding anything to hit. The two women spent about an hour there as Weeko learned drive and reverse, gas and brake. The whole time, Annie was talking about women victims of domestic violence. When she ran out of early historical references she started on movies. She told her about the Julia Roberts movie, "Sleeping with the Enemy," the "Betty Broderick Story," and even the Farrah Fawcett movie "The Burning Bed." It seemed Weeko was too focused on what she was doing to listen. She was going to learn how to drive today even if Annie talked her ears off while she did.

"Good, good," Weeko nodded her head, proud of herself for what she had learned so quickly. "I can do this."

Weeko put the car in reverse and floated the car between two spaces.

"Wow, there are people I know who have been driving for years, and don't do as well as you have done."

Annie was specifically thinking of Janet. She only rode with her a couple of times and decided no more. Janet would be driving down the road and see someone's flower garden, take her hands completely off the wheel and begin mapping out how they must have planted it. Or, she would see a new billboard and try to read every word, never looking at the road until she was finished. Even for someone like Annie, who had somewhat of a death wish, Janet's driving was a little much to take. Weeko was doing much better than that.

"You're a sweet, sweet girl," Weeko turned to Annie before she got out of the car. "Don't let your uncle make you feel bad. You're a sweet, sweet girl," she repeated.

"Yes, thank you. It was good to meet you," Annie watched as Weeko went inside the store.

Annie pulled out and parked across the street. Like a stalker, she watched to see what Weeko was doing, where she was going. Weeko left the store with a bag in her hand. Probably Jay's beer, Annie guessed. She watched Weeko top the hill and then disappear over the other side.

CHAPTER FOURTEEN

Annie wasn't looking forward to seeing her aunt Billie Jean and even less enthused about it now that she knew BJ had been talking to Jay. This was bound to happen sooner or later. She just wanted it to be later. It was only about a hundred and fifty miles from Jay's house to BJ's, not nearly long enough for Annie to come up with a decent plan on how to handle BJ if she refused to sign the deed. Dorie had warned her about Jay but not about BJ. Maybe Dorie had no idea that BJ and Jay were so close. It was hard to imagine that anyone could be close to him, even a sister.

Annie just wasn't ready to face it again today. She needed to recuperate and gather her thoughts. "Ah, right there."

She spotted it; the Hilton. As she pulled in, she noticed a huge bookstore with a large green roof. It was fabulous. How did this high-ticket hotel and enormous bookstore end up out here in the middle of nowhere? It was like an oasis.

"A good book, a good drink and a good night's rest," Annie sighed.

She looked at her cell phone – it was close to four. That would give her just enough time to find a good book, check into the hotel, get a few drinks and call Mary before passing out from exhaustion. She had promised Mary that she would check in from time to time to let her know how things were going. After today, she had a real story to tell. She wanted to let someone know exactly what had happened. She was hoping Mary could confirm for Annie if she was crazy or if the rest of the Cleaving family was.

The hotel was extravagant, and Annie felt ashamed for spending so much money on a room. She justified it by getting the weekday rate dropped by ten percent because she had arrived so late in the afternoon and would be leaving so early in the morning. She took a quick tour of the hotel before going to her room to put her things away. Once she spotted the hot tub with a bar right next door, she went to the gift shop and bought herself a bathing suit. Too tired to tromp across the street to the bookstore, she opted for a magazine instead.

Once inside the hot tub, icy drink in hand and magazine close by, Annie began to feel a little weird about calling Mary on her cell phone. Normally, she would just call her at work. Even though Annie felt a closeness to Mary, she wasn't sure that Mary felt the same. Good friends were hard to find and even harder to keep in Rayes County. First, you had to find someone normal and then that person had to be willing to sacrifice a few lunches a month to maintain the friendship. Annie, so far, had not been willing to sacrifice even one lunch to spend with anyone.

"Hey," the steam from the hot tub made Annie's voice crack.

"Oh my God," Mary sounded excited. "I was just wondering about you. How's it going? Are you making any progress?"

"Well, yes, I am making progress. I have five signatures and I've visited four aunts and one uncle."

"Wait a minute, that's five people," Mary did some quick math. "Does this mean someone wouldn't sign?"

"Yes, that's exactly what it means," Annie blew a long breath.

"So, I'm having a drink in the hot tub at the Hilton, and I thought I'd call to catch you up."

"Rough day, huh?"

"Very rough."

Annie told Mary all about Jay Cleaving a.k.a. Silver Tree and his young wife Weeko.

"I kept asking myself – 'did this really just happen? Am I crazy?'"

Mary laughed at Annie as she described her uncle, the situation and the weird visit with Weeko.

"Your family is nuts, girl. I wish I could have seen Uncle Jay or, um, I mean Silver Tree."

Annie felt relieved to have someone to talk to and really didn't want to hang up. But her drink had melted, and her skin was red from the hot water.

"Call me back and let me know in a few days how it's going," Mary laughed as she spoke. "I can't wait to hear more about your crazy Cleaving family.

"Will do," Annie smiled as she spoke. It was nice to hear a voice from home. "Talk soon."

*

Annie opened her eyes to the sun shining through the crack in the curtains. The air conditioner kept blowing the curtain back and forth – open and then closed – like a disc jockey's flashing light at a high school dance. She had only finished half of the second drink she brought back to the room with her. Half of it now sat on the night stand next to the remote control. Annie could smell the alcohol and the sour mix. It made her thirsty for water.

She didn't bother brushing her hair or even her teeth. She threw her hair up in a ponytail, but some sweats on, grabbed the newspaper next to her door and headed downstairs for breakfast. For some reason eggs actually sounded good this morning. Not over easy, of course, scrambled only. Annie scooped about a half a serving spoonful out. The rest of the plate, she filled with a waffle and some soup. She grabbed a small container of yogurt just in case she was still hungry after. She wasn't sure why she was so hungry, just that she felt like a bottomless pit, even more so than usual.

She was so happy to have some juice, a little coffee, and a lot of food; she must have been making noises as she ate. Her mother used to tell her when she would do it. Usually, it was after a full day of playing outside when Annie was her most tired or most hungry, or both. Most times, Annie never even realized she was doing it. "Mmmm, Mmmmm," she would moan. Ethan used to do the same thing. It made Annie wonder if he was just born that way or if he had learned the 'moan eating' by watching and listening to her eat.

A rather good-looking man was staring at Annie.

"Very good breakfast, aye?"

He was smiling wide at her, almost laughing.

"Yes, it is very good."

Annie could feel her face getting warm from embarrassment. She was sure now, by the look on his face that she had been making those eating noises again. She held the newspaper up so she didn't have to look at him again and so she could finish eating her waffles without being embarrassed.

The headline jumped out at her like someone had reached through the newspaper and smacked her in the face; then there was the picture and the sketch – it was unmistakable. Annie dropped her fork onto her plate. It made a loud clang.

Wife kills husband in Maplewood 'Burning Bed' style

Maplewood, P.A – The charred remains of Jaygar Adam Cleaving a.k.a. Silver Tree Cleaving, 62, of Maplewood, Penn., were discovered this morning after firefighters extinguished the blaze at his home on Green Road.

The manufactured home burned "quick and hot" firefighters said, "The home or Mr. Cleaving never stood a chance," said John Buelling, Maplewood fire chief.

Police are investigating the fire as arson and believe that Cleaving's wife, 33-year-old Weeko Boyet Cleaving, doused the area around his bed with gasoline before setting it on fire as he slept. Police are still searching for Weeko Boyet Cleaving, who is still at large. Police believe she drove the family vehicle, a 2001 Ford Ranger pickup truck to the Maplewood train station, where she stowed away. Authorities in Canada, where the train was heading, say it most likely came through early this morning and Weeko Boyet Cleaving could be anywhere between Maplewood and Toronto.

Since the release of the movie "The Burning Bed," in 1984, many women have committed copycat murders of abusive husbands. Statistics show about one a year in the United States takes place. For those unfamiliar with the movie, it is the true story of Francine Hughes, an abused wife who lived in her situation in Michigan until she decided to take matters into her own hands. She told her children to wait in the car, while she doused the area around her husband's bed with gasoline and then set it on fire. Maplewood Police Chief Nathan Flocking said this murder is eerily similar to that movie, the only difference being that Weeko Boyet Cleaving didn't drive to the police station to confess after allegedly murdering her husband; she instead kept right on driving.

The Cleavings had a history of domestic violence with several 911 calls coming from the residence over the past five years they were married. Jaygar Cleaving had been charged with domestic violence seven times since their marriage began.

Anyone who may have any information about the fire or where Weeko Boyet Cleaving might be, should call the Maplewood, Penn. Sheriff's Department at 555-2134.

Annie almost jumped out of her chair when her cell phone rang.

"Annie, Annie, It's Mary. I just got to work and got this story off the Associated Press wire service. Have you seen it? Annie, Annie?"

Annie couldn't speak. All she could do was stare at the sketch of Weeko and look at the photo of the crumbles and ashes that used to be Jay's trailer.

"Yeah, I'm looking at it in the paper right now," Annie's voice was weak. "Oh my God, oh my God. She *was* listening to me, Mary. She *was* listening."

CHAPTER FIFTEEN

Annie had showered and dressed in a hurry. She read the news story over and over. She even laid it near the sink while she was brushing her teeth and drying her hair. Maybe she thought it would change if she watched it long enough. It didn't.

She made no eye contact with anyone as she checked out of the hotel and retrieved her car from valet. She felt as if they all knew; they all knew what she had done. She felt like a criminal; like she had murdered Jay. She kept telling herself again and again that *Weeko* killed him, not her. It didn't make her feel any better; she felt that by teaching Weeko to drive, she had contributed to Jay's death, whether he deserved what he got or not.

She kept wondering why in the past five years Weeko hadn't asked someone else to teach her to drive. Why did she choose Annie? Why hadn't she ever just gotten in Jay's truck and drove away? Annie began to think that maybe she should just find an interstate south and go home. Maybe it wasn't worth all this. But she was so close to having all the signatures. If there was a chance to settle this once and for all, she should do it. Without selling the house there was no way her life was going to change.

She had seen the sign for the town of Peddy a few miles back. She was closer now, closer to BJs. She had to make up her mind – south or due east across Pennsylvania. There it was, Peddy nine miles the big green sign was almost shouting at her. Annie continued in the right lane, mile after mile. The right turn to Peddy, PA came quite naturally, after she'd convinced herself that there was nothing to left to lose by asking BJ to sign off on the deed.

Peddy was a small town, even smaller than Rayes County, or at least it looked so from the interstate exit. A couple of gas stations and three or four fast food joints served as the entryway. Not much further was a shopping center with only grocer and a big box department store. The rest of the shops were empty. As she drove through downtown, the evidence of what was once a vibrant community was still visible. Faded signs and dirty windows anchored the businesses still left there – a bank, a few attorney offices and four bars around the courthouse square. People walking around town looked like office workers – attorney's whose suits were too big for them; or, their pants were too short, or their socks the wrong color. It looked a lot like home. Annie was beginning to notice that wherever she went – it all looked a lot like home. The people were no different, the towns no brighter, no more cheerful – only the landscape changed as she traveled from place to place.

According to the directions Annie had gotten from Dorie, BJs house was just off the courthouse square in Peddy.

"Darton," Annie said aloud, when she saw the orange mailbox. "Just like Dorie said."

BJs mailbox was orange just like the color of a creamsicle. It looked like it had been bright orange at some point but just like the other colors here, it too had faded. Someone had scrawled with a black marker – B. Darton, 63 Washington Street, Peddy PA. It was the first house on the street, other than the one on the corner, just like Dorie said.

The house reminded Annie of something she'd seen on TV. It was tall and skinny – two stories. It had slim windows and a slit of a door. It was like it had been smashed in from either side. It was disproportionately stretched it seemed. The paint on the front porch was peeling and looked as if it had been that way for quite some time. Each step Annie made was followed with a creak or a squeak. The windows, just like the windows downtown, were dusty. Annie could barely see through them, but a moving shadow caught her attention. Annie got closer to the window and saw her aunt BJ. Her back was to the window, and she was sitting in the floor with her legs crossed. She had a large cardboard box in front of her and a lap full of papers. She was rifling through them, looking for something. Annie could see cigarette smoke billowing up above her aunt's fuzzy head. She could hear music and static coming from a small radio on the shelf just in front of BJ. It was country music, of course. Annie had to smile as she remembered her aunt dancing to country music when she came to visit once. The music sounded the same. It was that twangy type of music – the old country stuff – Conway Twitty, Merle Haggard and the like. Annie's mother used to listen to love it too. She remembered her aunt BJ calling it "good drinkin' music." No matter where Annie heard that type of old-style country music, that's what she thought of; what her aunt BJ had said.

Annie stared at BJ through the window, watching her lunge her hands in and out of the box of papers for several minutes. It seemed natural for some reason, seeing her rifling through papers in a box. Annie could almost see her mother sitting there next to BJ, helping her. Like everything else that reminded Annie of her mother, she couldn't quite decide if that was a real memory – BJ and Millie going through a box of papers – or if it was just Annie associating something or someone familiar with her mother.

BJ took a long draw off her cigarette, Annie could see her better now, and let out a big puff of smoke toward the ceiling. She had a highball glass sitting next to her. BJ gulped down the last bit. She put her hands behind her like she was about to try and lift herself off the floor. Annie quickly moved her face away from the window and stood straight as a toothpick in front of the door, like she was hiding. She began to tap on the door lightly then remembered that BJ was hard of hearing. She wrapped the next time a little harder and then even louder, pounding with the butt of her hand a bit, the porch rattling as she did.

Annie heard footsteps coming toward the door. The floors inside were creaking just as much as the floors on the front porch. Maybe that's why BJ hadn't heard Annie coming up on the porch. The creaking and squeaking must have been as normal as the sounds of the nearby wind chime coming from the house next door.

"Annie?" BJ wailed as she opened the door.

Annie couldn't answer right away; instead, she stood there looking at her aunt as if she'd never seen her before. Her hair was still fiery reddish orange just like Annie remembered it, but it was fuzzier and kinkier. Her roots were about two inches out from her head and were completely grey. It was startling to see it on top of her head like that, contrasted next to the red, curly fuzzes of locks. Her freckles were familiar to Annie. They were everywhere, just like Annie remembered them. Only now, many of them were hidden between the deep wrinkles in BJ's face. Her aunt had always been a tiny woman, even tinier than Annie. Now, she looked even smaller, more compact. Her belly bulged from her tight shirt and even tighter polyester pants.

"Yes, it's me. How are you?" Annie asked after a long moment of silence.

"Oh, my goodness," BJ said shaking her head from side to side. "You look just like your mama – just like her."

BJ reached her arms around Annie to hug her; the cigarette she held in her fingers still burning and smoking. Annie hated the smell of cigarette smoke but had prepared herself. She knew from the moment the front door opened that BJ was still a chain smoker.

"Dorie told me you might be headed this way," BJ gave a wide, yellow-toothed smile. "Come on in here and let me get a better look at you."

Annie stepped inside the smoke-filled, dingy living room. BJ actually could have gotten a better look at Annie if she had stayed on the porch in the daylight. The light inside hid itself well. The floor was covered with a faded navy-blue floral-patterned linoleum rug and the walls were painted a similar dark blue. Other than a floor lamp in the corner, there was no light at all. Even if there had been, the colors were too dark to provide much reflection.

"How have you been?" Annie followed BJ as she led the way into the living room. "I don't think I've ever been here to your house. It's charming, really."

"So sorry for the mess here," BJ gave a tired wave to the box and papers scattered all over the floor. "I guess you've heard about your uncle?"

Annie started to answer but then hesitated before she spoke.

"Uncle?"

Annie had already decided it was best to remain silent about the visit with Jay until someone asked her about it.

"Sit down here, Annie," BJ patted a spot on the dingy blue couch where she directed Annie to sit. "Your uncle Jay was murdered last night."

Before Annie could stop herself, she did it – with one simple word posed as a question, her lie began.

"Murdered?"

"Yes," BJ nodded, a look of despair pressing in on her face, "murdered."

Annie tried to convey her most puzzled look but said nothing.

"It's been all over the papers this morning and even on TV," BJ started to cry, her words breaking into pieces as she sobbed. "They contacted me last night. One of his neighbors told them I lived here in Peddy. She killed him, I knew she would. I could just see it in her when I went over there the last few times. I could just see it in her."

Annie told the second lie. Again, with just one word, one question, she was in deep.

"Who?"

As the word left Annie's mouth, a moment of fear struck her; death was not nearly as frightening as being locked up – conspiracy, motive – her chest felt heavy.

"Let me start from the beginning," BJ took a long drag from her cigarette. "About five years ago, your uncle Jaygar decided he wanted to get a wife off one of those Indian reservations ..."

As BJ spoke, Annie began to feel relief. Her shoulders became less tense and her teeth finally unclenched. BJ hadn't spoken to Jay before he died. Annie listened as BJ told Annie the same story, almost verbatim, the way Jaygar had told it to her just the day before, only with a little more class. Annie looked intently at BJ as her aunt told the tale of Jaygar meeting Weeko and then changing his name to Silver Tree. Her mind was wandering though – *is this how it starts? Is this how mom got involved in all this madness – with Roslyn, with Dorie? This family, just by being a part of it and being near them – they're all so screwed up,* Annie's thoughts raced between past and present, between her present and her mother's past.

"The police, Annie; the police – they aren't even doing anything," BJ cried into her hands, the smell of wet cigarette smoke made Annie's nose burn. "I know it's a domestic like they said, but my brother has been murdered, MURDERED! I don't even think they care."

BJ could no longer speak, she just cried. She did manage to place the newspaper in Annie's lap before going into the kitchen. It was a different newspaper, but the story was the same. Annie scanned the front page, reading the story of Jaygar Cleaving's murder for what seemed like the hundredth time.

"At the end there when they asked if anyone has any information about it; they don't really mean it," BJ emerged angry from the kitchen with two drinks. "Last night when they called me and told me what happened. I told them all about her; about her family and where they could find her father and her brothers. All they wanted to talk about were the police reports that had been filed."

"Police reports?" Annie was becoming rather accomplished at pretending to know nothing.

"Yes. Police reports with lies about how Jay had beat her up and the neighbors had called it in," BJ alternated between sniffling and smoking. "That's all they wanted to talk about – trying to get me to say that he beat her."

Annie could tell by the tone in BJ's voice that she didn't believe Jaygar had ever done anything wrong – that he was not abusive to Weeko. She was relieved that she had remained silent about the visit; about trying to get Jaygar to sign the deed.

"She wanted everybody to believe that she was good to him and that he was mean to her, battered her, beat her," BJ shook her head vigorously as if she were trying to shake some image out of her head. "It just wasn't like that ... her family they were like gypsies – thieves and swindlers."

BJ hadn't been happy at all with the arrangement between Jaygar and Weeko. She was suspicious from the very beginning. She told Annie she found out through other people she spoke to in the town where Weeko came from and that the family had a long history of prostitution and thievery.

"Weeko's father," BJ spoke in a sarcastic tone, "was actually her pimp – boyfriend," BJ rolled her eyes. "When she got too old to bring in much money, the two of them set out looking for someone for her to marry. They started running ads in men's magazines for mail order brides."

BJ remembered Jaygar first showed her the ad. There was an interview process for the pre-arranged marriage and an extensive application process. Jaygar wouldn't have it any other way than to go on with trying to get a young Indian wife; he became obsessed with it.

"Just like always, Jaygar lied about everything – his money, his house, his car," BJ lowered her head as if she was ashamed for her brother. "He even borrowed money from me to rent a fancy car to drive over there and meet her. He printed out his bank statements and had someone change the amounts. He took pictures of this mansion over in Pittsburgh and took them with him. He told them he was rich – international stock trader, who just worked so much that he never had time to find a decent woman."

After Jaygar met Weeko, he was hooked. He believed them – believed Weeko had never been married and that her father was just very particular about whom she would be with. Weeko's father said he wanted someone respectable and decent to care for his daughter. They took one look at his mansion, his bank statement and his car and immediately thought they could milk him for money for the rest of their lives.

"According to the police chief there where they lived, Weeko and company had interviewed many prospects before Jay was chosen," BJ's hand shook as she lifted her glass to take a drink. "It was con artist versus con artist – that's what I told Jaygar when he kept going over there."

Jaygar gave Weeko's father money with a promise to pay installments for the ranch in Mexico that would someday become Weeko's. He, in turn, gave Jaygar his daughter's hand in marriage in a ceremony that wasn't even legal. Once Weeko and Jay were gone, the father came to Pennsylvania to get the next installment payment. When he saw there was no mansion, he took off and left Weeko there.

"Police said they had been trying to catch the two of them at something for a long time," BJ picked up the newspaper, looking at the story again as if the words had changed. "They tried to get Jaygar to come to court but he wouldn't. Even after he knew the truth he still kept that whore there at his house and claimed her for his wife. They know she did it and it's like they're not even looking for her."

Annie sat there on the couch with BJ for a long time, listening to her story of woe and pain regarding Jay and his situation with the Indian wife. It took a while for it all to sink in but finally Annie was able to wrap her head around the whole saga. Weeko and her pimp were trying to scam Jay; Jay was trying to scam who he thought was Weeko and her father. When Weeko was gone and in the hands of Jay, her boyfriend ran off, probably with some other woman, to Mexico. She had no way out. When Jay found out she used to be a prostitute, he probably became abusive to her – if he wasn't abusive before, which Annie found hard to believe.

Drink after drink and cigarette after cigarette, the story got more and more vivid and tangled. By the time BJ was good and drunk, she had convinced herself that the police were somehow involved as well and that it probably had something to do with Mexican drug lords and international prostitution rings. Annie listened and nodded quite often, just to keep the peace. She waited for her moment to mention the deed, but it never came.

Annie was growing tired of being in that house. It was thick with smoke and stank of old hairspray and perfume. The bourbon BJ was gulping was making her sweat and smell like an old rotting apple.

"Would you want to go take a walk around town?" Annie patted her aunt on the leg. "Maybe it'll clear your head – I know I could use some fresh air."

Annie tried not to sound sarcastic, but subtlety was never her strong suit.

"Oh, I'm so sorry Annie. You don't smoke do you?"

"No, but I'm thinking of starting," Annie half joked.

"Don't you dare, child – this stuff will kill you," BJ held up her cigarette and her drink like an attorney pointing out exhibit A and exhibit B.

Once outside, the two of them opted for sitting on the porch rather than taking a walk. Annie took one look at her aunt in the sunlight and decided those bloodshot eyes didn't need to see anyone publicly. Her aunt staggered to the front porch swing and then burped loudly.

"Let's just sit here," Annie helped BJ hold the swing still while she sat down. "I think this will be just fine."

Annie had emptied the contents of her purse at the hotel and placed her belongings in the shoulder bag Reena had made for her. Usually when she changed purses, it took a while to get used to the newness – each time she'd reach for a new purse, it seemed foreign, like it didn't belong to her. But this bag seemed a natural fit for Annie. It felt as if she'd owned it all her life – the colors, the beading, and the threads all seemed familiar. She kept it close to her as she watched BJ in the swing. The deed with a pen attached to it was folded and inside the colorful bag. She knew she could grab it at any moment and give it to BJ. She'd learned by now that timing was everything with this Cleaving clan. BJ was quiet now, just swinging. Annie decided it was time to try and take her moment.

"So, Aunt Dorie told you I was coming around?"

"Yeah, she told me you'd be headed this way. She said she'd made you a promise that she would lay some groundwork for you before you got here."

"Yeah, she was great about the whole thing when I went to see her," Annie was hoping BJ would follow her sister's example.

"Yeah, Dorie told me the whole story about how the deed was all messed up. It doesn't surprise me any really," BJ was beginning to show intermittent signs of sobriety. "Mom never was a good hand to take care of business things. She understood a lot of things and what she didn't understand she just made up. She didn't need property law, she had Lucy Cleaving law."

Annie and BJ laughed, finding common ground while remembering a lot of other Lucy Cleaving laws over the years.

"So do you think she knew the deed was all messed up?"

"She probably did," ice cubes tinked inside BJ's glass as she swung back and forth in the porch swing. "She probably just thought she could get around it somehow. She was never one to follow rules, you know. I think that's what's wrong with the rest of us – always think there's an easier way; a better way; a way around things. That's what Jaygar always thought. That's how he always got himself into so much trouble – that's what killed him," BJ the swing had all but stopped and BJ turned and gave the back railing a push, starting it up again.

The air was only silent for a moment when BJ started to cry again. Annie knew she had to do something quick, or she'd be there for another two hours listening to her aunt go on about what a sad life Jaygar had and how he really didn't mean to be so cruel.

"So, do you think you could sign the deed for me Aunt Billie Jean?"

Annie could tell by the look on BJs face that she had overplayed her hand; laid it all out there too quickly.

"The thing about your aunt Dorie is she has money," BJ's tears dried quickly, her tone as dried as well. "She don't need nobody and she don't need nothing. But the rest of us ain't been so lucky as her. My momma and daddy never gave me nothing. When they died, here I sat. And I wondered why *did* Lucy Cleaving decide to give *my* inheritance to you? I was hurt, Annie – I'm still hurt over that. I just don't know if I can sign that."

Annie had wondered the same thing herself for many years.

"I'm sorry you feel that way, BJ," Annie tried to sound understanding. "I don't know why she gave me the house. She told Momma it was because I would need it most. After I moved in and had Ethan, I really just got used to living there and never thought anything more about it."

Annie hadn't meant to use Ethan's death as a hot button with BJ to get her to change her mind. She would never do that – sell Ethan's memory for even a mansion – let alone the rickety old Cleaving house. Nevertheless, the moment she said Ethan's name, BJ's whole demeanor changed.

"I had forgotten about your baby, Annie," BJ said. "I – I – I didn't mean to say anything about that."

"You didn't say anything," Annie interrupted her aunt. "I brought Ethan up and for that I am sorry. I shouldn't have even brought him into all this."

"I have no need of that old house and I don't know why you need it either – you need to get yourself out of that God forsaken place, Annie. Get yourself out of there," BJ started strong but then trailed off.

Annie knew better than to say she actually was trying to get out of Rayes County and sell the old Cleaving house. She had won this battle; BJ had agreed to sign. If there was one lesson in business that stuck with Annie it was this, when you're getting what you want, remain silent. And besides, she didn't want BJ to begin thinking that she might be entitled to a profit that would come with a sale. It was better for her to think Annie would just live there.

"I have it right here," Annie pulled the folded deed from her purse, the pen was still attached. "Here, sign right here."

Annie had no time for guilt, no time for shame. If BJ was willing to sign,

"Too much hatin' in the world anyway," BJ mumbled to herself as she signed. "We all just need to try and get along. Life is short – yep, life is short. I may be gone tomorrow."

Annie didn't mean to sigh aloud but she did. BJ noticed her relief.

"I can't even imagine going to see all our Cleaving idiots," BJ laughed at Annie's predicament.

"Well, it's been interesting to say the least," Annie was relieved that BJ was coming around now.

"INTERESTING?! HA!" BJ blasted a laugh. "With this bunch, I can't even imagine what bullshit you've seen, heard. I can't even imagine."

Annie was well past the point of being shocked by any of the Cleaving clan, but she did find it ironic that BJ was trying to figure out which Cleaving was most full of bullshit.

BJ took a long breath and propped her feet up on the porch railing, just next to the swing. It looked as though she'd sat there that way a thousand times before.

"Well, I talked to JJ on the phone before you got here," BJ laid her head back and then slowly brought it forward. "We're going to go ahead and have his services tomorrow – even without the body; well, really, there is no body. If they come out with anything after the investigation is over, we can bury him then. JJ and I think it's just best to get this all over with. Jay would have wanted it that way."

"Yes, yes – I'm sure he would have," Annie tried to muster up some sympathy for her uncle Jaygar.

"I want you to stay and go with us to the service, Annie. I know if your mother were still alive, she'd be here."

Annie wasn't entirely sure BJ's statement was true. She didn't believe her mother would have come to Jaygar's funeral. Annie immediately stopped herself – maybe she would have. Who knows? It's like I don't even know this woman anymore, she thought.

"Anyway, I'm sure JJ would like to see you, Annie. I bet he hasn't seen you for over ten years or more."

"It has been a long time," Annie agreed. "I can't really remember when."

"You know, your uncle Jaygar would have never signed that

deed," BJ acted as if she were letting Annie in on a big secret. "He told me never, never, never would he let it go. He hated that you were coming, and he hated that Momma gave that house to you while he sat up here in a trailer. You would have never stood a chance. Now you got JJ – he don't care about that house."

Annie's mind clicked quickly through all the heirs and the deed process. BJ was right; JJ would be the next one to convince to sign the deed. He'd be at the funeral tomorrow. As bad as she hated paying tribute to Jaygar Cleaving, she knew this would be the only way. She might never track JJ down again.

"I'm glad you didn't see Jaygar about this, Annie. I'm glad you never got to ask him. He was so angry about the whole thing. Honestly, him and me both had decided we wouldn't sign. But now, it all seems so stupid. It was like we just being contrary just to be contrary. Yeah, I'm glad you never got to ask him to sign," BJ stopped the swing with her one dangling foot so she could look Annie squarely in the face. "Maybe this is the way it was meant to be. I'd rather you have good memories of your uncle. So, tomorrow when you pay your last respects, you can do it with a loving heart."

BJ glared at Annie as she waited and watched for an answer. Was there even a question, Annie wondered? Then she realized that BJ wanted some validation that she had done the right thing by signing the deed. BJ wanted Annie to speak well of Jaygar so she would feel justified in defying him and helping her niece.

Annie forced a smile as she patted her aunt on the shoulder, "I will, Aunt BJ," Annie lied. "We all have fond memories of him."

CHAPTER SIXTEEN

Annie had been up most of the night with BJ as she continued to drink and rant about the police not doing their jobs investigating Jaygar's murder. She called the police station several times and event attempted to drive over to the department. Annie stopped her each time she'd try to get in her car. To try and put a stop to the nonsense altogether, Annie decided it best to take her to the police department and get it out of her system. The Peddy Sheriff's Department had nothing to do with the investigation, but Billie Jean had convinced herself that they would be more willing to help her because she had voted for the sheriff.

Annie took BJ to her car at about 5 a.m., after being up and down with her all night. The newspaper was still in the passenger's seat with the story about Jaygar and Weeko in full view. Annie was grateful at that point that BJ was drunk out of her mind. It gave Annie time to roll the newspaper up and hide it away in the glove box. As she pulled out of the driveway, BJ passed out. So, the Peddy Sheriff never got to get his earful that BJ had saved up for him. She helped BJ inside and was able to rest for a few hours before the alarm clock chimed.

BJ was wringing a bunch of tear-dampened tissues in her hands as Annie drove to the funeral home. She was more pale than usual but the sunlight on her grey roots and orange freckles at least brought some color to the otherwise dim canvas that was her face.

Annie knew alcoholism ran rampant in the Cleaving family and she was seeing it up close in BJ. BJ was always the fun one, the party girl, the one who was always laughing and having a good time. The results of her life-of-the-party role – had made her old, grey, pathetic, and helpless.

Annie couldn't stand the thoughts of ever being pathetic; she'd rather be dead. She owed more than pathetic to Ethan. He, at the very least, deserved a respectable mother, even after his death.

Annie's hands became clammy on the wheel as she saw the sign for the funeral home. She hated where the memories took her when she saw hearses. There were two funeral homes she had to pass to and from work each day. Wilman's, the one where both Ethan and her mother were taken, was the closest. Annie would go four miles out of her way every day to avoid having to pass them. Now, here she was walking right into a funeral home and for someone she didn't give one damn about.

The attendants were holding the doors open waiting for guests. Annie and BJ were the first to arrive. When the funeral director saw them in the lobby he stepped out and told them that JJ would be along any moment.

"He said to tell everyone to enjoy the photos he brought of his father," the funeral director said in a soft voice. "Step inside here – they're lovely, just lovely."

The parlor looked like a small church with just a few seats – four pots of flowers up front. Annie was relieved there was no casket, only a large glass frame with pictures of Jaygar. JJ must have pulled this together quickly. Annie remembered having to find pictures of her mother before her funeral. The cancer at least allowed for time, though. Annie began gathering the photos a couple of weeks before it all came to an end. But for Ethan, there was no time at all. Annie's mother managed to have many large portraits of him there. A friend of Millie's took care of it while Millie was trying to take care of Annie.

JJ stepped up behind Annie as she was looking at Jaygar's photos. He pulled a strand of her hair and she flinched.

"You remember me? Remember me at all?"

Annie *did* remember him –he was exactly the same. He looked as if he hadn't aged one day.

"How are you?" Annie realized immediately that was a stupid question to ask. "Um – I mean, I know these are bad circumstances …"

"It's okay," JJ put his arm around her shoulders and gave her a squeeze. "Really, I've made my peace with it. I haven't talked to Dad in over five years, not since he got in all that mess with that Indian girl. I knew something bad was going to happen. People in town would tell me all the time about the police being out there. It was just a bad situation," JJ stopped talking for a moment and looked at his father's photos and shook his head. "Something was bound to happen."

"You talk just like they do," BJ came across the room quickly and slapped JJ across the face raging at him. "The police act like it don't matter that he was murdered. I thought that at least his only son would care about his father."

BJ walked into the foyer and sat sobbing in a corner next to the entrance; she seemed to be waiting for someone to come and comfort her. The funeral hour had come – 2 p.m. – no one else had come.

"Maybe I'd better go over and talk to her," Annie started to walk toward BJ but JJ pulled her back.

"No, just wait. I have something to say to you," JJ looked

even more serious now. "I know you need a deed signed – Dorie told me last night when I called to tell her about Dad. I will sign it for you," JJ looked down at the floor.

Please don't think me insensitive about all this. My father – well, he only cared about himself," JJ looked at his father's pictures again. "There were a lot of things I couldn't forgive. He's been dead to me for a long time – this, for me, is just a formality. I lost him a long time ago."

Tears were starting to form in JJ's eyes. He quickly stopped them, clenching his jaw in anger instead.

"I'm glad I can do this for you, Annie. Your mother was always so good to me and my mom. Sometimes she was the only bright spot in this family for us. She was an angel among many devils in that Cleaving family."

Annie hugged JJ tight, "I'm so sorry for you, so sorry."

"Don't be sorry, just be glad it's over," tears rolled down JJ's face. "I knew what he was doing to Weeko. Whether she deserved it or not, it wasn't right," Jaygar's only son drew a long breath and looked around the room as he blew it back out. His eyes darted back and forth as he looked to make sure BJ was not within earshot of their conversation. "My father was a sick man. Now, he doesn't have to be sick anymore. So don't be sorry, just be glad it's over."

CHAPTER SEVENTEEN

Turning the knob back and forth, she stopped and listened for news on any radio station she could find it – nothing. Not a word about Jaygar's death had gone out since the funeral. She was relieved his death seemed to pass like a whisper between kindergarten friends then forgotten. Still, she was curious about what had happened to Weeko; where had she gone? Millie had always told Annie that sometimes just being in the wrong place at the wrong time could get a person in a world of trouble. Now, Annie understood the true meaning of her mother's statement and noted to herself that the phrase should also include, "with the wrong people." Annie was starting to see just how wrong and screwed up the Cleaving clan had been and still was, in so many instances. How Millie had managed to escape unscathed was beyond Annie's comprehension.

The drive through Amish country was calming and refreshing. Annie could feel the air getting colder day by day. If fall was turning to winter in Pennsylvania and Northern Ohio, it wouldn't be too much longer before Rayes County started to feel the effects as well. The holidays would come shortly. Annie's memories of Ethan's last Thanksgiving made her cry. He asked question after question about turkeys and Indians and Pilgrims – all things they were discussing in his preschool class. One afternoon, he came home with a brown construction paper headband with a feather attached to it. His class had performed a holiday skit. Ethan loved

being an Indian. He wore it until the feather wilted and was
insistent on wearing war paint well into December. Annie threw
the headband away after weeks of wear but kept feather. Now, it
was tucked safely into her favorite book, Harper Lee's "To Kill a
Mockingbird," the feather marked the spot where she had stopped
reading to Ethan.

"Boo is scary," the memory of his voice as soft as cotton in
her ear.

Annie found herself opening the book many times and
reading the same pages she'd last read to him then she'd gently pull
the feather across her face, "Momma, feel it. It tickles," she could
hear him in her mind; feel his breath on her cheek, his tiny hand on
the back of her head, urging her forward.

He had so many questions that year. Annie had even bought a
book – One Thousand Answers to Questions Children Ask –
"Where do clouds come from? What are they made of? What's in
the sky? How come birds can fly?" Ethan hadn't gotten around to
all of them yet, but he'd covered a good many. Annie always
wanted to be sure to tell him the right answer, so he'd be smart.
She couldn't stand the thought of him being embarrassed by not
knowing the right things. Annie remembered once in third grade
when the teacher asked the class if any of them knew anything
about thunder. Annie was humiliated when everyone, including her
teacher, laughed as she told them what her grandmother had told
her. "God must have been digging potatoes today and when he
filled his wheelbarrow and headed back to the house, he spilled it
all over the sky. Those big potatoes dropping in the sky make the
noise we call thunder." Annie had never said that to a large group
of people before – only family. Immediately, she was embarrassed.
She laughed with the rest of them, so they'd think she was making
a joke. They all thought it was funny. Annie remembered
wondering if her grandmother really believed that story or if she
just made it up for fun. After that day, she always double checked

on anything Mamaw Lucy told her. Usually, her mother had the right answer, so Annie began to rely on that as fact and what her grandmother said as mostly fiction.

There wasn't another Thanksgiving at the Cleaving house after Ethan died; it was too soon, and after that too painful. The sight of Cornish hens in the supermarket freezer always made Annie smile though, thinking of her little Ethan and his tiny turkeys. Sometimes she'd pick one up and hold it in her hand trying to fully recapture that day – poke her pinky at it to watch the frost melt away in just one tiny spot.

Today was worse for some reason, Annie missed Ethan – she missed his smiling face. She even missed looking at all his pictures back home. She had a few small ones in her wallet, but it wasn't the same as being at home, surrounded by wall to wall photos. She was so angry with her mother for not telling her that she and Buck Rosen had been together. There were so many times she could have said something – after the crash, after the funeral when Buck was there. It just didn't seem like something her mother would work so hard to keep from her. Even if it wasn't appropriate to tell Annie about Buck right after Ethan died then why didn't her mother say something when she found out she had cancer? It just didn't make any sense why her mother wouldn't tell her that she dated the man whose son had killed Ethan. Maybe Millie thought it wasn't worth mentioning. Still, it seemed significant, Annie thought.

Annie hated Jacob Rosen. She could never erase him from her mind –on that day when he crashed into her car and killed her son. She remembered seeing his blood-spattered face just in front of her spider-webbed, shattered windshield. His shoulder was smashed almost into the dashboard. He was just looking at Annie. He didn't speak, or maybe he couldn't speak. Annie knew he was conscious enough to see and know what he had done. The smell of alcohol was sickeningly sweet in the wet, morning air. He had been out all night drinking and apparently wasn't finished. They all laid there together for what seemed an eternity – Ethan, Annie and Jacob. Ethan wasn't conscious. His face and the new fall jacket Annie had gotten for him that weekend was splattered with blood. Annie could hear him struggling to breathe – gurgling. When Annie heard sirens in the distance, her heart filled with hope. She had been worried about work that morning – it was Monday and there would be lots of calls to make and more negotiating about the price of the new furniture for new stores opening all over the country. Suddenly, nothing mattered – only air for Ethan and someone to help her free him. Annie had tried to pull herself out and get to him. She could reach within a quarter of an inch of touching him, but despite stretching and struggling she couldn't grab even a fold of his jacket – he was trapped too. She would scream for help but out there in the field, it was hopeless. Her cries were absorbed by the fog and her voice quickly grew raspy and weak. She didn't want to look at Jacob anymore; she focused her attention onto Ethan as she prayed to God to let him be okay. She stared intently at him, directly into his closed eyes, as if trying to will him to live. Finally, his eyes opened – he was looking at her. "Ethan, Ethan – there you are," she spoke softly to him. "There you are. Mommy loves you – it's all going to be okay. Our car did a little flip flop, but the people are coming to get us out." She kept asking for acknowledgement that he heard her, "Okay? Okay?" she urged him to say something. He continued to stare blankly at her. Noise from the sirens and fire truck motors were a welcome interruption of the silence. Annie could see them working to get at Ethan. She could feel them tugging at her from the back. "No, stop," she screamed over and over. "Get him out."

The sounds of grinding and bending metal rang in Annie's echoed in and out of the car. She wanted to cover Ethan's ears, he was so small, but she couldn't. Jacob was freed first. It gave Annie hope, "Please God, let him live," she kept praying, hoping, pleading. The firemen worked and worked – pulling at the front of the car and at the same time pulling the side open as well. She heard someone yell, "STOP." He's wedged in there and that door is the only thing holding him together. Annie couldn't see what they were talking about, but she knew they were talking about Ethan. Jacob was already out; she could see him on a gurney, his father standing over him. When Buck heard the firemen yell stop, he came over.

"No, don't stop. You get that boy out of there whatever it takes!"

Buck came to Ethan's side of the car and reached in. "Oh my God," he gasped for breath. "Oh my God."

Annie knew in that moment it was bad. She screeched a small cry, "What, what?"

Buck held Ethan's hands up next to his chest and lay down on the ground next to him, holding him as much as he could. Time seemed to slow to almost a stop – noises, voices, everything stopped. Buck looked at Annie, he was crying. "I'm so sorry, Annie," his voice cracked as he whispered.

Annie knew the moment Ethan died. He was looking into her eyes; she was looking into his and the life just left. He was no longer there. In the moment when it happened, the colorful angel was there. It felt as if someone was hugging her, as if she were lying in a bath of warm covers fresh from the dryer. The angel's beauty and love took Annie's breath. Then, she wrapped herself around Ethan, looked briefly at Annie, their eyes locked in a long moment. She never spoke but she didn't have to – Annie understood. Then, as quickly as she came, she swooped Annie's baby away. His body was still trapped but it wasn't him. Annie knew exact moment he died – life left his face, his eyes. Buck was still holding onto him, crying.

The next thing Annie remembered, she was in a hospital bed,

her mother sitting in a chair nearby. She didn't have to ask what happened. She remembered it, everything.

The police charged Jacob with vehicular manslaughter but when the case came to trial; his blood/alcohol level test was inadmissible. The Commonwealth's Attorney couldn't prove beyond a shadow of a doubt that Jacob had been out drinking all night or that he was still drunk when he crashed into Annie's car. The defense argued that Jacob was an early riser and was most likely on his way to school to get some much-needed studying in before a big Monday morning exam. Everyone knew better. There was a big weekend party, and it wasn't likely Jacob would've missed it. Without the blood/alcohol test, there was no proof that Jacob wasn't the fine, outstanding golden boy his attorneys were making him out to be. The prosecution came back with evidence that Jacob had already skipped school more than a dozen times already and school had just begun. They said it was likely he wasn't going to school at all that morning but heading out to the lake to crash at his family's cabin, like he'd done so many times before.

The jury heard testimony that police, paramedics, firefighters and even Annie smelled alcohol at the scene. The hospital administrator, when called to the stand, told the jury his staff was more focused on saving lives that morning than tracking the handling of Jacob Rosen's tube of blood.

Buck Rosen's name came up quite often during the trial, but he never took the stand and never came into the courtroom. He did come to Ethan's funeral but didn't have much to say to anyone. Jacob, by this time was out of the hospital – banged up a little but well on his way to being perfectly whole again. He didn't come to the funeral, nor did any of the rest of the Jameson or Rosen clan, other than Buck. Annie couldn't figure out if Buck came to pay his last respects to Ethan because he was sorry for what his son had done or if it was because he was there during Ethan's last moments here on Earth. Annie was always curious if Buck had seen Ethan's angel. After the conversation with the social worker at the hospital, Annie didn't dare ask him. Annie had shared with her mother and a hospital-assigned social worker, that she had seen an angel take Ethan away. The social worker told her that hallucinations happen quite frequently to those who are involved in accidents, and especially those who had lost a child in the process. She said Annie's case was particularly traumatic because she watched Ethan die and she had been hanging upside down for quite some time until she was freed from the wreckage. This, she said, was most likely, where the angel came from. When Annie expressed an interest in asking Buck if he had seen it too, Millie and the social worker were quick to tell her that was a bad idea. They said Buck was dealing with what Jacob had done and the charges filed against him. They said it would just add fuel to the fire and nobody needed that so soon after the accident.

Again, Annie thought, that would have been a perfect time for her mother to tell Annie that she and Buck used to date. Why didn't she say something then?

Jacob would be in college by now, maybe even second year. That could explain why Annie had only seen him sporadically lately. She was glad she hadn't seen him much. Just after Ethan's death it seemed she saw him everywhere – at the grocery store, at the gas station or even just driving through town. Annie couldn't stand the sight of him; to her he was a disgusting murderer. Each time she'd see him, he was always with a big group of friends, laughing and cutting up with them. It made Annie even angrier to see him happy – just being a young man like Ethan should have grown up to be. So many times, Annie would pass him on the road in his new car, his second new car – it was everything she could do to not push the gas pedal to the floor and swerve over into his lane – killing them both. All the Rosen boys had new cars; Liz made sure of that. She was a Jameson before she married Buck – the wealthiest family in town – old oil and coal family. Then, when Liz's father took over the family fortune they became retail, restaurant, bank, and media people. They didn't own everything, but they had a good handle on most things in Rayes County. Annie's mother always said that since Buck married into the family, they were now law enforcement rich as well.

Again, Annie thought, that was another perfect time for Millie to tell me about her and Buck.

Annie would sometimes wonder what Ethan would have done with his life. She smiled as she thought of what his reaction would have been to the accident if he had lived. He probably would have wanted to be a fireman once he had seen them all in action. Annie regretted not getting to hold Ethan one last time before he died but she was grateful to Buck for holding him close when she couldn't. Maybe that was why she didn't hate Buck the way she hated his son; or maybe it was because she liked to believe he saw Ethan's angel too – and that they had that in common. Still, there was always something about Buck Rosen – Annie could never put her finger on it. Even beyond his badge, thick neck, and large frame there was always a certain sadness about him, maybe in his eyes – much like the sadness that had surrounded Annie since the death of her son.

CHAPTER EIGHTEEN

Annie had a few vague memories of Beulah and Lloyd. Beulah was just a couple of years older than Millie. Annie had heard for years that her husband Lloyd was a black eye for the Cleaving family. She laughed as she thought about that now. It made her wonder how bad one had to be to be considered a black eye to the Cleavings. At least he had to be worse than Jaygar and Billie Jean. Or maybe it was because he was an in-law and not really a Cleaving that made the others force him to rise to a higher standard.

Beulah was a drunk and as Annie was finding out, many of the Cleaving children had problems with alcohol. Much of it may have stemmed from the fact that Lucy Cleaving would sometimes make moonshine for extra money when she needed it. Annie had heard this tale from Lucy Cleaving herself. While it was not polite conversation for Millie, Lucy wore it like a badge of honor. She was proud to have been a moonshiner; and the fact that some of the Cleaving children participated in getting her shine into the hands of those who needed it, made her even more proud. She talked about it like it was a family business; and in many ways it was. From the stories Annie had heard her grandmother tell, the brutal mathematics of it all led Annie to believe it was more than just an occasional profession for extra money. If all the stories Lucy told Annie were true, the family business was elaborate – so much so that local police officers got their cut as well. This gave the Cleaving children a free ticket across the state line, which was something no one else had.

From what Annie's grandmother told her, Beulah liked the drink more than the adventure. While Lucy and the older children ran shine across the mountain for the money or the tall tales that came after a close encounter with the law, some of them, like Beulah, enjoyed the drinking the profits a bit more.

Annie remembered Beulah and Lloyd coming to stay with her grandmother from time to time. When they were in town, they'd come and spend time with Annie's mother and visit. The two of them would always reminisce about old times, driving across the mountain to deliver shine to Tennessee who had been busted up by the law.

Lloyd met Beulah while they were running shine. He came to Lucy asking if she had any work for him to do – odd jobs and that sort of thing. Lucy laughed at him saying there were too many of her own children who needed to work. Still, she put him on the road with Beulah. She told Annie it made her feel better to know that Beulah wasn't making those trips alone – carrying shine over and then money back.

What Annie remembered of Aunt Beulah had nothing to do with moonshine or adventure. Beulah was a large woman – tall and broad like a football player. She had a deep voice. Annie never knew if she was born that way or if it was the two packs of cigarettes a day that caused it. Nevertheless, she sounded like a man – even more than her husband Lloyd, who was as small as a horse jockey. At some point, Beulah had developed some facial hair and then to get rid of it, started shaving. Annie remembered asking her mother why Aunt Beulah had whiskers – Millie explained it the best way she could, saying that Beulah didn't know any better than to start shaving, so now she has to do it all the time.

Beulah and Lloyd, like most of the Cleaving clan had headed

north after the coal mines went bust. Both ended up working in a tire factory in northeastern Ohio. They worked there for a few years and then they both, Beulah first and then Lloyd, started getting disability. Lloyd developed liver problems while Beulah became diabetic but they both continued to drink.

Northern Ohio was not much of a change of scenery from Pennsylvania, for Annie. Though there were more places to stop and get gas and a cup of coffee. The little town where Lloyd and Beulah lived looked a lot like Stig. Annie wondered if no matter where a person goes, they end up gravitating toward familiar-looking things, even places. Annie was sure there was nowhere on Earth that looked like Stig, but here it was – Stig's twin, Mercury, Ohio. Beulah and Lloyd lived in a mobile home park. It was nicely landscaped, but the trailers were all very old and small. There had been a pool there and what looked like a state-of-the-art pool house at one time. The pool was now filled with stagnant rainwater and the pool house stuffed with junk and boxes. Annie had to laugh when she saw Beulah's front yard. She had cut and decorated tires for flower beds, just like Olga. She looked around to see if anyone else in the park had the cut and peeled-back tires. No, just Beulah. This, Annie thought, would be the one place most likely to have the tire flowerbeds – especially considering the town's history with the tire factories. Annie guessed it just never caught on up north the way it did in Kentucky.

"Oh, my word, child, we're so glad to see you made it," Beulah met Annie as she was getting her things out of the car. "We were getting a little worried about you – we thought you'd be here yesterday."

Annie told Beulah about Jaygar and the funeral. No one had bothered to call them. Beulah said she had heard that Jaygar was involved in something crazy. She said JJ tried to get her and Lloyd to come down and talk some sense into him. They couldn't – Beulah now had dialysis and Lloyd was sick with the cirrhosis.

Beulah was sad for a moment but moved on quickly to other subjects.

The trailer looked like something straight out of the 70s – thick, green shag carpet and groovy green glass votives in the chandeliers reminded Annie of a restaurant in Lexington – That 70s Spot. It was almost like Beulah had gone there and stolen their furnishings.

Annie saw Lloyd sleeping on the bed down the hallway. He was covered with a quilt and only his head was showing.

"He doesn't get around much, Annie. Don't be surprised if he don't even know you're here."

Beuhla's voice sounded just as course as it always had; her beard was now gray. She looked like she hadn't shaved in a day or two. Annie had felt her whiskers rake across her face as she hugged her and kissed her on the cheek out in the driveway. Strange how something as bizarre as a woman with a beard could bring back such fond memories.

"Give me that paper and I'll go ahead and sign it and then take it back to Lloyd and get him to sign," Beulah reached a hand to Annie motioning for Annie to give her the deed.

"Oh, I left them in the car," Annie had almost forgotten why she was there in the first place. Throughout the entire trip, she had been travelling purposefully – with deed ready and pen in hand at each stop.

"Don't worry about it, we'll get to it," Beulah waved her hand through the air in a "never mind" fashion.

"I'm so glad you're here. I hope you don't feel hard at us for not coming to the baby's funeral and then your mom's," Beulah stroked Annie's hair. "We really wanted to come but there was just so much sickness and we don't have any money to travel. We're lucky if that old Chrysler out there makes it to the clinic every day and back."

Beulah looked apologetically into Annie's eyes.

"I feel so sorry for you; you're so alone right now."

Annie didn't like for anyone to feel sorry for her, even if it was well intended. It made her uncomfortable. She reacted the only way Millie Cleaving's daughter would. She looked all around Beulah's trailer then looked her aunt up and down.

"*You* shouldn't worry about me, *I* do fine."

The moment she said those words, she regretted it.

Beulah looked around the house and her face turned red.

"Yes, I ... well I need to clean the place up a bit, I guess."

"No, I'm sorry Aunt Beulah I didn't mean to say it that way," Annie felt as if her own guilt had punched her in the stomach.

"Well, now that you put it that way, I completely understand," Beulah playfully slapped Annie on the arm. "Your mother was always proud that way too. Heck, all of us were – all us Cleaving girls – always too big for our breeches, too proud and too high to ask for help. But you know that ain't always good – not always."

Annie was glad Beulah didn't take offense to what she had said. It was such a habit to be on the defensive whenever old ladies were near. Growing old, scared Annie, she would rather just die. She guessed those were the only two options a person had, die young or get old. It wasn't the vanity part of it that made her worry about aging it was the living – living without anyone, living alone, without Ethan. She often wondered where people went when they died. Sure, Heaven, she thought. But Heaven could mean so many different things and she was sure Ethan would be in a special place, even too special for Annie to go there. That was what the only thing that scared her about death – that she still wouldn't see her precious baby when she left Earth.

"You know your mother taught me a lot about pride," Beulah scooted a chair across the floor for Annie to sit in.

"Really?"

"She came here when she was pregnant with you – came to stay and help out with the kids while me and Lloyd worked," a slight smile appeared on Beulah's face then ran away just as quickly. "It would have worked out real well too but we had some problems."

Annie never gave a thought that her mother would stay with Beulah and Lloyd. She couldn't imagine that the three of them would have much to talk about.

"She said she'd stay on with us after you were born and be our nanny. I was so glad to see her here, you just can't even imagine," Beulah rubbed her face hard, looking around at her dingy house again, "Oh, no, we didn't live here then – we had a big house over in York – that's where all the tire executives live now. Me and Lloyd we were on our way – big house, fine car … whatever we wanted, really."

"So why didn't she stay?" Annie tried to find a non-sticky surface to place her elbow on the table.

"It started even before she got here – about two days before she came – a celebration that we were getting a nanny. Well, Lloyd and me, as you well know, have a problem with the drink," Beulah acted as if she'd told this story a hundred times. "You remember the kids? Kathy and Lloyd Jr.?"

Annie nodded. She did remember Kathy and Lloyd – both had moved to DC after military service. Kathy had been in the Navy and Lloyd the Air Force. She always remembered their military photos; they looked so important – militant.

"Me and Lloyd went out drinking ... and the kids ...," Beulah stopped for a moment and swallowed hard. "They were only three and five years old. LJ was trying to cook some pancakes for Kathy 'cause they were hungry. Me and Lloyd figured they'd be alright, we told them not to touch the stove."

Beulah stopped, noticing Annie's confused look, "Didn't your Momma ever tell you about this?"

"No, she never told me anything about being here, but that really doesn't surprise me," Annie gave a sarcastic tone but got no reaction from Beulah.

"Yes, your mother was always a good secret keeper," Beulah forced a smile.

"What happened?" Annie was curious now.

"The whole place went up in smoke – gone, toast," Beulah emphasized the word toast. "But it was the best thing that ever happened to me and Lloyd. Can you even ... even imagine leaving a three- and five-year-old home alone to go out and drink?" Beulah was sounding preachy now.

Annie couldn't imagine it, but over the past few days nothing the Cleaving clan had done surprised her anymore. Annie had wondered about the scar on Kathy's face – she always thought it looked like a burn scar.

Annie pointed to her face, "Kathy's scar?"

"Yes, she was burned in that fire but the two of them got out – only by the grace of God," Beulah reached a hand to the sky. "A neighbor saw the kids moving around inside, broke the door down and got them out."

When Millie arrived, the social workers had already taken the children. Lloyd and Beulah had no money in the bank, so they had nowhere to stay. They were in a shelter at a local church. When Millie came and found out what had happened, she went and got both and then convinced the social workers and court system that she would oversee the household until they got back on their feet and into some sort of program for alcoholics.

"We did get straightened out and she got us an apartment with some money she asked Asher to send. We were so scared. We almost lost our babies, Annie. Did you ever have something that had such a hold on you that it could make you not even care about your babies?"

"No, I haven't," Annie couldn't hide the sick feeling that came over her. "I can't even imagine."

"Oh, I'm so sorry, Annie – I've put my foot in my mouth. I shouldn't have said anything like that about your baby ..."

"It's okay, Beulah, I understand the comparison you're trying to make – I understand."

Annie wondered why, if Beulah and Lloyd were so scared over losing their children, would they continue to drink after that.

"We lost our jobs, our home and our fancy car," Beulah waved a hand, letting Annie know those things didn't matter. "But thanks to your mother we didn't lose our children. She took us and got us some help. The kids stayed with Momma back over in Rayes County until we were better. Buck Rosen came up here and picked them up ..."

"Buck Rosen? You mean, the Rayes County Sheriff, Buck?"

Annie couldn't believe it – Buck again.

"Yeah, your mother called him and then left before he even got here," Beulah shook her head, still obviously confused by her sister's actions. "Oh, he loved your mother, even after he was married to that other girl – what was her name?"

"Elizabeth," Annie supplied the missing information right away. "Liz Jameson."

"He came here hoping to find Millie, but she had already left – wouldn't even tell us where she was going. She was afraid we'd tell Buck. I don't know what happened between those two, but your mother swore up and down that you didn't belong to him," Beulah shook Annie's arm a bit. "She didn't want to be around him, but he was the only she trusted to come up here and get the kids. The social workers would only release them to law enforcement to take them to Kentucky."

Millie had lied to the social workers and told them she was taking the children back home and that she and her mother would take care of them until Lloyd and Beulah could take them back.

"He came and got the kids and took them home to Momma," Beulah dabbed at her eyes with a dishrag from the nearby sink. "She took care of them until we could prove we could take care of them ourselves. We were able to get some other jobs – Lloyd got a job at the bakery, and I got a job waiting tables. It wasn't the kind of money we were used to making but it got us back on track."

Beulah saved up, got a trailer and when they passed inspection by the social worker, the children were allowed to return home.

"I can't believe Sheriff Rosen came all the way up here to get your kids," Annie felt she deserved a better explanation.

"Well, he wasn't the sheriff then, just a police officer. And you know, no matter what your mother said, she still had feelings for that young man – I could see it so clearly when she left here. I know she wanted to stay and see him; she was torn."

Annie wasn't shocked to hear Buck Rosen's name again in the context of a relationship with her mother. But now it was clear that Buck and her mother were more serious. A man doesn't keep picking up the pieces for a woman he has no feelings for.

"But he was married to someone else?" Annie wanted Beulah to tell her more.

"He had just married the girl – maybe even that week – but you know, Annie, you don't just stop loving someone because your circumstances change. Your mother and Buck had a special bond," Beulah clasped her hands together to demonstrate. "They always did. They were more like best friends than they were sweethearts – always there for each other. That doesn't just stop because circumstances change."

Annie tried to picture her mother and Buck but still couldn't. She could really never imagine her mother with anyone. "Why do you think she never told me – told me about her and Buck?" Annie sounded like a five-year old child.

"Well, if she didn't tell you I'm sure she had her reasons," even amidst the chaos of Beulah's messy trailer, her next few words were organized and clear. "Us Cleaving women are funny creatures, Annie. We keep secrets – from our parents, our children – especially our children. We all want our children to be proud of us and look up to us, think that we are good people. Just like my children never knew they were about to be taken away from us. They just thought they were visiting grandma because our house had burned down. I didn't want them to know that and for whatever reason your mother didn't want you to know about Buck Rosen."

CHAPTER NINETEEN

As a little girl, Annie could never tell Addie and Alma apart. They could have been the same person and none of the Cleavings would have known, except for their mother. Only when Annie grew up did she begin to see the subtle differences in their facial bone structures. Still, it wasn't easy to tell them apart unless they were together.

The Cleaving twins had always done everything together and they still did. They married brothers who were quite a bit older and had designed a car that was supposed to revolutionize the way people drive. The wheels could turn at a 360-degree angle. A German car company purchased the design for a huge sum of money but never used it. Annie remembered her mother telling her about the car design and how industrious "those fellas" were. When the big money arrived, the two of them – Bill and Bob, took the money and invested it in the stock market. They had enough money to keep them and their wives comfortably for the rest of their lives. Bill and Bob were free to tinker in a garage created just for their inventions. And tinker they did, for the rest of their lives. Addie and Alma became bored with sitting around the house while their husbands were engaged in life-altering work. So, the two of them decided to go to college and become schoolteachers. They finished at the same time and taught at the same school. After a few years teaching, they returned to school to get their library science certification. It was then they discovered their true calling and what them most happy in life – gathering history. They didn't care who the history was about if they got to experience the adventure of finding it. Millie often said that they were genealogists before genealogists were cool. When Bob and Bill died, Addie and Alma moved in together. Annie never knew which husband died first or whose house Addie and Alma chose to keep. Her only memories were of them together, no husbands, and living in the same house in Northeast Ohio.

When Annie spoke with them on the phone and told them she was coming, they promised her a day filled with information about the Cleaving family and asked why she hadn't come to them first. They were truly sorry they had missed the adventure.

The house looked so much smaller than Annie remembered it; the same, but smaller. The forest green trim gave dimension to the little place. It had wood siding that looked a lot like logs but flat. The flower garden reached all the way out into the driveway. Annie suspected Addie and Alma had done this on purpose so they wouldn't have to mow the grass. They had learned a thing or two from being married to Bill and Bob. If there was something to do, Addie and Alma were always looking for an easier way to get it done.

As soon as Annie stepped out of the car, she was met with the scent of cedar and pine. She remembered as a little girl playing on a swing just under an Oak tree at the back of the house once when she and her mother visited. She leaned around the corner of the house to see if it was still there, but a fence blocked her view.

"That's new," Annie's heels clonked across the front porch.

"Oh Alma, come out here. Annie's here," Annie heard through the front door.

"Well, she's coming in isn't she? Why do I have to go out," Annie heard Alma answer her sister and smiled as she remembered how the two of them bickered all the time. Millie used to tell them they sounded like an old married couple.

"Come in here, Annie, don't pay her any never mind," Addie hugged Annie as she stepped through the doorway.

"Oh, I didn't mean nothing about that, child. You know me," Alma got a hug from her niece despite her sister going first.

Annie wasn't surprised that the two of them still looked almost exactly alike; they were even wearing the same type of dress, only a different print. When Annie stared at their faces, she could see her Mamaw Lucy in there. As Addie and Alma had aged, they had become their mother. Annie wondered if her mother would have taken on those same characteristics if she had lived to be as old as Alma and Addie.

"It's so good to see the two of you," Annie faced them both then hugged them both together, which was easy. They were tiny women, even smaller than Annie. She felt like a giant standing over them.

Addie and Alma gave her a fresh tour of the house to show her what they had done with the different rooms. The two of them had added bedrooms downstairs, one for each of them and they had turned the upstairs into various project rooms. There was a sewing room, filled with half finished, just started and almost finished quilts. Colorful pieces of fabric lay all over the room. It smelled of cedar and pine, just like outside. Down the hall was the scrapbooking room, filled with pictures piled on tables, a trimming board and two easels sitting opposite each other. It was evident that the two of them had either done a lot of scrapbooking together or had intended to. Either way, someone had been working hard. There were books piled on top of books filled with newspaper articles, old pictures, wedding invitations and obituaries.

Then there was the family history room. This was the room Addie and Alma were most excited to show Annie. It was wall to wall Cleavings. The framed portraits didn't look anything like the people Annie knew them to be, but she recognized the picture of her mother right away.

"Wasn't she beautiful," Alma watched Annie as she stared at her mother's portrait. "Oh, she was so, so beautiful – her skin like a baby and her voice like an angel."

"Yes," Annie ran her fingers along the side of the frame. "She was beautiful."

Annie had missed seeing that picture. A copy hung in the hallway at home. She passed by it every day, never really noticing it until now, out of its element – far away from home.

"You miss her, don't you?" Addie put her tiny, wrinkled hand on Annie's arm. It was cold but Annie could feel the tenderness coming through her frigid touch.

The other Cleaving pictures were not as easy to associate with the Cleavings that Annie knew them to be. Asher, however, was a dead giveaway – those sideburns always wore him instead of the other way around but very recognizable.

One by one, Addie and Alma pointed out the family – Jaygar, who even at a young age looked like the Devil, Veda, who was striking in her own right – long, black, wavy hair and eyes that could pierce your soul if you stared at them long enough. She looked excited, ready and willing to take on the world. That woman in the picture was nothing like what Annie had seen over in Stig. It made Annie wonder how someone goes from being the person in that portrait to Veda, the Veda she met the other day – confused and lonely.

She looked over at Addie and Alma. They were the lucky Cleavings – they had each other. The two of them were busy finishing each other's sentences and trying to outdo the other regarding knowledge of the Cleaving history.

"No, Asher was 18 years old in that picture," Alma crinkled her forehead to express hard thinking, but her answer was sure.

"He was 17 and a half, I keep telling you," Addie argued. "This picture was in the fall, before he turned 18 that next year."

The two of them noticed Annie staring at them.

"Oh," Addie waved her hand in her sister's face, letting her know she no longer cared to argue. "Come over here and look at these. This is your uncle Jaygar – didn't you say you saw him before he died?"

"Yes, yes, I saw him, visited with him," Annie's mouth became suddenly dry. Her heart raced but then calmed a bit when Addie and Alma turned their attention to someone else.

"Here is one with Dorie, Cleda and Roslyn, all together," Addie pointed to a black and white, framed picture. "They were just like stair steps, those three. We used to call them the Three Musketeers. I'm so glad you got to see all of them. I keep trying to talk Alma into doing a visit with the family. She's afraid to leave this old place."

"I'm not afraid to do anything," Alma defended. "I just don't want to come home to an empty house. Somebody'll come in here and make off with everything we have."

"Geesh, Alma," Addie was disgusted with her sister's response. "Even if we came home to a bunch of splinters lying on the ground, it's all just bricks, wood and nails."

It was apparent that leaving their house to travel was a point of contention between the two of them and had been for quite some time. Annie could see that Alma was the worrier of the two – the one who took great pains to make sure everything was well preserved. Addie seemed to be the more carefree.

They had aged the same, in all the same places. The map on Addie's face was the same map on Alma's face. Both wrinkled in all the same spots, faded in all the same areas. Even the grey in their hair was spattered in the same strands. Annie wondered if it was because they were twins or if it was because they had lived almost the same type of life – shared the same concerns.

Their bickering was escalating, probably because they had an audience – an essential element usually missing from their performances of "I'm right, you're wrong."

Feeling she had to interrupt the argument, Annie walked over to two portraits she had never seen before. One was military – Navy; the other was a painting of a young boy.

"Who are these people?"

Annie and Alma stopped arguing immediately and the two of them raced over, seeing who could get to Annie first. Annie couldn't help but think about Tweedle Dee and Tweedle Dum, characters in one of Ethan's favorite cartoons, "Alice in Wonderland." Annie wished she had brought Ethan to meet these two women. He would have loved visiting here as much as she had when she was a child.

"Marsden and Kelvin; Kelvin and Marsden," Addie and Alma were both yelling the names at Annie.

"Okay, Alma, let's do this. You tell her about Marsden and I'll tell her about Kelvin, that way we're not screaming at her like the crazy old ladies at the nursing home at Bastion."

"Bastion?" Annie was puzzled.

Addie and Alma looked at each other and laughed at the same time, with the same tone, "We go visit the patients at Bastion Health – it's a place where they keep patients with dementia."

The two of them must have realized how silly they both sounded. They stopped arguing for a moment while they both took the pictures down from the wall. They urged Annie follow them to the scrapbooking room. Alma picked up a book labeled Marsden and Addie picked up a book labeled Kelvin.

Once inside the room, Annie's eyes were darting everywhere – there was so much to see. Piles of pictures and paper next to several stacks of books and fabric created a kaleidoscope effect as Annie moved inside the room. Once Addie and Alma retrieved the books, they were ready to go, ushering Annie out of the scrapbooking room as quickly as they had urged her to come in.

"Let's go downstairs and fix some lunch," Addie and Alma nodded in agreement.

"You can look at the books and then we'll give you a little history on the two Cleaving boys who didn't live long enough for you to know about them," Alma finished.

CHAPTER TWENTY

"Marsden was handsome – all the Cleaving boys were, before they got their age on them, of course," Alma looked to her sister for an Amen. She got it before the statement was even finished as Addie began to nod in agreement.

"This is one of my favorite pictures," Alma held the photo, tapping her finger on Marsden's face. Me and Addie are really the only two old enough to remember these boys. We were just children, but we do remember how the girls used to swoon over these two, especially Marsden."

Whether Annie wanted it or not, she was about to get a history lesson about two of the oldest Cleaving children – the only two who had never really concerned her regarding ownership of the Cleaving property. To her, it was like they never even existed. Still, she could see this was important to Addie and Alma and decided to embrace the family legacy for once. At least the atmosphere was cozy – the company entertaining.

"Mars, as everyone who knew him well enough called him, was very handsome. Even as little girls we knew that," Alma nodded at her sister, looking for approval. Addie agreed without speaking.

Mars worked at the Siler horse farm, a good walking distance from the Cleaving house. Sometimes he rode a bicycle he had bought wrecked for a few dollars and pieced back together one part at a time. By the time he was done with it, it was the nicest bike in Rayes County. All the other boys, even the ones who had cars, were envious of Mars' bike.

"It was bright red with white trim, and he had made a little license plate for it," Alma showed Annie an old black and white photo of Mars at the horse farm. She pointed to the bike. It was leaning up against a fence, way off in the background.

That was before having license plates on bikes was even thought of; Alma was excited about the possibility of her brother being an early innovator. "If he would have sent that into the patent office, he'd have been a rich man."

Annie looked deeper into the picture of Marsden. He was looker, no doubt about that – very rugged, tan and muscular.

"See, you see it too, don't you?" Alma smiled at Annie as if she understood exactly what she was thinking.

Annie nodded and handed the photo back to Alma.

"Who is the boy in the photo with him?"

"Oh, that's Ed Siler. Did you ever hear of him? He still lives in Rayes County, right there on that horse farm. Last I heard, he had old timers," Alma looked again at the photo, this time at Ed.

Mars and Ed were friends. Even though Ed's family was filthy rich, he would work right alongside Mars every day. Each summer Mars worked there; Ed would show up to work too. Except for the summer his family sent him to stay with an aunt in California. They wanted him to look at a college.

"He just did it to get to be near Mars," Alma pointed at Ed in the picture and then Mars. "A lot of people were like that about him. He was so charming and made everyone feel so special. People would do just about anything to get next to him."

Even though it was summer, Alma and Addie had gotten up early every day to make Mars lunch before he'd head out to the Siler farm. When they finished, they would sit at the table with him while he ate his breakfast. That was the only time they got to spend with him, alone – other than sharing him with their mother.

"When he'd get home from work, somebody would be waiting here for him every day," Alma smiled, still staring at painting of her brother. "And if they weren't waiting for him, they'd catch up with him on his way home and walk the rest of the way back home with him."

Addie and Alma agreed the only time they could have his full attention was before he went to work. If someone wasn't waiting for him at the house, they'd watch and hope to see him coming down the road by himself. He never did.

Alma turned page after page of the book she and Addie had made in Mars' memory. There were leaves and old pages from books that had been written on; and there were hand-drawn pictures as well.

"This is a picture I drew for Mars when I was a little girl," Alma turned to a page with a drawing. "I sketched this for him one day after he told us about his plans to join the Navy and sail all over the world; the seven seas, he'd say."

"So, he wanted to be like Kelvin?" Annie pointed to the other Cleaving boy's picture she didn't recognize.

"Yeah, I think so," Alma spoke, her sister still nodding quietly in agreement.

"Even if you're as admirable as Mars, I suspect you'd have to have someone to admire as well. I think Kelvin was Mars' hero. And, yes, I think he did want to follow in his big brother's footsteps," Addie interrupted Alma just before she could begin to speak about Kelvin.

Annie had to laugh a little at her aunts as each of them tried to inch over into one another's historical knowledge. They were concentrating hard on being ever so aware of the original agreement: Addie would give the history of Kelvin and Alma the history of Marsden.

Annie sent the smile away from her face and took a sip of her drink as if nothing had happened.

"Everybody wanted to be like Mars and Mars wanted to be like Kelvin," Alma flipped the pages of the book, uncovering an entire section of newspaper articles.

Women loved Mars, even the married ones. This was becoming more apparent as the story of Mars unfolded.

"That's what got him into trouble," Alma shook her head as if her concern from him had transcended the decades since his death. "That's what eventually got him killed."

"He drowned, right?" Annie was beginning to remember parts of the story now.

"Oh yes, he drowned. He drowned right down there in Rayes County at the Skeeting Lake. Ed was there, too – just the two of them on that day. I'll never forget it."

"Momma was in the kitchen and Sandy Jeffers came riding up on Mars' bike. She was screaming from down the road, trying to tell me something," Alma cupped her tiny, wrinkled hands over her ears as if she could hear the voices still. "I couldn't understand what she was trying to say. She was too far away. As she got closer, I could hear her saying something about Mars and Ed and that lake. She said Mars had drowned. She sped past me so fast the wind from the bike blew my hair. I can still remember that feeling. It always brings that day back to me when someone blows by me in a car or the wind hits my face in from that exact direction."

"Mars was an excellent swimmer," Alma removed her hands from her ears. Annie looked at Addie, who was nodding. "That's why he wanted to join the Navy. That's one of the reasons he would go to Skeeter's Lake, that's what everyone in Rayes County called it. Partly because the actual name was Skeeting and partly because in the Dog Days of summer the mosquitoes there would be so thick you could have hacked them with a machete."

"Mars would go down there at the lake and practice holding his breath underwater," Alma smirked. "He showed us a few times how long he could do it. He did it right there in an old washtub out behind the house. It would be mine and Addie's job to time him. And, of course, one or two of the pretty Rayes County girls would be close by for dramatic effect. They'd squeal and say things like, "Oh, Mars – you're going to kill yourself. Get your head out of there."

"I think he invited them to watch just so he'd have a captive audience," Alma scooted the book so Annie could get the full view of Mars and Ed. "As upset as they got, they didn't dare leave. They wanted to be with him no matter what. He knew that, too. There was never any reason for Momma to worry about Mars going down to the lake. In fact, most parents wouldn't let their children go unless Mars was there. They had elected him as sort of a lifeguard for Skeeter's."

Mars and Ed were both seventeen that summer and juniors in high school. Mars was all set to join the Navy; Ed wanted to be right behind him. But, his father had a different idea of what he should do with his life. James Siler wanted his son to be a lawyer. So, he kept sending Ed to different parts of the country where there were law schools. Even though Ed never really had a choice as to what he would do with his life, his father wanted to make it so Ed at least thought he was deciding for himself. He would make sure that each visit included pretty girls, lots of whiskey and the finest cars to drive.

"What he didn't factor in was Mars," Alma took a break from talking and let Annie flip through the pages for a moment. "He didn't realize how badly his son wanted to be exactly like Mars and do exactly what Mars was going to do."

"Remember how I told you that all the women loved Mars?"

"Yes, even the married ones," Annie had a pretty good idea about what Alma was going to tell her.

"Yes, you *were* listening," Alma was pleased with herself, "even the married ones," she repeated.

The summer Ed was away in California, James Siler took a trip to Europe to visit a horse farm hoping to strike up a deal for exclusive breeding rights on the Siler farm. It was big business in those days, to have the English breed their horses at your farm. Siler had bought two racehorses that hardly anyone knew about. His plan was to offer them for breeding to only the most elite horse farm owners in the world. This was one of the reasons he wanted his son to become an attorney. Agreements like those conceived in the horse world needed ironclad, loophole-free ink on them. James, being a businessman, decided it was better to own a lawyer than to hire one.

"James had left his wife Cecilia home alone," Alma's voice got lower, "alone with Mars, day after day that summer."

Cecilia had never been a woman who looked married. She was

always out driving around in her convertible, her hair tied neatly in a scarf right out of the latest and most stylish fashion catalog. Her dresses were a little shorter than other women in town were comfortable with and her hair a little longer, cascading over her shapely form.

"Momma waited years to tell me and Addie about what really happened to Mars. It was only after we begged and begged. We were both grown women when she told us – almost forty weren't we Addie?"

Addie nodded her head. Annie could see how keeping with the agreement to remain silent was wearing on Addie.

The aunt that Ed was staying with out in California let it slip that James had planned for his son to become an attorney and stay on with the Siler Horse Farm as its legal counsel. Ed was angry at his father for trying to deceive him and caught the first bus home.

"When he got home, he was so mad at his parents he didn't even bother to go inside," Alma turned the pages to reveal various newspaper articles. "He went straight away to find Mars. He knew he'd be there, somewhere on the farm."

It was only days after Mars drowned when Ed told police he had come home and seen Mars and his mother inside one of the horse stalls wrapped around each another. He told them he stood there and watched for a few seconds. He was going to confront them then but got sick and threw up.

"He waited for weeks, planning and plotting," Alma held up a newspaper article – *Siler confesses to drowning his best friend*

"How did you get a copy of that?" Annie asked as Alma showed her a copy of a police statement signed William Jenkins Siler.

"Somehow Momma got her hands on it," Alma shook her head as if she were still in disbelief that Lucy Cleaving could have managed to wrangle that out of the hands of law enforcement. "You know Momma, when she was determined ..."

The police report said Ed asked Mars to go to the lake. He knew he would be anxious to go because he always was. Ed said Mars had tried to tell him about what happened a few times, but would always stop after saying something like, "I need to talk to you about something ..." Ed said he would make up something about the Navy training or school or something. Ed said he just couldn't stand it anymore and began to wonder if that was the only reason Mars was his friend – to get to his mother. Ed told police that he held Mars down in the water for "a really, really long time" before he died.

"James returned home to find his son in jail and his wife gone," Alma held her hands out, conveying the final big picture. "She left because she couldn't stand the humiliation of everybody knowing what she had done."

Ed spent one year in the county jail and was released just in time for his eighteenth birthday. His father sent him to California. He became an attorney and took care of the Siler Horse Farm for the rest of his life. No one ever saw or heard from Cecilia again.

"Momma was beside herself for years," a tear escaped from the outer edge of Alma's shriveled eye lid. "She was so sad, so angry."

Although she had no idea her grandmother had gone through something so similar to what had happened to Ethan, Annie could certainly relate. Jacob Rosen spent no jail time either; he was now in college, enjoying life and Ethan was gone forever. Annie had always thought her grandmother had been cheated for not having known Ethan. Now, she decided, it was better that she died before he was born – before the accident.

"Why has no one ever talked about this?" Annie was puzzled by the lengths the Cleavings had gone to, to keep a secret.

"Nothing is ever black and white," Alma touched Annie's hand. "If anyone ever tells you there's nothing more to a story, then there usually is. Everyone, everything has a story."

Alma pointed to the doorknob across the room, "How many times do you think I've grabbed that doorknob in anger? And what are the stories behind that anger?"

Annie looked at the doorknob then back at Alma, wondering what the answer to that question really was.

"People are complicated, their lives are complicated. Behind every birth there's a story of love and behind every death, there's a story of pain," Alma gave Annie's forearm a squeeze with her tiny hand, her nails no larger in diameter than kernels of corn. "And as humans, that's all we really are – life and death, aren't we?"

Annie nodded in agreement; she couldn't remember ever hearing an explanation so simple, so direct.

Alma looked over at her sister as if to say, your turn now.

Addie wasted no time getting her book open. The cover was decorated with Naval stripes and patches. On the first page there was an old, yellowed telegram. It was long and slender, not on a full piece of paper. On the top the words, United States Department of the Navy was followed by, "We regret to inform you ..."

Annie had seen this before. She couldn't remember where, maybe on a visit to Addie and Alma's house. She ran her hands across the page, wondering about all the places that paper had travelled – the seven seas, she guessed, all the places Mars said the Navy would take him.

"Now, just as your aunt Alma said, with every story of life there's a story of love," Addie smiled at Alma. "Here, with Kelvin, we have a story of death and love or possibly a new life and love."

Kelvin was on a ship close to the Canadian border. He didn't want to be there but the only thing a young man in Rayes County could do was work in the coal mines or join the service. Kelvin chose the latter, thinking that when he got back, he would have enough money saved to marry his sweetheart, Virginia Root. Jinny and Kelvin had been in love since they were twelve years old.

"Momma said the day he left town, you'd have thought the two of them had melded into one person, they hugged so tight," Addie hugged herself, swaying slightly back and forth. "Momma always had a way with a turn of a phrase, you know. I've heard her say that hundreds of times when she would talk about Kelvin."

Jinny wrote Kelvin every single day while he was gone. Considering that he was on a ship with not much privacy, Kelvin wrote back as often as he could. Jinny had begun to talk to Kelvin about moving to Canada so she could be near him. He tried to tell her that it wouldn't do any good. He might be there now but there was no way of knowing where he might end up next. Then, there she'd be in Canada by herself.

In her letters she begged and begged for him to come home. She'd say she just couldn't stand it any longer without him. He would write back and tell her to be patient that he was saving money so they could be married when he returned.

"Momma said Jinny would come over to the house and ask to borrow Kelvin's things – a jacket, a shirt, pants – whatever she could get her hands on, really. She said it made her not miss him as much – made her feel closer to him," Addie raised an eyebrow of suspicion. "Momma said she started to think the girl was crazy but didn't say anything about it because she knew Jinny would be the mother of her grandchildren someday."

Kelvin's ship was moving closer and closer to port and a docking day was announced. Jinny headed off to Canada, taking all the items she'd gathered from Kelvin's closet with her. Before the ship could reach port, about 100 or so miles from the destination, it was blown up and sunk by a German U-boat. The U-boat captain claimed they lost contact with their home base and had been floating around unaware that the war had ended.

"I remember when Momma got that telegram," Addie ran her fingers across the words. "She was in the garden and me and Alma were outside playing. The men came and she tried to run from them," Addie stopped speaking for a moment then continued. "As little girls, we didn't understand why, but later we understood why she ran. She knew they were coming to tell her that Kelvin was dead."

"It was so sad that year, first Mars found dead and then Kelvin had been blown up on that ship. Momma was devastated," Addie ran stroked Kelvin's picture with the palm of her hand. "Me and Alma did our best to try and hold the house together. Then one day a miracle happened."

Jinny's parents had been looking for her to return home after the news of Kelvin had spread. When she didn't come, they began to do some investigating – making phone calls to anyone and everyone around that area. The staff on the bus line was questioned. The owner of the boarding house she stayed at was questioned as well. The police were told that Jinny didn't seem upset at all when she left, in fact, she was giddy. "That was the word Momma said they used," Alma looked excitedly at Annie.

"Jinny's mother began to search her room and found several boxes of letters in the top of her closet," Alma turned the pages to reveal several letters in Kelvin's memory book. "She brought them over to Momma and I remember they both sat at the kitchen table poring through them one at a time looking for any clue as to where Jinny might be."

After a few dozen letters the two women noticed a pattern between the *I love yous* and the *I miss yous* – Jinny and Kelvin were writing code in the PS line just below the main text. Notes like, "see you in the 20" or "hold my hand 35" and even things like "can't wait to take a dip in the cool water – only two months 'til summer."

"Funny thing was that when Jinny wrote those things, it was already summer," Alma's voice carried a tone of mystery now. "So, you tell me what you think might have happened?"

"I have a few questions," Annie felt as if she were playing a game of "Clue" with her aunt Addie. "Did Jinny ever come back?"

"No."

"Did you ever find the clothes Jinny took from here anywhere in her room?"

"No. Gone, everything except the letters," Addie looked at Annie as if all this were a brand-new discovery.

"Did he jump ship? Maybe and he and Jinny ran off together?"

Addie and Alma both started giggling.

"We think so – we hope so," Addie emphasized the word hope and then lunged forward a little, patting Annie on the arm. "Momma always said they probably did. Or Jinny would have come back home. Jinny's parents eventually chose to believe it too."

"Where do you think they went?" felt herself falling into the content of the letters as she skimmed over them.

"Oh, we had a pretty good idea that they stayed right there in Canada," Addie smiled.

"How do you know – why do you think that?"

"Well, there was an investigation surrounding Jinny's disappearance – it lasted several years," Addie, who hadn't touched her sandwich until now began tearing at pieces of bread. "In fact, the police were starting to conclude what we had suspected all along – that Kelvin had gone AWOL and Jinny was with him."

Just before Christmas three years after the boat had sunk, Jinny's parents got a picture in the mail of a baby. There was nothing else in the envelope, only the picture. The baby looked identical to Jinny and Kelvin.

"It had her eyes and his bone structure," Addie pointed to the photo with her twisted little fingers. "See here."

The picture was there, along with other photos of other children. Annie had never seen a picture of Jinny, but she was sure these children belonged to Kelvin.

"They look just like him," Annie was pleased the aunts had chosen to tell her this story last. It had a happy ending. Annie needed a happy ending.

"When we got the first baby picture, Jinny's parents stopped the investigation. They never gave the police a reason, just that they had resigned themselves to the fact that their daughter was never coming back," Addie flipped to the back pages of Kelvin's book

"Were they okay with that?" Annie wondered why Jinny's parents wouldn't still want her found.

"Well, no, they weren't – they hated us for years for that. But if Jinny had ever wanted to return home, she could have. But, she never did. I guess her mother and father eventually just had to accept that."

On the last page of the book, Annie's eyes lit up with surprise and her mouth gaped open. There it was. It must have been as shiny as the day they gave it to Mamaw Lucy – a Purple Heart, in recognition of the sacrifice and bravery of a fine young Soldier – Kelvin Bradbury Cleaving.

"Life's funny that way, Annie, just when you think you've got the crazy Cleaving family figured out, something else happens – something else *always* happens," Alma closed the memory book of Mars.

CHAPTER TWENTY-ONE

Although Annie had noticed that Roslyn and Dorie looked very much alike – and they both looked like her uncle Rubin, like most teenagers, she never really cared enough about the family history to investigate. Now, though, she was curious. Since her conversation with Roslyn, she had thought about it often. Rubin and Clive were her mamaw's stepsons; at least Annie had picked up on that over the years. Their mother died when they were little boys, then Adam had taken Lucy in to take care of the boys and the Cleaving house.

Clive, the older of the two boys, died over a decade ago, not that anyone would have noticed. Annie's mother told her that after Clive came out of the service, he just packed up his clothes and left home. Some say he built himself a little cabin in the Utah mountains. Rubin took the more industrious path and moved to Detroit where he worked in the auto industry it retired him. He must have made a pretty good living at it. Millie always said he was well off. Clive never married and never had any children. Rubin married an older lady, together they had two boys who moved to California when they got out of college. They started a small computer programming company and made a fortune together. When their mother died, they brought their families back to Kalamazoo so they could be closer to their father.

Annie had sent Rubin a letter since he wouldn't return any of her phone calls. She was on track to arrive at his house today. She hoped he was there – still alive and kicking, too. Roslyn said he was likely not answering Annie's calls because he wasn't happy about Annie's request of him to sign off on the deed to the Cleaving property. Still, Annie had no choice but to try and convince him to help her. Maybe she would get lucky and wouldn't have to ask him about her mamaw's "big love" as Roslyn had called it. Annie wasn't sure she even wanted to know.

The neighborhood wasn't what Annie had expected. For someone who "did well" the subdivision was rather ordinary. All the homes were small, red brick with one-car carports. The houses were all angled the same way and set the same distance from the road. Each of the homes even had the same size Oak tree just off center of the walkway leading to the perfect sidewalks lining the streets. The house numbers were the only visible differences. Annie had to look carefully at all the numbers so she wouldn't miss the house.

There was a car in the drive – a dark green, four-door sedan, just what she would have expected a retired older man to drive.

"Good, maybe he's home," Annie turned her wheels toward the driveway.

Once outside the car, Annie noticed the black lamp post. She remembered the lamp post from some photos at Addie and Alma's house. Each of Rubin's boys had been standing by this same lamp post in the pictures, both young men at the time. The lamp post was solid black then, now it had faded into the color of an already-spent brick of charcoal. Still, the bird perch on the front was exactly the same as the one in the photos. Annie was sure it must be the same one. She touched it with her fingers as she passed it – to get a feel for that piece of history in the tangled Cleaving mess. Just as she raised her hand to wrap knock on the door, she saw a torn piece of notebook paper taped to it.

NO VISITORS ALLOWED. OCCUPANT IS ILL.

The note was written in pencil and haphazardly placed on the door as if it was a spur of the moment decision. Annie was sure Rubin had put it there because he knew she was on scheduled to arrive today.

She knocked anyway. No one came. She knocked again. Again, no one came. After several attempts to get someone to the door, she decided to walk around to the back door. She hadn't come this far to just get in the car and go back now.

Just beyond the car port she saw a work building – a detached garage, big enough for one car, at least. She could see a shadow moving back and forth on the other side of the small front windows. Skeptical about trespassing, she began to tiptoe in the grass as if someone might hear her footsteps. When she got to the garage she started to knock on the small door at the side of the structure but stopped herself. Instead, she crept over to the window where she could see someone inside. There was a big black car parked exactly in the middle of the small space. She could see a white head of hair bobbing up and down on the other side of the forties model Ford sedan. Then, he popped up and began rubbing the hood of the car. His hair was as white as cotton, which made his skin look even darker. He was rubbing the hood of the car then dipping his rag in the can of wax, spotting here and there. His hands were covered in sunspots as well as his forehead. The folds of skin loose on his face jiggled slightly as he moved his hands back and forth across the car's hood. As he rose and looked toward the window, Annie moved over to make herself visible to him. He stopped for a moment and looked up at her. She waved excitedly as if to say, "Over here." Rubin looked down again at his can of wax, dipped his rag and began rubbing the car again.

"Hey, Uncle Rubin, it's Annie."

She repeated herself again, this time louder. He never looked up. She got louder and became even more persistent until he finally threw his rag on the car, never looking at her, and came to the door. Annie readied herself as quickly as she could. She knew this one wasn't going to be easy.

"Well, come on in," Rubin was annoyed at Annie for disregarding his attempts to keep her away.

Rubin turned around just as quickly as he opened the door and went back to the car and began waxing again, not even acknowledging Annie was there.

"Did you get my letter – my messages?"

Rubin looked up at Annie and nodded his head then went back to waxing.

"How have you been?" Annie tried to break the silence.

"You don't care how I've been, Annie. I know why you're here – just like you said in the letter – you want that old house."

"Well, I've been living in it, taking care of it, paying the property taxes on it for a great number of years," Annie tried to defend her claim. "I thought I already owned it, then I found out the deed was all messed up."

"A great number of years you say – a great number of years," Rubin repeated himself several times, mocking Annie. "You're not old enough to have done anything for a great number of years. This car has been around for a great number of years – but not you."

Annie did what her mother always told her to do in situations like this one, let the angry person vent and wait for the right moment.

"Yes," Annie agreed. "I guess you're right."

"I don't need you to tell me I'm right," Rubin tilted his head to one side and raising an eyebrow. "I know I'm right and you, little girl, are in no position to bargain with this old man. That house should have been mine and Clive's when Daddy died," he nodded his head as he spoke to make his point. "As far as I'm concerned, it still is our house."

Annie didn't say anything but wondered why, if Rubin felt this way, he hadn't come forward before now to put his claim on the Cleaving house.

"Even as little as I was, I knew that bringing her into our house was a bad idea," Rubin said, still rubbing the hood of the car as hard as he could. "She was nothing but trouble from the day she got there. I knew something was going to happen. My father, though, just like everybody else, couldn't keep his hands off her."

"Who are you talking about?" Annie was puzzled.

"Your grandmother, Lucy – that piece of Marsip trash over in Rayes County.

Rubin's words were like tiny daggers piercing Annie's stomach. She had never heard anyone speak that way about her grandmother before. She was hurt that Rubin would say such a thing; hurt for herself and for her grandmother. Still, she kept silent and let him go on. He was out of breath from waxing and beginning to sweat a little. He stepped over the bench at the side of the car and picked up a glass of water. His hands shook as he picked it up and slowly brought it to his mouth. He gulped hard and finished it off then went over to a sink at the back of the garage and filled it with tap water, drinking even more. Not knowing exactly what to do with the awkward silence, Annie stood there not daring to speak.

"Well, if you're going to be in here bothering me, the least you can do is help a little," Rubin threw a towel at Annie. She barely caught it as it fell toward the ground.

Annie quickly found a place for her purse in a corner shelf and rolled up her sleeves.

"I just want it on thin – just real thin, you know," Rubin instructed Annie as he sat on the bench sipping at his water and wiping his forehead with his handkerchief.

Annie began dabbing her towel in the can of wax and then ever so lightly rubbing the hood of the car, seeking Rubin's approval as she did. Her uncle nodded his head; she continued. He walked to the front of the garage and opened the big overhead door. Annie was relieved to have some air. The building was getting hot and stuffy in the afternoon sun.

"I guess I don't have to hide back here anymore," Rubin laughed. "You found me didn't you?"

"Yes," Annie stopped waxing for a moment. "I guess I did."

Rubin came back over and sat down at the bench again and pointed at the hood of the car.

"You go on ahead if you want to. You're doing a nice job."

Oddly enough, Annie was pleased that her Uncle Rubin was giving his approval to her waxing capabilities.

Annie examined her uncle as she slowly and lightly rubbed the wax in. He was looking down and shaking his head.

"You know your grandmother was good to me and Clive. She took care of us, even when sometimes we weren't so good to her. We missed Momma so bad. It was hard to let somebody else in with us."

Annie nodded her head in understanding, relieved to hear that Rubin's feelings toward his stepmother weren't all filled with hate.

"I was ten and Clive was twelve when she came to our house. Momma hadn't been dead but a few months. Do you know how old your grandma was when she married Daddy?"

"People have told me that she was only fourteen," Annie continued rubbing the car hood.

"Yep. Fourteen, only two years older than Clive," Rubin held up two fingers, again his hand shook. "She wasn't as big as a minute. She was a tiny little thing, always was a tiny little girl. I heard she died a while back."

"Yes, a few years ago, didn't anyone let you know?" Annie's voice softened.

"Yeah, your momma called me and told me," Rubin's eyes filled with tears, then he looked off out into the yard. Annie turned her attention toward the car again, as if she hadn't seen his tears. "I can't remember now what it was, but I had something here that I had to do – couldn't come to the funeral."

Rubin looked over at Annie as she raised her head.

"You look just like her, you know – just like her and just like your mother. Seeing you looking so much like her next to that car takes me back to when Lucy first came to us. Me and Clive didn't know what to think. She was different. She looked different from our momma, even smelled different."

Annie stopped working, remembering how her grandmother smelled.

"Like Lilies – a little dirt and a little flower – like Day Lilies," she said out loud, not meaning to.

"Yes," Rubin nodded at Annie, looking at her as if they had finally connected on some level. "A little dirty and little sweet – that was her."

Rubin sat there in silence, staring out the garage door. He sipped at his water, saying nothing, but Annie wondered if his thoughts were traveling somewhere back in time to a place where the old Ford once owned the Rayes County roads.

Rubin, being the youngest was much more comfortable with treating Lucy like a mother. With Clive, it was a different story. Not only was he only two years younger than Lucy, but he was bigger than her – much bigger than her. He didn't take too well to someone so close to his own age trying to tell him what to do. He and Lucy eventually developed an understanding with one another. He would stay out of her way, and she would stay out of his. It worked well, for the most part, especially when it came to chores and homework. Clive did what he was supposed to do so that Lucy would have no reason to chide him.

Adam was away from the house every day – he was the foreman at the coal mine. The Cleavings weren't rich by any stretch of the imagination, but they fared far better than the coal miners who had to live at the camp. Lucy's family was one of those. Adam had come to the camp from another mine in West Virginia, owned by the Chickory family. He had worked for them for many years and finally, they had given him the chance of a lifetime – to get his family out of the camp, get him out of the mine and run his own show, sending the Chickorys all the profits, of course. He had always considered himself a good businessman and the Chickorys had left him in charge several times when they were away. Adam was the only boy in his family to finish school. As the youngest of four brothers, he was able to elude coal mining long enough to at least get a high school education. This put him head and shoulders above the other men in the coal mine. Adam was smart and it showed. He emitted the kind of intelligence and confidence that someone like old man Chickory wanted at the forefront, not hidden away in some dark cave chipping out black rock. Adam was a hard boss with a profitable mine. When land in Kentucky became available, old man Chickory bought it just so Adam could run it. He knew the money would pour in – and it did.

For Adam, the chance to get his family out of a mining camp and into a real house was too good to pass up. Chickory let him choose a piece of land in Rayes County and then provided him all the tools he needed to build a house. Adam chose carefully where to put the Cleaving house. He didn't want it to be too close to the mines because he didn't want his family to feel they still lived in the camp. But he also didn't want to be too far away. He needed to keep an eye on things. Just above the mining camp general store there was a hill. Adam Cleaving put his house just below that hill on the other side of the mining camp then he proceeded to build a road leading from it that went straight into town. He commissioned the fiscal court to name the road after his grandfather on his mother's side, John Watkins. The first hard winter brought a dampness and cold to the hills of Kentucky never seen before. Adam's wife caught a chill and developed pneumonia. She died one night in her sleep.

The Marsip family had seven children and lived in the coal camp just over the hill from Watkins Road. Lucy was the oldest of the seven girls. Jacob Marsip had hoped for at least one boy but got none. It did him no good for Lucy to turn fourteen, the age most boys would be eligible to work in the mines. When Jacob heard about Adam's wife, he quickly offered Lucy as a solution for the Cleaving family. When the agreement was made, both men knew exactly what the other wanted. Adam, not used to being alone, wanted a wife and Jacob, in debt for several hundreds of dollars at the general store, wanted relief. Lucy's mother, naïve and hopeful for a miracle, agreed to give over her oldest daughter for work in return for more money in her husband's paycheck and forgiveness of the debt at the store. It would be a fresh start for the family.

Lucy was supposed to work Monday through Friday and then return home on the weekends when Adam could be home with the boys. When that first Friday came and Lucy didn't come walking over the hill, she knew what had happened.

A week later, Adam and Lucy were married right there at the Cleaving house. Lucy's father was proud to have his daughter married to the boss; her mother was heartbroken that her husband would arrange such a sad life for their daughter in exchange for money.

Lucy was unhappy but Adam was decent to her and rarely asked for special nights in the bedroom. It was as if he would wait until he absolutely could stand it no longer before he would ask. Lucy never told him no, grateful for the long reprieves in between.

Adam and Lucy had only been married a few years when old man Chickory decided one Kentucky coal mine wasn't enough. He sent Adam away for a few months to help take over a mine and get it up and running. Rather than uproot his sons, who were now in high school, Adam packed a suitcase and left his family. Lucy's father took charge of the mine in Adam's absence and Lucy took care of the home place.

"When Dad left is when it all started," Rubin came out of his trance. "Clive and Lucy would play together outside – tag, ball, whatever they could do to be together. I knew something was different about Clive – he acted different toward me and toward your grandmother.

"I could hear them at night in her room. I guess they didn't know I was listening. I was old enough to know what was going on."

Rubin told Lucy's father what he suspected was going on between Clive and his daughter. Even though almost everyone at the camp, including Jacob, knew there was an affair going on,

Jacob, afraid of losing his extra money and his new standing at the mine, told Rubin he was being ridiculous and to go back home and not to say anything. He told him that his father would be angry at him if he told.

"That next winter, your grandmother gave birth to Roslyn," Rubin looked at Annie, waiting for a reaction. "Funny thing was, she looked a lot like my mother. How do you think that happened?"

Annie could feel all the blood draining from her face. She had stopped waxing a while back and was leaning across the hood of the car as far as she could to listen to what Rubin had to say.

"Oh my God," Annie had no idea she was speaking out loud until she heard her voice. "And, what about Dorie – her too?"

"Yes, I'm pretty sure her too," Rubin glared at Annie with certainty.

Adam suspected Roslyn was someone else's child. He fired every Cherokee-looking miner in the camp that spring, though he never said why, everyone knew. One by one, anyone who even had a hint of Indian in them, was sent packing with their families – the youngest ones went first. The gossip in the camp was thick but Lucy's father rallied behind Adam, leading him to believe he was doing the right thing. If Adam couldn't come up with a reason to fire someone, Jacob was always waiting with a complaint at the ready.

"I saw good men leave with their families with nothing more than a sack of clothes and food for a week," Rubin blew a short breath of disdain. "Everybody knew what was happening but Jacob told them all if they said anything that my father would shut the mine down and they'd all lose their jobs."

Clive and Lucy knew better than to let on while Adam was

home. They reverted to their old habits of staying out of each other's way so as not to bring any suspicion.

"Clive never paid any mind to any of those other children, but Roslyn was different," Rubin shook his head in disgust. "He would get close to her any chance he got – I even caught him holding her one night. When Lucy caught him and saw me watching she yelled at him to put that baby down – just for my benefit, I'm sure."

Summer came, and again, old man Chickory sent Adam to oversee the takeover of another coal mine. He felt safe leaving this time, knowing that whoever Lucy had fallen in love with was gone. Even though his marriage to Lucy was an arrangement out of convenience, Adam loved her – even cherished her at times. She was beautiful, even after giving birth to six of his children. She made him feel whole, like he belonged somewhere. His first wife viewed him as a chore to be done. It wasn't her fault; it was the culture of the Native Americans to be aloof and distant. But with Lucy, she cared about what Adam felt, what he thought. She could tell when something was bothering him and would ask him about it. There were times that Adam would start to feel like a father to Lucy. He hated those moments but making love to her would quickly diminish any fatherly love he had for her. He was heartbroken when he found out she had been with someone else, but neither he nor his wife mentioned it to one another. They just went on like nothing had ever happened. He couldn't bear the thoughts of throwing her out. He knew he could never take care of the children; and in some small way he had expected her to go astray when he left. She was so young, so alive – desirable.

"It wasn't a day or so after he left that second time that your grandmother and Clive started again," Rubin shook his head in disbelief. "Everyone had almost gotten over the shock of the firings, the gossip about Clive and Lucy – it was all but gone. Then I saw them again. He was with her in the barn. It was good for me to see it, though. I had wondered if she did it with Clive the way she did with Dad – you know, because she had to."

Annie was embarrassed at the turn of the conversation and Rubin cleared his throat several times before continuing, obviously uncomfortable as well.

"Well – I'll just say this, they were in love," Rubin put his hand slightly over his mouth as if that were the worst thing he told Annie during the entire conversation.

Adam returned home happy to find his wife pregnant and thinking their marriage was back on track. Then winter brought another Indian-looking child into the Cleaving family – Doris, who would later be known as Dorie. It was then that Adam began looking beyond the camp and into town. He spent his days asking around about Indian families nearby and then someone told him that Indian blood sometimes skips a generation. It was then he turned his attention back toward the camp. He and Jacob began looking for people with Native American ancestry.

One drunken coal miner, feeling he had nothing left to lose, told Adam the truth about his wife and about his son. He told him that everyone knew and that he needed to stop beating the bushes around the camp and start looking under the covers at home. In a fit of rage, Adam nearly beat the drunken miner to death.

"It wasn't too long after that Clive joined the service," Rubin's raised a shaky hand and gave a sarcastic salute. "I remember the day he left. Lucy was crying after him, telling him she loved him and saying it right there in front of my father. I saw my brother shed a tear or two as well that day. Everyone at the camp came to the top of the hill and watched what was happening. The children were all screaming. They had no idea what was going on – just that their mother was upset. Dad had to drag her away as Clive walked down the road. Strange thing was that he comforted her – told her everything would be alright."

Annie was trying to picture her grandmother and Clive in love. It made her happy to think that her grandma had been so in love at one time. She wondered if she would ever feel that way about anyone.

"Poor Clive," Annie blurted out without thinking.

"Yeah, poor Clive, poor Dad and poor Lucy," Rubin had a hateful sarcastic tone. "They ruined all our lives for a little roll in the hay. None of us were the same after that, especially Dad. And, I missed my brother. I had always thought we would run coal camps together – all my dreams just stopped after that. All I wanted to do after that was get out of there, that God awful place. Thank God I did."

Clive never contacted his family again – even after Adam died, he never came to the funeral.

"I got word a few years back that Clive had died," Rubin pulled a handkerchief from his pocket and wiped the sweat from the back of his neck. "He evidently stayed in touch with an old high school buddy of his around Rayes County – a boy by the name of Jameson."

"I don't really know what to say other than I'm sorry you feel that way," Annie tried to offer some comforting words.

"Nothing you can say now," Rubin threw his hands up in the air. "What's done is done."

The name Jameson brought Annie hurling back to the present and out of a tangled Cleaving past. The Jamesons, she thought, again so much a part of everything. Even as far away as Michigan, Annie couldn't escape their golden, intrusive reach. She had tried to catch a moment to ask Rubin about signing the deed. It never came. He must have said a hundred times, during his story, how grateful he had been to get away from Rayes County; that was something the two of them had in common.

"You know, Uncle Rubin. I'd like to leave Rayes County as well – that's why I need your help with this."

"I know you need my help but if I have this one chance to get my father's dignity back then I'm going to take it," Rubin tried to convince Annie that his intentions were honorable. "Don't you think my father knew exactly what he was doing when he left his estate that way?"

Annie knew the answer to that question, and she also knew where Rubin's line of reasoning was headed. If Adam Cleaving's intent was to make sure that Lucy never had the chance to own the property outright, then no court of law would dispute that the property belonged to all the Cleaving children – not just Annie.

"He wanted all of us to have to approve of Lucy's actions after his death if she wanted to stay there. My mother and father built that house from the ground up – I was there, I saw them do it. They worked hard to make a family. They worked until their fingers bled and their mouths were so dry, they could spit dirt," Rubin looked at Annie as if she were a stranger. "They built that house to get our family out of the rat-infested coal mining camp. I can't let your grandmother's wish for you to have that house, override the memory of my parents."

Annie could understand Rubin and why he felt the way he did. Still, she wasn't happy that he wasn't going to cooperate and sign over his rights to the Cleaving house. He obviously felt no attachment to anyone in the family other than his estranged brother, the late Clive. There was no way Annie was going to change that in only one afternoon.

Annie had waxed and buffed the entire car by this time. Her arm was tired and limp. Rubin got up to inspect her work.

"You've done a pretty good job here young lady," Rubin patted her on the back, his old hands shaking.

"Yep. I'd say I have done a good job here," Annie smiled after a moment of inspecting her own work.

"Let's go inside and have some good old fashioned sweet tea, what do you say?"

"Sounds good to me," Annie pulled her purse from the corner shelf and followed her uncle inside his house.

When Annie pulled the back door closed, she found herself in Rubin's kitchen. It looked like a widower lived there – everything completely clean and free of debris – no cute decorations – no cows, ducks or daisies cluttering up the counter space; just clean, white surfaces in every direction.

"Come on in here in the sitting room and I'll get us some tea," Annie followed her uncle into the living room and sat on the sofa. Rubin opened the front door and removed the note he had taped there before Annie came.

"Sick, huh?" Annie made light of the note he left for her benefit.

"Yeah, I really didn't want to get into all this today. But I'm glad we had our little talk. I'm glad you don't just think I'm some mean old man who doesn't want you to have that house. Now you know I have my reasons."

Annie nodded, accepting that fact that she was going to leave with an unsigned deed. She sank back in the couch enjoying the comfort of air conditioning for what seemed like the first time all day. Across the room she saw the family portrait wall and got up to get a closer look.

There was a picture of her grandfather. She had seen a picture of him before but never one where he was this young.

"This your mother?" Annie pointed toward the photograph as Rubin handed her the tea, ice cubes clinking against the side of the glass as his hands shook.

"Yes, that's her," Rubin stood close to Annie. "She was a true Native American –half Cherokee. You see it don't you?"

Annie nodded; her attention now focused on another picture.

"Clive?" she pointed to another photo.

"Yes – that's my brother."

"I think Addie and Alma have this picture of him?" Annie remembered seeing it in their house.

"Yes, I believe if anyone could come up with a copy of this picture it would be the two of them," Rubin laughed. "I believe that's an old school picture of him."

Annie studied Clive's jaw line and his nose. She looked closely at his hair and forehead. Then, she turned her attention back to her grandfather's first wife.

"What was her name?"

"Shazuan – but everyone called her Betty."

"Betty? How did anyone ever come up with that name?"

"I think she just wanted a name that sounded very American, and Betty was it – of course, I always just called her Mother."

Annie studied the pictures closer. She could see Roslyn and Dorie in the face of their father, Clive. He was much more Native American than Rubin.

"I know," Rubin must have been reading Annie's thoughts. "We don't look that much alike. Clive always took after Mother and people always said I looked like Dad."

"I can see that," Annie examined Rubin's face then looked at the photo of Adam Cleaving.

"You got a long way to travel yet?" Rubin patted Annie on the back.

"Well, I am going to make one more stop but as for my deed-signing adventure, you were my last visit."

"Sorry I couldn't be more help to you," Rubin walked Annie to the front door. "But I hope you know now that I really would if I could. I just can't do that to my father. It would be like what Clive did to him in a way – giving up all we have. I need to keep my part and take it with me. I know that's what my mother would have wanted, even if my father was weak when it came to your grandmother."

"I understand," Annie pulled the deed from her purse. "But, I want to leave this here with you. The address and my phone number are here," Annie pointed to the small slip of paper clipped to the back of the deed. "If you change your mind, you can just sign it and send it on to me."

"No need to leave that thing here," Rubin took the blue paper. "I made up my mind a long time ago."

"You do realize that by not signing, all you're doing is forcing me to stay in that house?"

"No matter, you know my reasons," Rubin held his hand up conveying no further discussion was necessary.

"Thank you for the story," Annie nodded her head toward the portraits hanging on the wall on the other side of the room. "I feel like I know my grandma so much better now. I only wish I could go home and talk to her about it."

Rubin gave a slight wave as Annie backed out the front door. For no reason Annie could explain, she felt compelled to give the old man a hug.

"Thank you, young lady and thank you for the nice wax job on my car," Rubin was smiling from as Annie stepped off the porch. "You feel free to come and visit me anytime up here in the great white North."

"The interstate runs both ways you know," Annie opened the car door, got in and rolled down the window. "If you want to own a piece of the Cleaving house then maybe you should pay your little spot a visit sometime."

"Maybe I'll do that," Rubin shouted so she could hear. "Maybe I'll do that."

As Annie pulled out of the driveway, she knew her fate had been sealed. There was no getting rid of the Cleaving house and there was no running away. An unexplainable sense of relief came over her; she had no more decisions to make. Whether to leave or stay in Rayes County was no longer up to her. It had just been decided for her, and oddly enough she found comfort in that. There was one more stop to make – Asher Cleaving had some explaining to do.

CHAPTER TWENTY-TWO

Determined to get to Asher as quickly as possible, Annie was angry at herself because she had to stop and get a room midway through her trip. Michigan to Virginia is a long haul and she just couldn't stay awake last night to finish it. She made good use of her time at the hotel, writing down all the questions she had for Asher so she wouldn't get lost in conversation and forget. Getting information out of Asher was no easy task; he was easily distracted. When she visited with him at the Sunshine camp before, she attributed his short attention span to a lifetime of drug use. After having time to think about some of the things he'd said during those seemingly unfocused moments, she decided that maybe he hadn't been trailing off to somewhere else accidentally but had been trying to stray Annie away from certain topics about her mother.

Then, there was the dream when she spent the night at Cleda's house. When she woke up, she attributed it to potions and smells of potions coming from the kitchen but maybe, just possibly, she thought, there might be some merit to this particular dream.

She was in the woods with her uncle Asher. Barefoot, she had stubbed her toe. If not for the pain she felt, she might not have looked at her feet at all. They were small feet – child's feet, but not a baby – a larger child, a toddler. They were dirty as were her small legs. Her fingers were throbbing as she held tight to pieces of the horse's long mane. Her little hands were clenched tight to the few hairs that would fit inside her tiny fists. She was sliding back and forth as the horse strolled on. It was so tall, and she felt as if she were going to be bounced off at any moment, hitting the rocky ground far below her.

"Hold on tight, Annie," Asher looked back from in front of the horse. He was leading it with a rope. His face carried that same, warm smile that Annie remembered from her visit at the camp. But he was younger, his hair had no gray in it at all and it was thicker, bolder. His face looked alive, ready for adventure, not tired and finished. "This path is a little bumpier than what you're used to. I don't want you to fall off this horse. Your mother would kill me."

Annie nodded her head – a head that was filled with grown up Annie, but still little Annie somehow existed there too.

"Why can't we ever just go without her getting mad?"

Annie heard her voice as she spoke and it startled her, but she stayed inside little Annie just listening. It was a child's voice – small and innocent, just wanting to know the answer to a simple question.

"Old Red Penny is well … old and sometimes she can be cantankerous," the younger Asher explained. "Like most women, she's a little moody. Your mother is afraid for you to ride Red Penny, afraid she'll throw you off."

"What does cantankerous mean?" Annie heard the small child's voice again.

"Mean," Asher's answer was short, but one Annie understood. "You ask me this every time we take this horse out."

"I do?" Annie continued to sway on the horse with every trot.

"Yes, you do," Asher looked affectionately at his niece.

Asher stopped walking and untied the horse. He rolled the rope up around his arm, the way he always did – at least little Annie always knew he did, the big Annie looking on from above now wasn't sure if he ever did it at all.

Then, he climbed on the back of Old Red Penny just behind little Annie. She wasn't scared anymore. She let go of Penny's mane and let her tiny little fists relax as her hands rested on Uncle Asher's legs on either side of her.

At that moment, Annie realized she was dreaming. But just before she woke up, she watched from above as Asher and little Annie rode Old Red Penny fast through the woods. Even though she was no longer with her former, smaller self, she could feel the wind on her face and the butterflies in her stomach as Penny made long strides over the rough path. Annie woke herself laughing out loud – cackling like a child.

CHAPTER TWENTY-THREE

Even during the day, the Sunshine camp was hard to find. Annie stopped at the same store where she had met Reena and her man. It seemed different now – she knew where she was going. As she took her wallet from her colorful bag Reena made, she felt a twinge of excitement that she'd be going back to the camp. She gassed up for the long drive but with no one to follow into the camp this time, she made several wrong turns from the highway and then several more down dirt and gravel roads before finding the spot. She parked near the other few cars and vans on the grassy hillside, hoping there were no nails or glass. This was not the place she'd want to find herself stranded with a punctured tire. She remembered thinking when she left the last time how careless she'd been not to think of it before. But she was on a mission and not much else mattered at the time; just getting the signatures and selling the house.

She was disappointed that she would never be able to sell the old Cleaving house, but it didn't mean she couldn't leave Rayes County. She'd just have to do it with a lot less money. Other than a car payment, she was debt-free to begin with. Still, it would have been nice to tuck away some money or invest in another home rather than throwing money away on rent. It just simply went against her very nature to rent – like such a waste. But, if buying meant a long-term commitment to anywhere, Annie wasn't sure she was ready for that. What if she hated this new town, what if she hated her new job? Maybe, she thought, it would be better to test drive this new situation of hers and not get all tied up on owning a home just yet or moving her 401k to the new company.

The Sunshine camp looked deserted. Annie didn't see anyone out milling about and Sunray wasn't there to greet her at the first tent. She walked down the rugged path until she heard voices in the distance. She stopped and listened quietly to hear which direction they were coming from.

"A gathering, somewhere at the gathering," Annie made an audible sarcastic note to herself and laughed as she walked toward the voices.

She could hear people talking louder and louder as she walked. Then she could see the tops of their heads just over the hill. They looked like pussy willows, all bunched up together moving as the wind pushed them around. They were all gathered at Phoebe's med tent. Annie rolled her eyes and shook her head.

"What miracle is Dr. Phoebe about to perform today?" As Annie was walking, looking ahead and trying to hear and see what was going on, she stumped her foot on a rock.

"DAMMIT! DAMMIT! GOD DAMMIT!" she screamed and sat down on a nearby boulder.

Most everyone was looking toward the pink tent with red corners, but a few heads turned after Annie screamed and cursed the rock that had interrupted her mission to find Asher. She pulled off her shoe and started rubbing her throbbing toe, sitting down on a nearby boulder.

"Hey, what are you doing back here? I thought I took care of your business already."

Asher came over and sat down next to Annie.

"Hey," Annie greeted her uncle while still rubbing her toe.

"They said you were over here, but I thought they were imagining you from the other day," Asher's raspy laugh now sounded comforting to Annie. "You know that tends to happen to a misused brain sometimes. You forget what happened mostly, but there are times when you imagine what did happen."

"That's *so* deep," Annie's tone smacked of sarcasm.

"Wow Annie, your aura is glowing red today ," Asher held the palms of his hands up as if to shield himself from Annie. "You need to calm down; you're a fiery red and even white hot. You're angry right?"

"Yes, you could say I'm angry."

"Whoa – there little girl, enough with the sarcasm, have I done something?"

"You lied to me. You just outright lied to me," Annie pointed her finger at Asher to drive home the message. "And I want to know why. Why it was so important that you not tell me that Momma and me stayed with you after I was born?"

"I didn't tell you anything about that," Asher was noticeably confused. "Wait a minute, I didn't tell you or not tell you, *really*, anything about that."

Annie blew a sigh and a long breath to show Asher the level of her aggravation with him.

"I know you didn't tell me that we *weren't* here longer," Annie tried to calm her voice a bit, so not to confuse Asher again. "But you did say my mother left after I was born."

"Well, technically she did leave here after you were born," Asher stood in front of Annie now ready for her confrontation.

"Well, no matter how you said it, you lied to me," Annie folded her arms. Asher's folded his arms to mock her. "And I want to know why it was so important that you not tell me the truth."

"I think you're being a dramatic about this, Annie. And I'm not sure I like your tone of voice with me. I came here to get peace. I got it and I aim to keep it."

"You 'aim' to keep it," Annie laughed at Asher. "Now you sound like a good ole Rayes County boy."

"Well, really Annie, I have nothing more to tell you," Asher shrugged his shoulders. "I'm sorry."

Annie knew she was about to lose Asher. She had pushed him too hard. But now that she was here, she knew she was right – he *did* know something else. He now had turned his back to her and was staring off into the woods.

"What ever happened to Old Red Penny?" Annie said quickly as if poking him with a stick.

He peaked over his shoulder to look at Annie then turned to face her.

"Did your mother tell you about Old Red Penny?" Asher was confused.

"Nope."

"Well, who told you about …?"

"I remember, Asher – I remember Old Red Penny. I know I was here, here with you."

Annie took a chance on whether that horse was real or just a dream. Now, she knew Penny was as real as the young Uncle Asher who was leading her down the path.

"You were only two – how on earth do you remember …." Asher stopped mid-sentence. "I guess the good things and the bad tend to stick with a person no matter how young they are, don't they?"

"Yes, I guess they do," a calm rushed over Annie. She now had Asher at least admitting to some of the truth. It was a good start.

"What else do you remember about me?" Asher sat down on the boulder with his niece.

"Well, I remember you looked a lot younger. You didn't have any gray hair."

Asher laughed as he grabbed his long, gray ponytail and pulled it through his hand and around his shoulder.

"Yeah, I guess I have grayed a little."

The crowd at Phoebe's med tent began cheering and yelling. Asher stood up.

"He's here."

"Who's here?"

"The baby, c'mon," Asher started walking toward the pink tent; Annie quickly slipped her shoe back on and followed him.

"Well, wait for me," Asher was walking fast toward the group.

Asher fought his way through the crowd to the tent's front flap. He went inside, leaving Annie among the rest of the Sunshiners. Annie looked around and saw no familiar faces but people were greeting her as if they had known her all her life.

"Hello Angel, so glad you're back," an older woman in a colorful dress grabbed Annie's arm.

"I heard you were here the other night, and I caught a glimpse of you but … well, I know you don't remember me," she said and then hugged Annie.

"Isn't this exciting?" Annie heard Reena's silky voice next to her. She touched Annie's shoulder bag that she had made only days earlier, "Beautiful," it was as if she had never seen it before.

Asher emerged from the tent with a rolled-up blanket in his hands then lifted it high to the sky.

"IT'S A BOY! IT'S A BOY!"

"A baby," Annie repeated herself. "A baby?"

Asher carefully brought the baby down from his lofty moment of ascent; made sure he was tightly bundled and then placed it in someone else's arms. The child seemed satisfied, not crying, and not wiggling, as the crowd passed him from person to person. Without warning someone turned around to place the infant in Annie's arms.

"I, I, I don't need to hold him," she tried to escape.

It did no good. As soon as she saw his face, she couldn't help herself. She brought him in close and cradled him next to her. His little brown eyes were looking all around; his mouth would open and then close while his little lips searched for his mother's breast.

"Oh," Annie whispered. "Oh."

The emotion came quickly, and she couldn't stop them. She closed her eyes as the hot tears rolled down her face and thought of the first time, she ever held Ethan in her arms – so soft, so peaceful. She looked up to see Asher standing in front of her and quickly realized that this moment must have been much like the moment Annie was born; much like the first time her mother held her. Everyone was smiling as they ooohed and ahhhed over the new baby. And just like that, someone took the child from Annie's arms, and he continued to make his way through the crowd. Annie felt blanketed by closeness to these people she could neither describe nor understand. She stood there with her arms still in the infant cradling position until Asher hugged her. She hugged him back as tight as she could, not understanding what was happening to her. The tears wouldn't stop, and she sobbed hard into Asher's shoulder as he held her.

"There, there, Annie," Asher rubbed and patted her back. "Hey now, come on, it's okay."

Asher pulled Annie away from him so he could see her face.

"Are you alright? I wouldn't have had you over here if I thought you …"

"No. I'm fine," Annie began trying to wipe the tears from her face, only more were taking their place. "I'm sorry; I didn't mean to cause such a scene."

Asher shook his head as if to say, "Don't worry about it," and took Annie's hand, leading her to the spot where they sat and talked during Annie's first visit.

Asher's eyes were filled with tears as he motioned for Annie to sit on the rock. He stood for a few moments looking out into the trees. This gave Annie a moment to gain some composure over her emotions.

"Oh," he gave a long sigh and turned to Annie. "Days like this bring back so many memories of you and your mom – the day you were born to us."

Annie was nodding her head, "Was it just like that? Did I get passed around through the Sunshiners just like he did?"

"Yes, yes you did, Annie. Only difference is there were a lot more of us then."

"It's really intense, isn't it?" Annie looked back toward the crowd, still passing the new baby hand to hand.

"It is intense, it is.," looked back over at the crowed. "But as third world as it may seem, it's important for our community to feel responsible for each and every child born to us. We all need to look out for them and be connected to them – for life."

Annie never realized how wise her uncle was until this very moment. Maybe a few more communities out there could benefit from the Sunshiners' approach to child rearing.

"I guess it would make the world a better place," Annie agreed.

"You got it, Annie," Asher turned, looking out into the mountains again.

"You know Annie, when your mother came here to us, her soul was torn in half," Asher began. "She was broken and weak. I had never seen her like that."

Annie had a feeling she was about to get her answers but now wasn't sure if she was ready to hear them.

"I know she had been through a lot," Annie took note of Asher's apprehensiveness about telling the story.

"A lot would be an understatement," Asher corrected his niece and then repeated, "certainly an understatement."

Asher paced back and forth in front of the sitting rock several times with his hands on his hips. He kept looking at Annie as if he was about to speak but couldn't. He took one long, last stare out over the trees and then turned to Annie. Finally, he had something to say.

"What I'm about to tell you will change your life, Annie. Are you sure you're ready for that?"

Asher was suddenly different, worldly sounding and certain like an old college professor.

Annie nodded her head slightly but still wasn't sure. Then the words came to her, "Yes, I want to know."

CHAPTER TWENTY-FOUR

Rayes County spring 1965

Graduation day came and went. Millie was feeling the pressure not only from Buck and his family, but also from her mother and the rest of Rayes County.

"So, when will you and Buck be tying the knot?" people would ask almost every day.

It wasn't that she didn't love him. They'd been together since ninth grade. Of course, she loved him. She just hadn't seen anything yet – never looked out over the ocean, never saw a building taller than the Union Bank but she knew they were out there. She'd been reading about them in books and looking at pictures of them since she was old enough to turn a page.

When she mentioned the trip to her mother, all she got was, "Oh my goodness, Millie, one of these days you're going to have to settle down and stop all this dreaming."

It was the typical Lucy Cleaving answer to everything – if she could keep her eyes on you then you were always safe. No matter though, Millie was eighteen now and she'd saved her work money since she was in the eighth grade – babysitting, canning for the old ladies and picking pole beans. She had enough saved and enough to spare. She had been dreaming of this trip all her life. She wasn't about to let Buck, her mother or anyone else keep her from going to Washington DC and over to the Jersey shore. She had written to the lady in DC about the boarding house first and then found someone on the shore who would rent a room for the rest of the summer. The bus would take her exactly where she wanted to go. She had tried to get Nancy to go with her, but she was getting married that summer. Millie couldn't wait to get her toes in the sand; to see The White House and to catch a glimpse of President Johnson. Before President Kennedy died, he said the nation was changing. He was right and Millie wanted to see it for herself.

Buck was plenty mad but no matter what, Millie was going. He kept saying he wouldn't be there when she got back. Millie knew better than that. He had gotten a job at the police department starting out at a pretty good salary. She knew he'd be there when she got back, and she agreed to marry him in the fall when she returned. Whatever this was – jealousy over her trip, insecurity about her finding someone else, well, he'd just have to get over it. Millie wasn't worried at all.

CHAPTER TWENTY-FIVE

Rayes County late summer 1965

Millie was glad to be coming home. Buck must have been mad at her; he hadn't written to her, not even one letter. She jotted a letter to him every week, sometimes she'd mail two a week, but she never heard back. She had called her mother a few times and asked about Buck. Her mom would always say that Buck was working hard and probably just didn't have time to answer the letters right away. She could always hear her sisters screaming in the background, "let me talk to her, let me say something to her." Lucy never would, her frugality insisted that long distance phone calls be kept short and that only necessary things talked about over the phone lines.

Millie couldn't wait to throw her arms around him and give him a great big kiss. She was ready to get married and ready to settle down with Buck. She had stuck her toes in the sand and looked up at the windows of the Whitehouse. She had walked the steps of the Capitol just like the pictures of people in books she had seen. She wondered if someone had snapped her picture as she walked those same steps and she might end up in a picture book someday too – some young country girl dreaming of being just like her. Millie had gone on a real adventure; something she would tell her children about when they were old enough. The whole rest of the bus ride home she imagined their little white house next to

Buck's mom and dad's. It had black shutters and a yellow door, like a cute little Bumble Bee. His parents had been stocking it with furniture over the years. They knew Millie and Buck would live there someday. Everyone in Rayes County knew Millie and Buck would live there someday, their children playing in the backyard with their little Collie they might name Lassie.

When Millie got off the bus she expected Buck would be there waiting for her. He wasn't. In fact, none of her friends were there – only her mother.

The drive home was silent other than pleasantries about the trip – "how was the weather, did you get to see the president?" Silly things that made Millie think something was wrong. As they passed by Buck's house, there were strange cars there and it looked like someone was living in the little Bumble Bee house.

"Stop Momma – stop here."

Lucy knew what had happened but was hoping to hear her daughter had met someone else. She kept prying about all the activities of her daughter's trip, but no young men were ever mentioned.

"I mean it Momma – stop the car! STOP NOW!"

Lucy screeched the car to a halt and held Millie's arm so she couldn't get out.

"I must tell you something, Millie. I wanted to tell you on the phone so many times. I had hoped you met someone else."
"What do you mean met someone else, I don't know what you mean," Millie started crying and yelling at her mother. "Let go of me, I'm going to see Buck – I said, let go of me."

Millie broke free from her mother's grip and ran toward the house where she saw Buck's car.

Buck's mother was screaming from the yard at Lucy, "DIDN'T YOU TELL HER?! WHY DIDN'T YOU TELL HER?!"

Just as Millie reached the front porch, Elizabeth Jameson stepped out from the front door of the Bumble Bee house; she was wearing a maternity dress. She wasn't showing much but perched her hands tightly against the top of her belly to reveal the slight protrusion. She smiled at Annie as she turned slightly sideways to make her point. Millie could see Buck standing behind his new wife in the shadows with his head in his hands. He looked up momentarily and his eyes met with Millie's. He swiftly turned and disappeared into the house.

CHAPTER TWENTY-SIX

"That was the first time your mother came to find me. I had only been gone five or six years – long enough to know I didn't belong in the world of high finance and lucky enough to find the Sunshine Family of Peace," Asher held his palms upward and outward in presentation of his peaceful kingdom. "Momma thought I was still in New York making other people money. What she didn't know, I thought, couldn't hurt her."

Millie got back on a bus and headed straight to New York to look for her big brother. When she got to the bank, they told her Asher hadn't worked there for three or more years. One of the employees at the bank knew where Asher had gone and gave Millie a phone number to call and find out where the Sunshine people were staying. They were in the Blue Ridge Park.

"Momma came looking for her and found out what I had done," Asher now had a sheepish grin like a guilty teenager. "She was plenty mad at me for a long time. She worried herself to death that Millie was going to be a Sunshiner, too."

"So did Buck ever say why he did that?" Annie couldn't help but wonder how different Rayes County would have been if Buck had married her mother instead of Liz. Who would Annie be or would she even exist at all?

"Liz had tried at different times to bust your momma and Buck apart. She saw her opportunity when Millie took her trip," Asher waited for Annie to speak but she didn't. "Buck and some of his friends got drunk because he was so mad at your mom for leaving that summer. Liz showed up at the party and – well, there you have it."

Millie stayed with Asher for no more than a month and went back home, accepting that Buck and Liz were now married, and a baby was on the way. Still, Buck and Millie kept running in to one another all over town. Millie still loved him; she just couldn't help it even though she knew it was wrong. He and Liz had one more child and then trouble began.

"Your mom and Buck really never got over each other and Liz never really got what she wanted – his undivided attention and undying love," Asher pounded his fist into his chest lightly. "It was only your mother who had that."

Annie tried to think back in her mind about a time when she saw Buck differently – maybe the way he looked at her mother, maybe he hung around a little too much. She just couldn't put her finger on anything.

"I never noticed any …"

"…out of the ordinary? Well, you wouldn't have," Asher finished Annie's statement. "It was all over after – well, even before you were born."

Millie and Buck started having a relationship shortly after he and Liz had their second child. Liz had accepted the fact that her husband would always love Millie. She stopped sleeping with him and they split the house right down the middle, taking separate bedrooms. Neither of them sought divorce. The Jameson family had, by that time, elected Buck sheriff. He was making a comfortable living for his family and Liz didn't want to rock the boat. Her family was so large they could have elected Buck sheriff even if no one else in Rayes County voted. This also meant they could vote him out if they wanted to.

"That's sad Asher," Annie thought about how many times she wondered why her mother never married. "... for both of them, all of them, especially Mom."

"That's the way it was back then. You got married and you stuck by it, no matter what," Asher linked his forefingers together to illustrate the point.

Asher began pacing nervously again. He would put his hands on his hips and pace five feet or so and then drop them to his sides and pace back. He would stop and look at Annie over his seventies-style wire rimmed glasses, start to speak and then pace again.

"What is it?" again, Annie was asking for the truth but was afraid to know the answer. "Is there something else?"

By this time Annie had a clear picture of what her mother's life had been like. She was the queen of bad luck and if Cleda were making potions back then, Millie sure could have used one. Asher stopped pacing and started speaking again.

"Your mother and Rosen went on for years just like they were dating or even married," Asher stopped and waited for Annie to speak. Again, she didn't. "Your mother said sometimes she'd even forget about Liz and the children. It was just like she and Buck had always been together."

The affair went on for over six years before everything changed. And in the meantime, Buck and Liz somehow saw fit to have one more child.

"When Millie got here, she was seven and a half months

pregnant with you," Asher held his arms out in front of his stomach to demonstrate the size of Millie's belly. "I couldn't believe it when I saw her. I just couldn't believe it.

"Of course, I thought the baby – you – belonged to Buck but she kept saying no, you didn't – that she had met some guy, a military guy. At least that's the story she told everyone."

Annie's blood ran cold, "That's the story she *told* everyone? Are you saying it's not true?"

Asher began to pace again, stopping and starting then staring at Annie.

"STOP IT! You're killing me with the pacing," Annie screamed at her uncle.

"Boy, you're a load to deal with you know that kid."

Annie *had* been a load, but Asher had no idea about the accident, about how Ethan was killed by Buck's youngest son. If he did, Annie didn't dare tell him, he would have never taken Annie this far with the story.

Annie remembered Jacob from that day like it was only moments ago. She saw his face coming at her as the cars collided. She remembered him being pulled out of the car, still drunk from a party which, she heard later, had lasted into the wee hours of the morning. She and Ethan were going to get some breakfast at his favorite fast-food restaurant just before a Monday morning at school. He loved school; he loved books and even more than books he loved to learn. Now, Annie could barely stand to see his school. She would even drive two miles out of her way to avoid seeing the place Ethan loved so much. No wonder her mother never said anything about dating Buck, no wonder she never mentioned it. How awful to even think about the possibilities.

You could smell the liquor all over the grass, all over the car. Buck was there, he had his arm around Ethan when he died. He reached his other arm across Ethan through the wreckage to hold Annie's hand. She never forgot him for that. He was the one connection between Annie and her son on the day he took his last breath.

The day of the trial Jacob took the stand and swore he was sober. The lab results had been conveniently lost but everyone who was there knew better. Buck sat there and watched his son tell lie after lie, saying that Annie had swerved to his side of the road. He and his attorneys somehow convinced the jury it was Annie's fault that her son was dead and that she had no one to blame but herself. They said she looked away from the road to get a book for Ethan and that's when she "lost control."

She knew the Jamesons were helping him cover it up. No one came forward and said anything to the contrary, but no one admitted it either. Jacob walked away from the crash without a scratch, and he walked out of the court room the same way.

"Buck had no idea your mother was pregnant when she left Rayes County," Asher squatted on the balls of his feet in front of Annie. "She had gone to the sheriff's office to tell him, only *he* wasn't there, someone else was. She never got a chance to let him know they were going to have a baby, Annie. She never got a chance to tell him they were going to have you."

CHAPTER TWENTY-SEVEN

Rayes County 1974

Millie was worried. She hadn't had a period in two months now. She kept waiting and waiting but it never came. She hated to make the decision to go over to Stig to get a test, but she certainly couldn't do it in Rayes County. Patient privacy had somehow managed to elude the doctor's offices and even the Rayes County Hospital. For years, the local AM radio station would sound the list over the airways of who was in the hospital. Finally, they stopped telling the masses *why* people were in the hospital, but they still broadcast who was there. Lucy said it was a good thing that people know when their neighbors were sick. That way they could send flowers or visit. Millie never saw it that way. If she was ever in the hospital, she didn't want everyone in the world to know – or even just everyone in Rayes County for that matter. If her family and friends knew she was in the hospital that would be enough for her. It seemed as if nothing in Rayes County was private. She was sure if she took the pregnancy test at either of the doctor's offices there, everyone in town would know even before she left the building.

Waves of different emotions would wash over her – happiness at the thought of having Buck's baby would make her smile and get butterflies; then reality would come quickly with fear as its messenger. There had only been a few times when she thought of her relationship with Buck as cheating. It never really seemed that way. *She* had Buck first; he loved *her* first and still loved her. It was only trickery and fraud that landed him with Liz. If life had been fair and just and Liz had not been underhanded and deceitful then it wouldn't matter that she was pregnant now. She and Buck could be happy and count the days until their new arrival.

She and Buck had talked so many times about being together, getting married. But both knew the Jamesons would destroy Buck if he and Millie ever actually did it. They had even talked about running away in the night, but as an elected sheriff, there'd be no hiding if he just disappeared. The headlines would be bold, they were sure, and it would spread like wildfire over the news wires. Either way, Buck would be ruined. He hated being with Liz, but he loved his children. He knew there'd be scant chance of ever seeing them if he left her. Millie had always loved him enough to know that being without his children would kill him but now things were different. They were about to have their own child. Millie had always been willing to sacrifice her own feelings for Buck's boys, but she wasn't willing to make that choice for her unborn child. No. Her child would have a father; her child would be the one playing tag outside in the yard. She had seen Buck and his boys so many times, playing ...

She had waited long enough and wasn't about to let another week go by without telling him. Today was going to be the most special birthday Buck would ever have. She had come up with a plan for them and hopefully it would work. He would resign from his post at the sheriff's department then ask Liz for a divorce. Leelo Johnson, the sheriff over at Stig had been a family friend for a long time. Buck could take a pay cut and go over and work as a deputy. They'd ask for the divorce case to be moved to Stig County because of the Jameson family's strong political ties in Rayes County. There had to be at least one fair judge in Rayes County who would agree to a change of venue. Buck and Millie could then be married, and he'd still get to visit his children.

Millie had become accustomed to getting sick every morning for the past six weeks or so. But today it was almost six o'clock and she still hadn't fully recovered from that morning's bout of nausea. Even so, she had to pull herself together. She wanted to look her best when she told Buck the news. She wanted it to be special; she wanted to make sure she remembered the exact words they'd say to one another when she told him. She imagined he'd hold her close and put his hands on her belly, saying hello to their child for the first time. When they were married, she could sleep in his arms every night with the bassinet close by in case the baby cried. She just knew Buck would be the first to rise, pulling the baby from its bed with his enormous hands covering most of the infant. He would hold the baby close to his face and say all the right things that a father should say to calm his crying child.

It was Friday, Buck's third night shift for the week. The county was running low on money which meant no funds for overtime. Since Buck was salary, he got any and all shifts not covered by a full-time deputy. He didn't mind working, it meant he and Millie would get to see each other even more. She'd bring him supper and they'd eat together at his desk and then close the door. It was during those times he and Millie would pretend they were married. They never talked about Liz or the kids during those times.

Millie pulled into the lot and saw his cruiser there. She was nervous but excited all the same. She checked her lipstick in the rearview mirror. She decided to leave his supper in the car for now; she would come back out and get it later; no distractions, no interruptions, just Buck and her talking about their baby.

"Hey, Millie," she heard a voice from the back of the building. "He's not here."

Danny came walking to the front counter from the hallway.

"His cruiser is out there," Millie pointed toward the window.

"Oh, yeah, that – she picked him up about an hour ago and I came over to fill in," Danny gave a sexy wink.

"She picked him up?"

"Oh, did he not tell you?" Danny was sarcastic. "He and Liz are having dinner together tonight; I think it's a birthday dinner for Buck – the whole Jameson family took him out."

"Oh, well, I guess – I don't know maybe he did tell me," Millie was trying to save her dignity. "I can come back later."

"Oh, no need to do that," Danny shook his head. "He said for me to take the entire shift, he won't be back."

Buck had to tell Danny last year about he and Millie and the way things had happened between them over the years. It was nice to have someone on their side. Danny, who had been one of Buck's best deputies over the years, had developed quite a crush on Millie. She would come over and copy down the arrests for the local newspaper. Their reporters really appreciated her work. She could get more information from Buck than they could. The newspaper paid her, and it was a decent part-time job; but even if they hadn't she still would've come to see Buck. It was the perfect excuse to be at the sheriff's office anytime she liked and near the man she loved. Danny had flirted with Millie over the years, not realizing that she and Buck were in a relationship. He even started asking Buck to fix the two of them up. He became relentless in the pursuit of Millie's affection, enough so that Buck finally told him to stop making a fool of himself, she was taken.

After that Danny stopped flirting quite so much, but still there was the ever-present wink and smile that he would shoot Millie's way ever so often. Millie sloughed it off as innocent most days, but there were times it made her feel a little uncomfortable. She never told Buck about it. She and Buck had such little time together as it was, she didn't want to waste it on petty complaints.

Millie couldn't help herself and started sobbing right there in front of Danny, the only person who really knew the truth about her and Buck.

"There, there, now," Danny walked over to Millie and held her in his arms. "I'm sure it's not as bad as all that, now."

Millie cried as Danny held her tighter.

"I'm sorry, Danny," Millie sobbed as she pulled away from him. "I don't know why I'm so upset."

"You need to see him and he's with his family," Danny pretended to sound sympathetic but knew his words were like knives in Millie's heart. "That's enough to upset you, I would think. You know Millie he *does* have to spend time with his family."

"Yes, yes, I know," Millie continued sobbing.

"Did he know you were coming over here tonight?"

"No, he didn't. I just thought I'd drop by."

"Well, you're looking awfully lovely tonight in that tight sweater and those with big red lips," Danny gave Millie a wink.

Millie suddenly felt strange and uncomfortable. Her tears dried and she became panicky.

"Well," Millie quickly picked up her purse and placed the strap in the bend of her elbow. "I'll come back by later tomorrow. It's not a big thing."

She smiled trying to act normal, but something about Danny's demeanor was scaring her.

"What's your hurry? C'mon Millie," Danny pulled her close again. "You know how I've always felt about you. Why can't we just try and see. Buck's married; he's never going to leave his family. I would love you, like you've never been loved by him." Millie tried to pull away from him, but his large hand had wrapped almost completely around her arm.

"You know I don't feel that way about you," Millie tried to sound sympathetic through her fear. "I'm just going to go, and I'll come back tomorrow."

"Don't pity me," Danny was angry now, his grip tightening around her arm. "*You* are the one who's pitiful. You come here night after night waiting for Buck. He don't give a damn about you. He's married to somebody else. You're just a different kind of roll in the hay for him."

"STOP IT DANNY! You're hurting my arm," nothing else had worked and Millie decided it was time to be assertive with him. "LET GO AND I MEAN IT!"

"Awww, look at you," Danny was now condescending toward her. "What are you going to do, tell Buck on me – he's with his wife, Millie, his family."
Danny walked to the front door, pulling Millie by the arm he moved quickly. She tried to break free from him, jerking this way and that, but couldn't break his grip. Maybe he was going to throw her out the door; maybe he would just push her out. Millie froze when she saw him click the deadbolt to the right. He turned and looked at her with that smile, that creepy smile.

"Buck's never loved you like this," he winked at her again.

Millie fought and scratched then realized it was doing her no good. She braced herself for what was about to happen. His breath was wet and he smelled of onions.

"BUCK WILL KILL YOU!!" Millie was finally able to scream.

"Buck ain't gonna kill me, you're nothing more to him than an old whore anyway," Danny pushed into her. "Maybe you'll be part of my Christmas bonus. I'll just take it a little early."

Danny didn't speak after that. Millie closed her eyes and gritted her teeth until it was over. As he perched over her, his eyes rolling back in his head, she felt him get tense. She knew this was her moment to escape. She kicked him hard and ran for the door. The lock that was normally sticky opened right away for her. She didn't dare look behind her, but she no longer felt his presence around her. She slammed the door hard behind her just in case he was there.

"The keys are in the car," Millie reassured herself as she sprinted to the sedan.

Once inside, she locked each door and then turned the key in the ignition. Her tires screeched as she pushed the gas pedal all the way to the floor. She didn't even look behind her to see if anything was coming.

"OH MY GOD!" OH MY GOD!" Millie couldn't stop shaking. She held her hands tight on the wheel to get them to stop but they wouldn't. Suddenly she felt sick. She pulled the car into the church parking lot, opened the door and began throwing up. She was afraid he was watching her; afraid he was nearby. She didn't even let herself finish throwing up before she shut the door again and quickly locked the door.

She was wet with vomit now and Danny's sweat and semen. She shivered and shook uncontrollably; her teeth were clacking together; her legs were shaking uncontrollably. She nervously

looked around the parking lot and saw no one. This scared her. If
he was watching her and waiting to come for her again, it was too
isolated. She had to go somewhere, she had to find Buck.

Millie calmed herself enough to drive again. She was
determined to find Buck, to tell him what Danny had done to her.
She drove slowly up Main Street to see if she could see Liz's car
anywhere. She found it, exactly where she thought she would, in
front of Jameson's Restaurant. She pulled next to Liz's car,
panicked now about what to do, what to say once she got in there.

She looked around cautiously to make sure Danny wasn't
there, then stepped out of the car quickly and ran toward the front
door.

She froze in front of the big front window as she caught sight
of Buck sitting in front of a birthday cake, getting ready to blow
out his candles. He was wearing a goofy pointy hat; he was
laughing – all of them were. She could hear them even out on the
sidewalk. It was there that she also caught a glimpse of herself in
the glass. Her skirt was dirty and wrinkled and buttons were
missing from her top. Her hair was tangled, and her face was
swollen, dirty with mascara; her lipstick smudged down her chin.

Liz's whole family had come to Buck's birthday celebration.
They were all around the table. Liz's father patted Buck on the
back and Liz stood behind him with her cheek near his. He looked
up and kissed her lightly on the lips just before he turned to blow
out his candles. There were cheers and laughter; Millie could hear it
even out on the sidewalk.

She heard Danny's voice inside her head, "You're nothing
more than an old whore to him, he *has* a wife … he *has* a wife …
he *has* a wife …

Millie slowly turned from the window and walked away.

CHAPTER TWENTY-EIGHT

"That was the second time your mother came to find me – well, not right after that," Asher seeming more willing now to finish the story. "She first went to stay with some of the other girls; visiting, she said. But I knew better. She was running away only she had no idea where she was going."

"Oh my God," Annie was past the point of tears now and trying to imagine what her mother must have been thinking. "If she had told me about this I just …"

"Annie, if your son were alive and you were in the same situation would you tell him?"

Annie thought for a moment about what she would say to Ethan and at what age would be appropriate to say it. She would never have wanted Ethan to think of her as anything other than a loving mother. She decided Millie did exactly what *she* would have done under the same circumstances.

"No, I guess I wouldn't. It's just that I feel like I know my mother better now than I've ever known her before," Annie was crying now. "I can't tell her it's okay."

Asher came over and sat next to Annie.

"Your mother was afraid when she got here – afraid of her

own shadow. She slept for days in the Mill Tent before ever reemerging as even half the person she was. It took a while, but she told me bits and pieces here and there about what happened. I guess she told it as she was moving past it. She told me about Roslyn and Mason, Cleda and Edward and what Dorie had done. Your mother, in addition to dealing with her own pain, had taken on quite a bit of pain from the other girls as well. She was emotionally exhausted."

Annie looked around the camp and then back at Asher.

"I can see how someone emotionally spent might end up here," was beginning to feel quite comfortable among the Sunshiners herself.

"I tried to get her to go back home and talk to Buck, but she wouldn't even hear it," Asher was still confused by Millie's unwillingness to tell the father of her child what had happened to her. "She said she could never go near there as long as Danny was there – she'd never think of it – of taking you back to the same town where it happened, as long as he was still there."

Asher warned him never to tell anyone.

"I left one little bread crumb for Buck, though I probably shouldn't have meddled," Asher's voice was just a bit louder than a whisper as if Millie could possibly hear them. "But it did no good. I guess your mother was right – it was better left alone."

"What do you mean bread crumb?" Annie was curious.

"Oh, a little note I sent without your mother knowing about it," Asher made the motion of writing. "But he may never have even gotten it, who knows? After that, I decided to mind my own business and let fate take a hand. If that little bread crumb was supposed to be found it would have been found."

"What did the little bread crumb say?"

"Eh, just that the deputy had done what he done. But that's not what your mother needed from me – to meddle in her business. She was so ashamed," Asher looked down at the ground. "When she got here, she was a hollow person, nothing inside. She regretted the affair with Buck, and she was humiliated by Danny and Edward to the point that I wasn't sure I'd ever see my Millie again. It was like she was gone."

"Did she ever come back the way she used to be?"

"She healed but there were scars she carried with her for the rest of her life," Asher looked into Annie's eyes. "The Millie you knew was not the Millie I knew. By the time you were born, she was different; her voice was no longer loud and proud, she was convinced no one cared what she had to say and if they did, they were only listening so they could make fun of her later. So, she kept quiet, never voicing her opinions, keeping her light hidden from view – afraid someone might blow it out again," Asher mimicked holding a candle and blowing it out.

Annie remembered so many times watching her mother stare out into space. It was like she was in a constant state of deep thought about something. As a child Annie would ask often just so she could hear the answer, "What'cha thinkin' about Momma?"

Annie's mother would always say, "Rainbows and cotton candy, Baby. That's what I like to think about."

Annie would stare off into space and think as hard as she could about eating cotton candy under a rainbow. As Annie got older, she resented her mother for never getting angry, never speaking her mind or asserting an opinion. When Ethan was killed Annie was beyond angry and Millie should have been too, knowing what she knew – knowing that Jacob was Ethan's uncle, Buck his grandfather. Annie could never understand why she didn't want to kill all of them, all the Rosens. Annie could have set their house on fire with all of them in it and never looked back. Millie accepted what had happened as "meant to be" when Ethan's body was placed in the ground.

Asher could see Annie's frustration, "Annie, your mother was broken. The whole time you knew her that wasn't really her."

Annie remembered glimpses of someone else, someone reckless and mischievous. Sometimes when they were out of town, Millie and Annie would do something spontaneous like slide down a stair rail or run up an escalator. But those moments faded fast, and the smile would run away from Millie's face when she'd see someone watching.

"She was afraid to be herself," Annie let the thoughts from her mind exit her lips.

"Exactly, Annie. Your mother had seen a self she couldn't live with, so she chose to become someone else. No better, no worse, just someone else – the someone *you* knew."

Annie hadn't forgotten her initial question, the question that urged her to stop and talk to Asher before going back home.

"How long *did* we stay here, Asher?"
"You and your mother were here until you were a little over two years old."

"Why did you lie to me? Why was it so important for me to believe that we left just after I was born?"

A smile came across Asher's face, "Actually, Annie, since your mother didn't even tell you that she was here when she was pregnant with you, do you really think she'd want you to know you lived here and were a Sunshiner – born and bred?" Asher laughed as he looked Annie up and down in her well-groomed outfit. "I don't know – I guess I was just holding on to that old lie we always used to tell. I thought that I could still protect Millie, somehow, by telling you that even though the two of you were here, you didn't stay very long."

Annie thought for a moment and considered Asher's logic.

"I'm still not sure I believe you, but I'll accept that answer for now," Annie looked at him suspiciously.

"So, we left because my mother decided this was no place for a child?" Annie questioned as she looked across the path at some children playing in the woods.

"Well, there was more to your departure than that. I had no idea how bad Millie wanted to go home. She would pretend that she never wanted to go back there but I found out quickly that wasn't true. It was a hard winter, but we did okay, camping around the Florida Everglades. I went into town one day for supplies and saw a headline about Rayes County."

"Really?" Annie was surprised to hear the rest of the country even knew about her little town.

"Yeah, I couldn't believe it, Rayes County made national headlines – there we were – right there on the banner," Asher waved a hand through the air as if to display the headline.

"Escapees from a funny farm, a young couple, shot and robbed a convenient store guy in Knoxville and ended up in Rayes County. Buck and that deputy of his went after them; they were camping up on the mountain."

"Were they Sunshiners?" Annie was making a joke, but Asher didn't laugh.

"There had been a bunch of snow that winter up there," Asher continued, giving Annie no consideration for that last attempt at humor. "Buck and that deputy went into the woods and found those two. Buck was the only one to come out of the woods that day. Story was that the deputy shot the girl and then her boyfriend shot the deputy then shot himself. When Buck got to the top of the mountain, they were all dead."

"I don't think I've ever heard that story," Annie was sure that if Rayes County had ever made national headlines it would be displayed proudly somewhere – maybe in the local history museum.

"Your mother wasted no time packing up and going home to Mom. I guess I just never really knew the level of fear she felt – the horror she had been living with. I guess she just couldn't stand the thoughts of ever seeing him again. It was almost like she was giddy that he had been killed."

"The bastard deserved to die," Annie yelled. "She should have gone back there and killed him herself and castrated him, too."

Asher nodded in agreement, "Yeah, but I think Millie was just relieved to get to go home. She never realized how much she loved home until she had to leave it."

Annie knew that feeling well, now.

"I wish you could remember that day," Asher looked into Annie's eyes as if willing her to remember. "She was so excited – couldn't even flesh out a coherent sentence. We were passing through there that spring, so I dropped you guys off at Mom's."

Annie imagined she and her mother – the hippie and her little child, heading back to see home again. Even if she didn't understand her mother, she understood the need to go home – the tug toward the familiar no matter how bad it had seemed in the past.

CHAPTER TWENTY-NINE

Rayes County Winter 1977

The front door slammed shut just as the bell rang, *again*. Buck looked up from his desk.

"How'd do, Buck," Jim took off his cap and nodded at the sheriff. There was no time to respond before Jim started talking. Buck had just hung up the phone – another call from yet one more Rayes County busy body claiming to have seen the couple Buck and every other law enforcement officer in the country had been looking for. Winter was usually a slow time for the sheriff's department. People stayed in and minded their own business for a change. The snow-covered mountains had a way of insulating their little town from the rest of the world. Usually, Rayes County hibernated – but not this winter. Jim Danes had lived in Rayes County all his life as did his father and grandfather before him. He'd tell anyone, if they cared to know, that he knew these mountains better than the bears who owned them. Even though he worked at the local hardware store bidding jobs and negotiating prices for what little construction went on in the county, he considered himself a tracker. He said he had Native American ancestry – his great- great grandfather had taken a wife who was "full blooded." Buck had expected Jim to show up before now to let him know he had figured out where the fugitives were hiding.

"How'd do to you too," Buck stood up from his desk and extended a hand for a shake.

"Well, Buck I wanted to come in and tell you that over on the far side of the mountain – over above the flood wall – you know, where the path starts – I seen some broke branches."

"Oh?" Buck lifted his eyebrows, pretending to show interest in Jim's story. Jim was always trying to help Buck find clues to solve crimes or conspiracies where there were none.

"I went over and took me a little look and see and there were tire tracks going up that path," Jim was nodding deeper now, to show his assuredness that there was foul play on the mountain.

"Tire tracks?" Buck furrowed his brow. "That path's not wide enough to get a car up in there."

"Oh no, I didn't say it was a car," Jim was proud of himself for fooling the sheriff. "I said *tire* tracks. I think they belong to a motorcycle."

As if Buck didn't have enough to do, now he was going to have to climb the mountain to satisfy Jim that there was no one up there.

"You know, these kids are always doing something up there …" Buck started but Jim interrupted.

"No, now, I know – I just got a feeling about this, Buck. Those two are up there; I just know it in my guts that those two murdering thieves are up there."

Murdering thieves was not the image Buck got when he first saw the description come through on the fax machine. They were both of age, but barely. The girl had just turned 18 and the boy was just a tad shy of 20. He had busted her out of a mental institution. She had been there, Buck had on good authority, because her father had abused her so severely that she would cut herself up with knives, razor blades or whatever other sharp items she could get her hands on. She had tried to kill herself more than once but really hadn't been a threat to anyone else, until now. Social services took her away after years of abuse and placed her in a mental hospital in Knoxville just last year. Although no one told her this, she believed when she turned eighteen, she would be released. When she found out she'd have to stay, the boyfriend showed up to rescue her. The media had taken the story and run with it, as usual. They had portrayed this couple like cold-blooded killing machines. It made for better headlines. Buck wished he didn't know the background story; he might have been a little more eager to catch them. Instead, he found himself feeling sorry for them. Still, they had gone into that convenient store, robbed it and killed the owner in the process. He had come at them with a ball bat – still had it in his hands as he lay there dead on the tile floor. Law enforcement was sure now that the boy had a gun and if anyone believed headlines, the two were "Armed and dangerous killers … the girl, identified as Mary Jane Waters will only answer to the name Reena. The man she is traveling with is yet to be identified."

Buck rubbed his hand back and forth against his forehead hard. He closed his eyes tight trying to imagine it was all a dream and when he opened them, Jim would be gone and there'd be no fugitives to chase. Able to escape for no more than thirty seconds or so, Buck opened his eyes and Jim was still there with that look on his face that said, "Do something."

"Got a headache, Buck?" Jim innocently asked, having no idea that he *was* the headache. "I can go get you something over at the drug store."

"No, no, I'm fine," Buck sat down in his chair. "I'll get on that right away, Jim. I'll have someone out there shortly."

"Now, if you want me to go up that path, I'll …," Buck interrupted Jim.

"No Jim, don't you go near that path," Buck tried to use terms he could relate to. "It's evidence now and if you tamper with evidence even if we do get 'em then they could throw it out of court."

Buck was lying shamelessly trying to get Jim to let go of the notion.

"Oh yeah, I know," Jim agreed, as if knowledgeable about

evidence and legal matters in criminal cases. "I know about them courts and all that. You're right, Buck. You're right. I wouldn't want to tamper with this case. It's way too important."

Buck, relieved that he had gotten through to Jim, stood up and shook his hand.

"You know I appreciate all you do for us Jim. We'll get right on that. Don't you worry."

The doorbell rang as the door slammed again. Buck sat back down in his chair, rolled it back away from the desk and watched out the window as Jim got in his truck and drove away. The sun hadn't been out for days but today the sky was blue and clear, and the sun brought blinding light as it reflected against the eight inches or more of snow which had fallen over the past four days.

Buck rolled himself and his chair back under the desk. He opened the folder again and read the file. The last report Buck had gotten only two hours ago was that Knox County police believed the couple had crossed the state line and were headed somewhere near Rayes County. Buck was sure they had passed right on by. Still, he had a duty to follow up on every lead he got and report back to Tennessee State Police about the findings. As he read over the reports again, he couldn't help but notice the boxes of other files piled in front of his desk. Not criminals, but files nonetheless that had to be taken care of. County workers had brought them over in a pickup truck – boxes and boxes of old records and information. Judy Stowe had died suddenly of a stroke last month – the county, short on cash, decided not to replace her. She had been a staple at the Rayes County Courthouse for as long as Buck could remember. She was the keeper of the keys and the guardian of the files. Judy had a key to every building in the county; she also knew exactly where to find whatever anyone needed. She was the go-to person for just about anything – completely indispensable. She had no prior health-related issues that anyone knew about. She was sixty-four years old and the picture of health. Most were surprised to find out she looked much younger than her years. Her little brother, Danny, had no knowledge that she had any health problems either. The coroner said it was just one of those things – silent killers, a small clot that tried to pass through the brain. They found her lying next to her desk in the same outfit she had been wearing the day before. She never made it home from work that night. Danny said he was comforted she had gone quickly – at least that's how the coroner described her death.

In addition to taking care of just about every elected official in the county, she always took care of her little brother, too. She made sure, after their parents passed away, that Danny finished high school and went to the military just like all the other men in the Stowe family had done. When he got out, she made sure she had secured a job for him in the Rayes County Sheriff's Department. Buck was happy to bring Danny on with him. He certainly needed the help and Judy had always been good to Buck over the years. When he first took office, Judy immediately became his Pit Bull, his protector against anyone who might even hint at letting an unkind word escape their mouths when it came to Buck. There was never a truer statement than the last thing the former Rayes County Sheriff Ray Hunter said to Buck before he and his wife left for Florida, "Now you take good care of Judy and she'll look after you right."

It wasn't long before Buck understood why Ray left Judy in an office at the courthouse rather than bring her over to the sheriff's department. Judy kept Buck in the loop about all the comings and goings of everyone in that courthouse in addition to what was being said and who it was being said about. Buck imagined that without Judy, his office and the politics surrounding it could become isolated quickly and those who had always salivated after the sheriff's seat might try to oust him. But Judy kept the wolves away by keeping Buck informed of complaints and those who might have ill feelings toward the sheriff. After all, he did have to do his job which meant someone was always going to be unhappy about the outcome.

Buck was not looking forward to taking care of his own files and his own paperwork – he hated the idea of it and just like everyone else who had huge boxes of papers staring them in the face, he fought for a replacement. But there was just no money; Rayes County was broke and barely keeping Buck and one deputy on the payroll.

In some ways though, Judy's death had been a relief for Buck. For months he had been seriously considering firing Danny. The drinking had gotten way out of hand and Buck had recently had reason to believe Danny was abusing his authority as a deputy. One of the magistrate's great nieces had been visiting from out of town when Danny pulled her over for speeding. She told her uncle the officer reached into the car to get her license and grabbed her breast, telling her he'd let her go if she'd do him a couple of favors. She immediately told him who her uncle was and Danny, she said, tried to play it off like it was an accident. Still, it was more than just that. Danny's drinking was starting to embarrass Buck. Danny would go out into the hollers where he knew the parties took place on Friday and Saturday nights, Buck had heard on pretty good authority. He would confiscate any alcohol, pot or other drugs he found and then bring it all back to his place. Girls were starting to flock to Danny like flies to a rotting carcass. It was hard not to notice the frequent stops and visits he was getting from these girls. Buck had a pretty good idea that Danny had been supplying the girls with drugs. One of their mothers had come by and told Buck about a situation her daughter had gotten herself into with Danny. She said she thought that as sheriff, Buck ought to know that his deputy was fooling around with young girls around town in exchange for alcohol and drugs. If the girls were of age, there wasn't much Buck could do without proof; but consuming evidence confiscated from parties would be enough to get him out the door. Buck had not been looking forward to breaking the news to Judy.

It was almost time for Danny to start his shift. He was now

working from 11 a.m. to 11 p.m. every day. Buck was supposed to be working the 12 a.m. to 10 a.m. shift but was spending many more hours than that on paperwork. Now, it was about to get worse – even more hours would be spent shuffling papers.

The bell clanged and the door slammed.

"Hey boss, what's up?" Danny bounced over to Buck's desk.

Most days, Danny was a likeable guy. Buck could tell today was one of those days. He didn't reek of stale bourbon from the night before. He had come to the office just like this for the past few days. Buck had hoped that his sister's death had made him think more responsibly. At this point, though, it didn't matter how much Danny was changed. There was the matter of the magistrate's niece to consider. Buck was expected to do something.

"Listen, I'm going to have to work a little while longer today," Buck pointed at all the boxes of files around his desk. "But I need you to go and check something out for me."

"Oh yeah? What do we got?"

"Jim came over and gave me a *tip* about the couple everybody's looking for," Buck shook his head and rolled his eyes. "You know how Jim is. But we gotta go check it out. It *is* a lead."

Danny took the notes and grabbed the keys to the one cruiser the department had left. Buck turned his attention back to the boxes of files around his desk. Maintenance workers had emptied Judy's filing cabinets and brought them over as well.

Buck was fascinated by all the folders from the former sheriffs and deputies, ones he knew as a child. The files led all the way up to his and Danny's tenure. He had taken too much time looking at the historical documents of Rayes County law enforcement, but it was interesting, addictive even. Buck had never really been unhappy about how much money he made even though he knew other sheriffs in other places made more. He and Liz were comfortable, everything they had was paid for and they wanted for nothing. He felt better about his pay looking back over the old files and seeing that some of the Rayes County law enforcement officials worked for mere dollars a week and that their healthcare plans consisted of the mandatory physical each year.

"My God, Danny," Buck said out loud, as he took Danny's personnel file from the box.

It was a good six inches thick with papers and made a loud thud as Buck plopped it on his desk, sitting down to crack it open.

"Daniel Arthur Stowe ... let's see what all this is," Buck opened the cover.

Employment agreement, law enforcement certification, CPR certificates, and then Buck stopped when he saw the first one – FORMAL COMPLAINT – DEPUTY DANIEL ARTHUR STOWE. Buck skipped to the third paragraph, to the details. "Officer allegedly touched female inmate inappropriately while in transport to court proceedings." Buck flipped to the next page. "Officer questioned female and threatened incarceration if she didn't comply with officer's 'inappropriate' request." The next page was the same type of accusation. "Teenager's mother reported officer Stowe tried to force himself on her daughter as she was walking home from school. She was charged with jaywalking and resisting questions from a uniformed officer."

Page after page after page, Buck found the same type of accusations. On each page of complaint, the section labeled, "ACTION TAKEN" was signed off on by Buck. But it wasn't his signature, it was Judy's. Pages of lies: "sheriff's investigation of claim against Deputy Stowe found officer's actions to be within guidelines of the law."

Buck couldn't stop combing through the file. The phone rang relentlessly; smacking it off the hook; he let the receiver fall in the floor. Page after page, "Buck Rosen" had "investigated" and found Danny to be "honorable in his intentions" with each offense. Judy had done her homework to ensure the wording was exactly what the state would expect to see if they ever audited the files.

Every time Buck saw "his signature," he got madder. He slammed his fists on the desk and cursed Judy's name. Danny had always had a problem with women. People tried to tell Buck about Danny. Their sheriff wouldn't hear it. He knew Danny; they didn't.

Buck closed the file and picked it up with both hands slamming it down on the desk and beating it with the side of his fist. The folder's worn edges began to tear enough to reveal a small note that had fallen toward the side of all the rest of the pages. Buck saw the name Ashes, written in pencil.

"Ashes?" Buck was puzzled. He picked up the little note written on the back of a store receipt. There was only one Ashes that *he* knew of.

The note read: "Your deputy raped my sister and she left. She's having a baby soon. Ashes"

Buck turned the note over and saw the receipt – Blue Ridge Mountain Café and More – .30 coffee. The date was barely readable though the ink had not faded completely: May 21, 1965 – seven months after Millie left Rayes County.

Buck got up from his chair and threw the phone against the front door; glass shattered like ice across the tile floor. He pulled his gun from its holster and made sure it was loaded. He got extra bullets from the drawer and left the office. Even though the glass was shattered, out of habit, he locked the door as he left.

CHAPTER THIRTY

Asher and Annie began walking the path to her car. Unlike Annie's last departure from the camp, she was sad to leave Asher. She watched him as he walked beside her and wished for a moment to be inside his skin, inside his head – to know the Millie Cleaving that he knew.

She felt a love for him she hadn't felt for anyone, at least not any male person who had ever been in her life. She was protected again, like he would always be there for her, even if she had to find him in the woods somewhere. Asher caught her staring at him and as if he were reading her thoughts, ran up the path in front of her and stopped, holding his arms out for a hug. She ran to him and hugged him tight and for no reason began to cry. Asher pulled Annie away from him by her shoulders so he could look her in the face.

"You're more like your mother than you know," Asher, grasped her arms tighter and shook her a bit. "The things you say – your curiosity, your boldness, Annie. You are so much like her."

Annie smiled and tried to think of her mother as being right there with them, right next to them holding Ethan.

"I can appreciate that," Annie hugged Asher again. "C'mon,

let's go, I'm ready, now."

Annie's car looked oddly modern among the Sunshine motorcade, but she was glad to see it still sitting there like a faithful servant waiting to take her home.

"So, now you know everything. You're in a very unique situation, Annie. What you do with this information is entirely up to you. But may I make one suggestion?"

"Just one?" Annie pulled out a last bit of sarcasm for her uncle.

"Yes, there's only one important thing to remember – live, Annie – just live. Stop worrying so much about the past and see every day for the gift that it is," Asher lifted his hands straight up toward the sky and made a scooping motion down to his mouth. "Drink it in, Annie – drink it in."

Annie couldn't help but laugh at him. All day she had seen glimpses of someone else – a *normal* person – stressed, frazzled and bent, just like her and everyone else she ever knew. Now, he was back – good old mellow Asher without a trouble in the world. It was good to see him again.

"You know I can't live here," Annie was certain she was invited. "It's just not me, but God – oh God, I wish I could."

Annie knew she would miss Asher and even Sunray and his little pink polyester skirt, but life was waiting to be lived and the Cleaving house was calling to her. She could feel the knob in her hand and hear the familiar creak of the porch.

"You're too unique to be a Sunshiner," Asher smiled at his niece.

Annie gave a slight wave without saying a word and looked at her favorite uncle and smiled a good-bye. Asher began walking away but turned around one last time and shouted.

"The horse, Old Red Penny you asked about?"

"Yeah," Annie yelled back.

"I don't know what ever happened to her, she was never ours we just stole her from across the fence when we wanted to ride."

ABOUT THE AUTHOR

Melissa Newman, Ed.D. is an award-winning journalist, a novelist, and professor of communication. She has committed her career to making Kentucky's Appalachia a better place to live, work, grow, and thrive.

Melissa earned her doctoral degree in Educational Leadership & Policy Studies from Eastern Kentucky University. Her master's degree is in secondary education and her bachelor's degree is in business management and communication, both from Union College. Her ongoing research, rooted in Kentucky's Appalachia, studies methods of raising hope in communities through the erosion of negative stereotypes and reveals economic implications for individuals and regional populations.

"House of Cleaving" is her second novel, originally published in 2010 and re-released in 2022 under a new imprint.

www.melissanewman.net
www.martinsisterspublishing.com